Copyright © 2015 by Kristine Ireland Waits. ISBN 978-0-692-32659-6. Cover and interior design by Stephanie Greenlee. Photograph by Amanda Meberg Photography. Books available at KristineWaits.com and EndurancePublishing.com

This book is a work of fiction and is not intended as a substitute for medical advice of physicians. The reader should consult a physician in matters of health and fertility.

JULIA'S FIGHT

A battle with infertility

by Kristine Ireland Waits

ENDURANCE
publishing

Books available at www.EnduranceBooks.com

JULIA'S FIGHT

A battle with infertility

by Kristine Ireland Waits

Books available at www.EnduranceBooks.com

DEDICATION

My first book, a non-fiction project called *Every Drunken Cheerleader: Why Not Me?*, was based on a journal I wrote during my battle with infertility. Since the publishing of that book, I have received the most wonderful support from readers. I am reminded of the saying, "my cup is so full I am drinking from the saucer."

I asked many of the women who contacted me to share their story, insights, heartaches, and uplifting moments. I was overwhelmed by the depth and honest disclosure of these responses. With permission, I have folded their words, like ingredients, into the batter of these pages.

I dedicate this book to the following women who became the muse for Julia's Fight. Their names appear in alphabetical order and without last names to protect identity. Amanda (both of you), Carrie, Cassie, Cheryl, Christina, Dannette, Elana, Emily, Erin, Jannory, Jen, Kim (both of you), Kelly (both of you), Kerry, Krista, Lisa (both of you), Mel, Melody, Nicole, Purvi, Rebecca, Sabrina, and Stacy. I hope you will find glimpses of your story within these pages and know I am grateful for your trust.

I also have to thank Laurie Taylor, Sarah Andrews, Quinn Baldwin, Stephanie Greenlee, Leslie Baldwin, and Mike O'Neil who helped in countless ways to make this novel better.

Finally, a dedication to my husband, Matt Waits, and our three children. I love you each more than life.

Comparison is the thief of joy.
Theodore Roosevelt

CHAPTER 1

"Are you drunk," she asked.

"No, I'm not drunk," he said, picking up his red wine, the Cab Sav blend that had recently become their favorite. Holding the stem, he swirled the mahogany liquid in his glass before taking another sip, his head slightly tilted to one side, his dark brown hair framing his face and strong jaw, his stare fixed intently on her. He has beautiful eyes, she thought.

"I'm on my second glass of wine, sitting on the back porch with my lovely wife, enjoying this perfect spring night."

He was right about that. The unpredictable weather that suggested spring one second and blew cold north winds the next seemed to have finally retreated. The days had become a steady stream of upper 70s, leaving the evening air crisp enough for long sleeves but not cold enough to nag the skin for more layers.

And the daffodils. Where had they come from? Yesterday, it seemed as though the gray, naked landscape was destined for a colorless future. But today, there they were, the beautiful hope of spring and color surprising with blooms of yellow and white. Sprouts of expectation and encouragement.

She had noticed the first daffodils next to a park bench during her lunch hour. She fingered the soft, vivacious blooms, savoring them for a moment, and then reached for her phone to call David at work. She asked him to pick up two steaks on his way home. She'd grab the wine. They worked compatibly like that.

"Okay, so you're not drunk, but you are... What are you?" she said. "You have a wild look in your eye that tells me you're up to something."

He stared into his glass, studying the way the red hue glowed in the soft yellow light coming through the kitchen window. From the street their house appeared small with large shuttered windows looking into the living room. But what the house lacked in width it made up for in depth, reminiscent of the shotgun style from the turn of the last century but built only ten years ago. The selling point was the trees that hung low over the back porch providing shade during the hot summers. It was where the couple sat most evenings.

David took a drink and nodded his head as if confident about something.

His glass made a heavy sound as he placed it on the metal table. He sat forward in his patio chair and took both her hands in his. "Let's do it," he said.

She furrowed her brow, unable to tell what kind of mischief he was creating. "Do what?"

"Let's have a baby," he said.

"What?" she said, releasing his hands, warm within hers. "Where did this come from? Did someone at work just announce they're pregnant?" The taste of something metallic rose at the back of her tongue.

He reached for her hands again and she placed them in his palms, a silent surrender to hear him out.

"It didn't come from anywhere," he said. "I just love you, and I want to have a family with you. We've been married for two years. I'm not going anywhere, and neither are you. Let's start our family."

"Whoa, David," she said, taking her hands from his again. "Are you serious?"

"As the day I asked you to marry me," he said. "I want to be a dad, and you'll be a great mother. Let's do it."

At the word "mother" her heart began to race. She gulped

her wine searching for composure. She hadn't been around kids the way David had. What if she ruined the perfect little child with the baggage she carried from her own childhood? Or what if they brought a special needs child into the world? How could she handle that. She was far too selfish and self-centered a person. And what would a baby do to her career? She had been hired as the managing coordinator at the health department only a year ago.

David knew her fears, most of them anyway. He knew better than to ask this of her already. What was he thinking?

"This is just too soon," she said. "I know you love kids . . ." she trailed off, her thoughts exploding with thousands of tiny tendrils looking for something stable to hold onto.

David sat back in his chair watching his wife, the seasons of emotion changing her face. He took another sip of wine, allowing her time to settle.

"You are right about one thing," she said, finally. "We've only been married two years. We haven't done so many of the things we said we'd do. What about going to Italy or climbing the walls of the Grand Canyon? I bet babies can't do that."

"We'll have nine months before the baby's born. We can travel then. And from what I hear, they don't stay babies forever. They actually grow into people."

He leaned in with a tender kiss of confidence, his love for her warming her entire body and ever so slightly thawing her resolve.

At that moment, she saw something unique in his eyes, a shine of excitement. Looking at him deeply, soaking in his request, she realized the look was of hope.

"I'm scared," she admitted to herself and her husband.

"This will be the best adventure of our lives," he said, getting out of his chair and down onto his knees in front of her. "Julia Katherine Ellis, will you be the mother of my children?"

It was a beautiful gesture. With tears streaming down her face, she kissed the most romantic man in the world and then led him to the bedroom.

CHAPTER 2

"You are amazing," he said. The pillows had been thrown to the floor. The comforter and sheets were pushed to the bottom of the bed, leaving it bare except for the exhausted bodies that lay side by side. The idea of a baby had made him ravenous for her.

"We're pretty good at that," she agreed, reaching for his hand and rolling to her side to face him. "You really want to have a baby?" she asked.

"I really do," he said. "I love you so much, and I want to share our life with a child. Maybe two or three."

"And do you really think I'll be an okay mom?"

"Better than okay," he reassured her, gently rubbing his fingertips on her cheek. "You're compassionate and strong. You are loving and smart. Not to mention a total knockout."

"You're just saying that because I'm lying here completely naked." The delight of her body felt like a blanket of euphoria covering her physical imperfections. She hated to wear a bathing suit in public, but lying next to David, exposed like this, she was unconcerned about the dimples in her thighs or her any of the flaws that were so undesirable in the light of day.

"True, but I'm sure a lucky guy. If we have a girl and she looks anything like you, she'll wear a ski jacket even in the summer."

She laughed, enjoying the idea of a little girl with her blonde hair and his dimples. Julia could almost see the full

10

pink lips of the little girl's smile.

The idea of a baby began to take form. There were hundreds of books about parenting, if not thousands. She could read those. And daycare was invented for people just like her to have both a career and children.

She thought of the time she and David had attempted a ropes course together. Fifteen feet above the ground, she had frozen with fear, as the only thing that separated her from the plummet was a few wires and a harness. David had talked her through the last ten steps of the obstacle, encouraging her with patience. He would be there for parenting too.

Not only did she have David at her side, she would have Sarah also. Her best friend had been thrown into motherhood and had flourished with the task.

Just as she had on the ropes course, Julia decided to trust David and follow his lead.

"So what should we do to make it official?" she asked.

"I think we just did." And there was that contagious smile, the same one she saw on the little girl.

"The last time you got down on your knee and asked me a question, we had a giant wedding and exchanged rings in front of our friends and family."

"I don't think we should invite our friends and family to this," he laughed. "Can you imagine?"

"I've got it," she said, jumping up. "Come on."

Tugging his hand, she pulled him into the bathroom. In the top drawer next to her toothbrush she found the pink, rectangular pack of pills that she had taken every day of her life since she was nineteen.

Julia remembered the cramps she had as a teenager, doubling her over in pain and forcing her to miss school. She was humiliated as her mother walked her into to the gynecologist's office and then took the birth control prescription to the pharmacy. Julia had felt complete embarrassment as her mother gave her the pills and the instructions. She was sure the pharmacist thought she was a girl with both loose morals and loose underpants.

Opening the pills, she counted the twelve remaining.

She handed the pack over to David. "Flush 'em."

He popped each pill out of its aluminum confinement and into his hand. The snap of the tablet breaking free was a sudden and exciting sound. He tossed the empty container into the trash and took Julia's hand.

"Ready?"

She hesitated, taking a deep breath. "As I'll ever be," she said. Though she was worried that the cramps might return, she thought it would be liberating not to be tied to this medication.

She had never been skydiving, but imagined throwing her arms out, screaming into the wind, and leaping with faith into the air, hoping the parachute would open. Exhilaration, fear, trust, and hope—she was feeling all this now.

He turned his hand over and the twelve tiny pills plopped into the bowl.

"With this flush, I thee make babies," he said, and pushed down the handle. Julia smiled at his play on their nuptials. While it was corny, there was also weight in the act, as if they were stepping over the threshold of something grand and deeply important.

Julia bit her lip as together they watched the medicine swirl around the toilet and disappear.

David pulled her naked body to his. How appropriate, she thought, that we would do something so significant while being this exposed, this vulnerable.

His kiss was deep and warm. His fingers found their way up her back and into her hair as together their passion rose. Breathing heavily, she asked, "Can we do this again?. Leaning her head back she let him kiss her neck. They had never had consecutive sex only minutes apart, and she worried that her body was becoming too greedy with expectation.

He moaned a seductive yes, pressing himself against her. In one motion he picked her up and set her on the bathroom counter. The cold granite gave a painful bite, but the heat of her desire warmed it quickly.

He leaned over her body, kissing her neck as he pulled himself to her. Oh, this wonderful man, she thought.

Her back arched, one hand pressed overhead against the mirror and the other around his neck. Her body shook, enraptured, until they both let go.

To her surprise, he picked her up as if to carry her over the threshold. "Let's get you horizontal while my swimmers do their work," he said.

They spent the rest of the evening watching a movie in bed. He jumped up to serve her when she wanted a drink of water, encouraging her to lie still for the entire movie. The uncomfortable feeling of wet between her legs and the thought of motherhood distracted her from the drama on the screen.

This was real. She was lying in bed, next to her husband, actually trying to have a baby. They were actually going to do this.

Please, she thought, let the parachute open and don't let my mothering be a terrible disaster.

CHAPTER 3

After her morning shower, David gave Julia a love tap on the rear. "Good morning, Mama," he said, his hair disheveled and his smile electrifying.

"I think we did some good last night," he said with a wink.

Without looking at him directly, she smiled. Julia feared her gaze would give away her anxiety about this leap into parenthood. She needed some time to think about what they were doing before she could put it into words for David.

"It's going to be perfect," he said.

"You're not going to start calling me "Mama" already, are you?'" she asked.

"Maybe," he said with a light kiss as he stepped into the shower.

She could barely keep her eyes on the road as she drove to work. She daydreamed about how she would tell each of her friends. The thought of an actual baby was too much to comprehend. She didn't want to picture the diapers or the late nights. But the excitement of revealing the news of her pregnancy was exhilarating and fun to plan.

Of course Sarah would need to know as soon as the test showed up positive. Then maybe she would call her mother, who would probably do some kind of weird blessing to the Earth.

David's mom would alert the entire family using the phone

tree method. That woman was nothing if not a well-organized pipeline of gossip. Julia was grateful for the distance when her in-laws moved three hours away to be near Stacy, David's sister, and her kids.

David would have to beat his mother to Pops, his grandfather. He wouldn't want the news coming from anyone else. She could picture the way Pops would put his large, strong hands around David's face as he declared his love. Julia could imagine how proud David would be in that moment. She made a mental note to video everything she could regarding the announcement of their pregnancy and imagined watching the reveal with the baby each year as they celebrated her birthday.

A baby, she thought. A real, live, beautiful baby.

She pulled into Flavors, the local coffee shop, and ordered a skinny double shot cappuccino. She loved that this dive didn't have a drive thru. There was something refreshing about seeing the barista face to face as she ordered her drink. Sure, it took longer here than at the big chain coffee shops, but this place gave her an opportunity to see her friends, glance over the day's newspaper dependably sprawled across a table, and say a quick hello to the gray-haired man who occupied the same chair every day.

These common, ordinary things, the things that can be counted on, were a comfort to Julia and helped start her day on the right foot. Not to mention the coffee was delicious. The barista, Sasha, had come to know that Julia liked her drink with an extra Splenda and a little whipped cream on top.

Julia thought of life as a carefully balanced act of existence, just like her "skinny" coffee was perfectly juxtaposed to the extra calories in the whipped topping she requested.

This morning, none of her friends were at Flavors; it could be hit and miss. She tipped her head and smiled toward the gray-haired man then ordered her drink. He wore his pageboy hat slightly askew, hair exposed at his temples betraying his age, a well groomed beard of silver stubble covering his face. Julia thought he must be European and was probably handsome in his earlier life. The texture and lines of his face led Julia to believe he'd lived a hard life. But the brightness in his eyes suggested an altogether different story.

She was handing her credit card to Sasha when she heard the high-pitched, fearful squeal of a young child at the door behind her.

A woman was trying to maneuver into the cafe pushing a baby stroller with one hand and holding the hand of a toddler with her other. With her elbow on the door, the mother tried to let go of the toddler's hand, sending him into a loud, whining fit.

Obviously embarrassed, the mother grabbed for the boy's hand as large tears rolled down his cheeks. She used her elbow, hip, and foot to open the door wider while trying to squeeze the stroller and the toddler inside. Watching the woman negotiate the entrance was like watching someone using a spoon to hammer a round peg into a square hole.

Julia took a couple of quick steps and pulled the front of the stroller inside.

Studying Julia, the young boy regained control of his tears. For some reason the scene made Julia think of the birthing of a whale she saw on The Discovery Channel. The huge animal had to twist and wriggle, contorting itself in a painful looking display until the calf was free and peace returned to the sea.

Maybe the whale had been breech or had experienced some other medical obstacle. Surely that had not been a standard birth, just as this could not possibly be the way this woman walked into every store. Nature couldn't purposefully allow such difficulty to be the standard. Could it?

"Oh my gosh, thank you so much," the woman said.

"No problem at all," Julia said, finally able to look at the kids. "How far apart are they?"

"About a year and a half." The woman beamed. "Best surprise of my life."

Julia was taken aback by the answer. The mother looked like she hadn't had a full night's sleep in eighteen months.

Her hair was pulled into a low ponytail, and her makeup was minimally applied at best. Her sweatpants suggested she lost the need to care about her appearance and was doing what she could to keep the hours moving forward. Other than a shot of caffeine, Julia thought the woman would benefit greatly from a deep breath and a getaway weekend.

David's words came to her like a reality flash, "maybe two or three." He had actually said he wanted two or three kids. There was no way she could handle that. Look at this disheveled woman using all her body parts just to open a door. Julia didn't want to be this woman.

The fact that the kids had been a surprise widened Julia's eyes and increased her apprehension further. Motherhood was beginning to sound like a mud slide, a slippery slope that took you unaware and propelled you into the unknown.

"May I?" Julia asked, indicating that she wanted to pull the fluffy, pink blankets down from around the baby in the stroller.

"Of course," the woman said. "She's a precious one."

The little girl's dark hair stuck out from her head at all angles. Her skin, an olive color, was almost iridescent in its perfection. Her tiny pink lips and delicate nose were angelic. But most magnificent about this little girl were her blue eyes. Like crowning jewels, they glistened with depth and understanding. But something else, another truth was begging to be shared by those beautiful eyes.

Julia caught her breath. It was the promise of the future.

Tears welled below the surface as her fears of motherhood vanished like a whisper in the wind, replaced by a truth so substantial it took the form of thought. I get to be a mother soon. I get to have one of these perfect creations, and hold her in my arms, and protect her, and love her. I can, absolutely, do this.

"She is beautiful," Julia said, masking her emotion. "Congratulations."

"Thanks. They say God doesn't give you more than you

17

can handle. There are days I cling to those words like a life line," she said. "But it's all worth it." Beaming, she flattened the hair of her son and pulled him closer to her leg.

As the women smiled at one another, Sasha called Julia's name, and set the cappuccino on the pickup counter.

"Have a great day," Julia said and left the coffee shop, floating on the high of possibilities.

When she got to the Health Department, she looked over her schedule for the day, and a shot of energy flooded her body.   She felt as though hers was the kind of job that helped the community and stimulated her better self. There were going to be several meetings in the conference room to discuss the new vaccinations they would offer in the fall. There was a child-rearing class at noon and another at five. Hearing screenings would take place that morning. And the walk-in clinic would be open as usual.

Her job was to organize and maintain the operations and scheduling of the facility. It might seem mundane to some, but she loved the work, the people she helped, the causes they promoted. Her bachelor's degree was from the business college, a major in general business. Those four years of general study made her envy the people who knew who they were and what they wanted to become. With diploma in hand, she had felt adrift when looking for work. Though she had always been driven and organized, her employment search seemed more like throwing spaghetti at the wall and waiting to see what would stick.

When she had applied for this job it was overly ambitious of her to assume she was qualified. During the interview process she realized how much the job fit her and her determination to get the position grew like a well watered seed.

After the interview, she tediously researched Health Departments in other cities and states comparing and contrasting services. Then, based on her research, she composed a list of suggestions and ideas that might improve the marketing of services and flow of patients. She mentioned an available grant and potential support from local organizations. She mailed the letter three days after the interview; by the end of the week she had the job.

During the first six months of her employment, however, she was afraid she would be unable to manage the chaos. The naiveté of her expectations became abundantly clear, if only to her. There was always so much going on at any one time she was unable to keep up. But the hectic office pace was juxtaposed with the slow acceptance of the changes she had recommended and the approval of grants she had submitted. She had felt like a piece of ice in a blender, spun and chopped and then set out to melt in the hot sun.

She knew the staff had quietly scoffed at her youth and inexperience when she was hired. She, too, wondered if she could handle the volume of work and level of leadership the position required.

In time, she found a way to color-coordinate the office schedule and discovered software that would allow the entire staff to communicate more efficiently, relieving the problem of double staffing and double booking rooms and events. Eventually, Julia found her pace and place within the office and grew to love the women who worked there.

Now it was spring. The need for flu shots had diminished as did the number of sick people who came in needing care. There was a glow about the office that resembled optimism.

By noon, her stomach rumbled and she walked a couple of blocks to a nearby deli. She called Sarah on the way, eager to share the news about David's pregnancy proposal.

"You've reached Sarah Beckett. Obviously, I didn't answer my phone in time. Make it a great day."

"Hey, it's Julia. Call me as soon as you can. I have news." She said the last word like a song, the rest of its beautiful melody waiting to be heard.

The walk back to work after lunch allowed a sense of peace to settle in Julia's heart, and the feeling led her to think about the most recent conversation with her mother, Beaty. The conversation had been about finding harmony with nature and being wholly in the moment that surrounds her—very Zen. At least her mother was into that last month. Julia thought she might call her to tell her about this walk. Some moments are more vibrantly alive when shared.

She decided against it. Beaty had an overly mothering way of getting involved, and somehow she would sense something was going on. Julia wasn't yet ready to tell her the news, until there was real news to share.

All of this bliss evaporated the moment she stepped back through the double sliding glass doors into the Health Department.

She smelled the situation before she saw it. The putrid odor of vomit attacked her nostrils and instinctively forced her hand to cover her nose and mouth. A mother in the waiting room was apologizing to a nurse as she held a wad of paper towels to her child's mouth. The towels did little good as a majority of the mess laid in splats and chunks on the gray linoleum floor.

The boy responsible was around a year-and-a-half old. He had wide, terrified eyes as he continued to separate his stomach from its contents. The mother held him tightly on her lap and consoled him the best she could. It was obvious from the circles under her drooping eyes that she hadn't had much sleep. Nonetheless, her face registered genuine concern, even fear, for the child in her arms.

The janitor always took a late lunch and would be gone until three, so it would be up to her to handle this mess. Her euphoria sank like a rock in water.

The mother positioned her son on her hip and rose to follow the nurse into an examination room. All Julia could do was watch as, with the sudden sound of pain and relief, the little boy let loose his bowels. His gray sweatpants and his mother's blue shirt were covered in a foul brown liquid. The levy that was his diaper was no match for the volume of his excrement.

The mother burst into tears. She put her forehead against

20

the sweat soaked temple of her son. "Oh, Jacob. Oh no, honey." She looked to the nurse weakly. "I just don't know how to handle this," she cried.

For what felt like forever, Julia cleaned the floor with every soap and potion she could find in the janitor's closet, but the smell lingered like smog in Los Angeles.   By the time she got home, she was exhausted and ready for a glass of wine. Her phone showed that she had missed Sarah's return call— no message, typical. The exciting news of flushing the birth control pills last night somehow seemed a little less joyous, having been diluted by the reality of motherhood that had unfolded at work.

After pouring herself a glass of wine, she sat on the back porch and studied her hands still lemon scented and raw from the day's events. If she were that mother, holding a miserably sick child in her arms, how would she have handled herself?

The answer was discouraging. There was no way she would be able to operate on zero sleep because of a crying kid. And there was absolutely no way she could cope with wearing an outfit of throw-up and poop. She would have frozen, immobilized by helplessness and disgust.

She worried about how David would take the news. How he would react when she told him the truth? Their fights had always been a flash in the pan, but this was bound to be different. In college, when their relationship had become less about drinking and kissing and more about their future together, David revealed the true reason behind breaking up with his last girlfriend.

"She couldn't have kids," he told Julia. "She was born with some kind of medical problem that prevents her from having kids, and I want a family. Pops always says 'make proud the family name.. How could I do that without kids of my own.'"

At the time his words seemed logical but distant, like looking at a trail on the map that she didn't have to negotiate. For all she knew, her body was in working order, and thinking of children was a future so far ahead her map hadn't yet charted the path.

"Make proud the family name," had been the exact thing Pops had said to Julia after walking down the aisle. Like his hands, the words enveloped her, reassuring her of her position as a member of the family.

Now, she thought about David's ex-girlfriend and how painful the breakup had to have been because of the reason. She wondered what would happen when she told him. We're married, she thought, he couldn't break up with me. Would he want a divorce?

"I brought you a flower," David said, surprising her out of her thoughts. Smiling roguishly and leaning on the door, he held out to her a single yellow daffodil.

Like the mess she spent all afternoon cleaning up, the words spilled out before she could stop them. "I can't be a mother," she said. "I saw this woman today, and I just can't be her. I can't, David. I'm sorry. I hate puke. I hate poop. I can't change diapers and clean up nasty messes all the time. I need my sleep or I get super grouchy. I can't be a mom, David. I just can't do it. Please don't divorce me." The words poured from her like lava from an exploding volcano.

"Whoa, whoa, whoa," he said, pulling her to him. "I am never going to divorce you. Now, take a deep breath, and tell me what happened."

As she spoke, he laughed, picturing the scene. He continued to hold her hand as he told her stories he had heard from friends about their kids' embarrassing bowel explosions. They were all obsessed with the color and consistency of bowel movements, "BMs" they called them. Before long, they were laughing together.

"Why do you think they are so wound up about this stuff?" he said.

"Beats me," she said, shrugging her shoulders. She thought the question was rhetorical and smiled at him, feeling as though her fears and concerns were understood, comforted by knowing he too didn't understand the point of parenthood and all the disgusting stuff that accompanies it.

"Love," he said and looked at her with serious eyes. "They care because they love. That woman today was exhausted because she spent the night worrying about a tiny baby who called to her when he was scared. They care about poop because they want their baby to be healthy and live a long, happy life. They love their children the way I love you."

She looked down, contemplating his words feeling selfish.

"Will this be hard?" he asked. "Yes. We will lose sleep, but we will gain something more amazing than either of us can ever imagine. You are brave and beautiful, and you will make a wonderful mom. You can do this. We can do this."

She hugged him tightly. Her cheek resting perfectly against his neck like puzzle pieces that had found their way back together. "I love you," she said, meaning it with all her heart.

CHAPTER 4

"Why haven't you returned my calls?" Sarah asked, stealing Julia away from the crowd at Yvette's baby shower.

Sarah was in a mid-length floral bohemian skirt and pink tank top that screamed "stylish spring." Somehow, Sarah always looked like she'd jumped out of prime time television. Once on a float trip down the river, everyone else was in grungy gym shorts, bathing suits, and ponytails. Sarah wore frayed, trendy jean skirt, a skimpy yellow bikini top, and a large brimmed hat. She could have been posing for the cover of a summer issue of Vanity Fair.

Not only that, but her shoes were usually fabulous too. Her arms were toned from exercise and her hair was always in that messy styled look that Julia couldn't create no matter how much or how little she tried. If Julia didn't love her best friend, she'd hate her.

The topper to Sarah's style was the way she did it all with a small child on her hip. Joshua was the sweetest thing Julia could imagine. If he came with whipped topping, she might just eat him up. He followed his mother's high style and usually trotted around the playground in a collared shirt and top-siders, but he had his dad's silly streak and loved to make people laugh.

How Sarah managed to keep it all together was beyond Julia's comprehension.

"I've just been busy," Julia said, trying to deflect. "Sorry."

24

"I don't want sorry," Sarah added. "I want your news. Are you pregnant?"

This woman had ESP. "No, I'm not pregnant," she said with a sly smile, and looked in both directions trying to make sure no one was listening. A friend's baby shower was no place to talk about her private, personal life. "I'll tell you later."

Julia had spent the last several days thinking about what David had said about loving a child. She tried to write a pro and con list, detailing what she'd be giving up in the "con" column and what she'd be getting in return in the "pro" column. She had done the same thing when deciding which college to attend and, once, when choosing between boyfriends. When she was done with her self-analysis, she would rip the list into as many pieces as possible and distribute the evidence into two trashcans. She didn't want anyone to uncover her work.

Pen in hand, she realized how ludicrous the list would be and abandoned the plan.

She had watched television thinking how she would handle the parenting situation on sitcoms versus the childless freedom of so many reality shows. There seemed to be two parallel story lines—one centered entirely on the parent/child interaction and obligatory comedy of errors, the other on the liberated single hanging with friends, making for poor choices and good drama. There was never an intersection in these story lines. Take your pick—children or freedom.

She had gone to bed wrestling with the thought of being like her own mother, wondering if that was a good thing or not. She and her mother had had many seasons in their relationship, not all of them spring.

Being true to herself, she wanted to make sure she was jumping into parenthood because she was ready and not just because David was.

She remembered about a year ago her college friend, Kate, had moved in with her boyfriend. The next day the two bought a dog and named him Rascal. Kate was not a dog person; Quinn was. She agreed to the dog out of love for her man.

Eventually Quinn moved out, but the dog stayed. Nowadays Kate's Facebook status consistently included some incident with the dog eating her shoes or pooping in the hall. Rascal fully lives up to his name. Julia didn't want to feel about a child the way Kate felt about her dog.

With the baby shower in full swing, Julia hugged Yvette, her church friend now bursting with pregnancy. Before they were married Julia and David had gone to the same church as Yvette for about four months. It had allowed them to meet a few people and warm up to the pastor who would preside over their wedding. A few months after their honeymoon, however, their attendance dwindled. Now they almost never woke up early on a Sunday. Yvette was the one friend she had kept in contact with.

This was the third baby shower Julia had been to since January. All her friends seemed to be starting families, as if spring had arrived on their biological clocks. Hit twenty-six and boom, the seeds start sprouting all around.

"You look beautiful," Julia said.

"I look like a beached whale," Yvette said. "But thank you."

"When are you due?"

"Four weeks. But it feels like four centuries." She put her hand on her belly. "He's ready to escape if you ask me. Wanna feel?"

Julia had never touched the stomach of a pregnant woman before. She surrendered her hand to Yvette who placed it on her rounded belly, low and to the right of her bellybutton. Julia waited an uncomfortable moment, not feeling anything, thinking how awkward it was to be touching someone like this; it was almost too intimate. She wondered if she should look Yvette in the eye or off in the distance. Which would be less awkward and remove her from the uncomfortably private touch?

Then it happened. A tiny movement beneath her hand. A flutter. Julia's eyes snapped to Yvette's. She sucked in a small, surprised breath. "Is that him?"

"Yep, the little man has been kicking all day."

He moved again in the same spot and Julia was awestruck. A spark ran from her palm up her arm and warmed her entire body. Her heart ached with pure joy. It took all her willpower not to put both hands on Yvette and ask to stay there all day, waiting for more proof of life.

She knew right then and without question that David had been right. She did want a child. The conflict within her perished, as if its time for consuming her had expired. With that one little kick, fear vanished into the nothing from which it had come.

She wanted to experience what Yvette was experiencing. She wanted small arms to wrap around her neck like Joshua's did when he hugged Sarah. She even wanted to hold on to a crying infant, loving him to health even if it meant sacrificing her own. It was as if the film of fear about parenting had been stripped away and the clear picture of motherly love was unveiled.

She wanted to make proud the family name. She could taste the desire and, like an atomic fire, it consumed her in an instant.

"It's time for Yvette to open her gifts," the hostess announced.

Julia sighed, reluctantly releasing her hand from her friend's pregnant belly.

Yvette opened one baby blue jumper after another. Passing each one around, Julia was struck by their size. She had been to several pink and blue showers, going to support girlfriends and eat chocolate-covered strawberries.

Today, however, she saw the experience with entirely new eyes. When a package of tiny socks passed into her lap, she quietly swooned with longing. She cupped the socks in both hands and hugged them to her breast.

Sarah, sitting next to her, caught the action, eagle-eyed. "What's going on with you?" she whispered.

"I can't help it," Julia said, looking around. She hoped no

one else noticed her crazed obsession with the tiny socks.

"Let's pee," Sarah said. Without waiting for an answer, Sarah took Julia by the hand and led her to the bathroom. Of course neither one of them needed to use the bathroom, but Sarah wanted answers and this was a prime spot to talk.

"Spill it," Sarah said, closing the door behind her and folding her arms. Her body language and the fact that she was standing in front of the door made it perfectly clear to Julia that she was not going to leave this room until she had given full disclosure.

"I just had great sex again last night. That's all," Julia said, a bit coy.

"You are married. Talking about your sex life is not that exciting. Plus, it doesn't make you hug socks." As the last words rolled off Sarah's tongue, and the truth struck her. "Holy crap! Are you trying?"

Julia could hardly muster a smile before her best friend flew at her with a hug. The true comfort of a friendship like theirs was knowing you don't have to say a word to be perfectly understood.

Once, when the girls had gone out for a glass of wine to unwind after work, Sarah was confronted by Jane, an associate from her insurance firm. The company was going through restructuring, and Jane was aghast at the choices upper management had made. Unbeknownst to her, Sarah had been given a top-tier broker's position she had fought for tooth and nail. Jane obviously wanted to pry into who would go and who would move up.

Julia read Sarah's shifts in posture and lack of eye contact with Jane. Her friend needed an emergency exit. Julia worked up a few sniffles and wetted her eyes as if she had been crying. "Excuse me," she said to Jane in as pitiful a voice as her acting skills allowed. "Can you pass me those napkins? My grandmother just passed away, and I was just filling Sarah in on the funeral details."

Jane apologized profusely and excused herself. Under the

table, Julia and Sarah gave each other a high five.

This bathroom hug felt just like that high five, a touch conveying the bond of deep friendship. Julia had read once in college that daffodils are the "easiest and most dependable of all the families of flowers." The description fit her friendship with Sarah perfectly—easy, dependable.

"This is huge," Sarah said.

Julia knew Sarah would instinctively understand the gravity of this decision. As a couple, she and David had verbalized many times their desire to quest before settling down with children. Concerts, road trips, and a beach vacation were all things they wanted to experience together. To make this choice before the adventure . . . Sarah knew Julia had done some serious soul searching.

Sarah hadn't had the luxury of choice when it came to Joshua's birth. A few months after her wedding, Sarah started throwing up. As with so many things in her life, she handled the unplanned surprise with elegance, calling the pregnancy "an act of grace." How could Julia not be best friends with a woman like that?

"Yeah, it's pretty huge to me," Julia said.

"When I saw the plus sign on my pregnancy test, I burst into tears," Sarah said. "We were newlyweds for God's sake. I thought everything was going to be ruined by a baby."

"You never told me that," Julia said.

"I've never told anyone that. Joshua is a blessing, and the second he was born I felt like an ass for thinking anything different. There is no greater moment than when your child is placed in your arms. You are about to experience the best thing in the world," Sarah said.

"Thank you," Julia said, wiping a tear from the corner of her eye.

With Sarah's vow to keep silent, the girls left the bathroom hand-in-hand. Their shared secret a knot in the rope of their friendship, their smiles conspiratorial.

CHAPTER 5

"Jules," David called walking in the front door with the newspaper under his right arm and two packages in his left. He kicked the door closed behind him. "There are gifts on the front porch."

Julia stretched out of the warm comfort of the bed and followed David's voice to the living room.

Julia loved David on Saturday mornings. His gym shorts and ratty t-shirts made him less the impressive executive he exuded during the week and more her familiar counterpart. He would make a pot of coffee and sit on the back porch reading the news with his feet propped up in the chair opposite him. This was her David, the one no one else knew.

He held out the presents and gave his wife a look of false surprise. "Let me guess," he said. "You told Sarah about us."

With her signature gold wrapping paper, Sarah had snuck over to the Ellis's house in the middle of the night to leave two packages. One rectangular and thin with only the word "Dad" written in script, the other a shirt box with the "Mom" emblazoned on top.

David opened the "Dad" package while Julia went to the kitchen and poured two cups of coffee. She heard the paper rip followed by her husband's laughter.

"What is it?" she called from the kitchen.

"The note says 'to help your swimmers,'" he said.

She hurried into the living room embarrassed that, in four

little words, her best friend had disclosed to her husband the details of her description of their first night of trying.

David's laughter was proof of his forgiveness, and she joined in when she saw him sitting with a purple kickboard on his lap.

David and Julia had known each other in elementary school before David's dad moved his family to Illinois for work. The two kids had been in a swimming class together the summer she was six and he was seven. Many of their friends knew how to swim, so it was an embarrassment to both that lessons were still needed. They made a pact to keep the swim class a secret.

Together, along with the tiny five-year-olds, they jumped into the pool and held on to the side. After several hours of instruction and assisted practice, the kids were told to let go of the side and swim across the pool alone. Julia did so without hesitation or trepidation. Her arms outstretched like a rocket and her feet masterfully kicking water into the air. David, on the other hand, got two strokes from his starting point and panicked. "I need a kickboard! I need a kickboard!" he hollered over and over. Julia swam to his rescue.

When they reunited in college and finally made the connection, Julia didn't let the kickboard story drown. She brought up her superiority at swimming lessons whenever he needed to be bested.

Once, when David was driving them on a long distance road trip he swore up and down that he had made the correct turn at a fork in the road. Julia had said, "I think it's left, but do whatever you're going to do." The comment ignited a fight over his stubbornness and her passive-aggressive ways. When the sun had set and it was abundantly clear they were lost, Julia said to David with a smile, "Pull over at the next gas station and I'll go in and get a kickboard."

"What in the world will Sarah have gotten you?" David said.

Julia set down her coffee to uncover the shirt box. She

opened it just a crack and saw red silk. She closed it quickly and looked at David with devious eyes. "I think I'd better open this one alone," she said, eyebrows raised seductively. "I'll be right back."

His protest echoed in the sparsely decorated living room and then fell silent.

Two minutes later she appeared in the doorway, her back against the frame, one knee bent. The red silk nightie hiding only the necessary parts and nothing more. Bending her knee a bit more would cause the slip to slide up for full exposure.

"She has good taste," David said, enjoying the exceptional view of his wife.

Thirty minutes later, Julia shot her friend a text.

Thanks for the gifts. Mine worked. We will see about David's.

The response was instant.

Late night run to Target. Enjoy ;)

David kissed Julia's shoulder. "I love you this way," he said.

"What way?"

"Free. Fun. I don't know. Sex on a Saturday morning. If I knew trying was going to be this fun, we would have started a long time ago."

Laughing, she threw a pillow at him. "How long do you think it will take?" she asked.

"To get pregnant? I don't know a month or two probably."

CHAPTER 6

"I had a dream about you last night," Julia's mother said, instead of "hello."

"Mom, it's 7:00 a.m. on a Sunday. What do you want?"

"Wow, it's already seven. That's great, I was afraid I was calling too early." Julia recognized this tone of voice. It was the one her mother always used when she was excited about something new. She had used it when she had discovered hot yoga in February and when she learned about the medical benefits of wheat grass shots in March.

"Did you hear that ocean water will naturally remove wrinkles?" Julia said. Poking fun at her mother's hippie-esque nature was done partly out of humor and partly out of annoyance.

Beatrice Meyers, "Beaty" as her friends called her, had recently fallen in love with all things natural, organic, and Zen. As an oversized woman in her mid 30's, she had taken great pride in losing 75 pounds, and now she looked for remedies and stamina boosters in the world around her. The problem with inner peace and communion with nature was that it required silence. Beaty, however, was Type A by birth.

"Oh you," her mother said, dismissively. "No, I had a dream," she paused for dramatic effect and lowered her voice. "A sexy one."

"Mom, gross. Really? We should never, never go there."

"It wasn't gross. Not that kind of sexy. It was wonderful,

like magical or something."

Julia covered the receiver of her cell phone and nudged David. "Mom had a dream about us trying."

"Uh huh," he moaned and rolled a pillow over his head.

"Well," she heard her mother ask. "Do you have any news for me?"

"Yes, Mom I do."

"Ha! I knew it. Your dad said not to call but I told him there was something big happening at the Ellis house. So, what is it? What's the big news?"

There was no way Julia was going to tell her mom that she and David were trying to conceive, certainly not this early into the whole thing. Her mother would probably have her meditating in the woods while she flamboyantly danced around her with a chicken... or some other crazy baby-making ritual she found online.

She did have to admit, however, that this communing with the world thing was working. How else could her mom know something had changed?

"The daffodils are in bloom," Julia said, smiling at her cleverness.

The heavy sound of exhausted air came over the phone. "Okay, fine. Don't tell me. But I know something big is going on. When you are ready, Dear, I'm here."

"Thanks, Mom," Julia said.

Was it that easy? Could you just flush your birth control pills down the drain and in doing so send a magical signal into the universe that let it know you were ready for Act Two of your marriage? Julia had been blowing off her mother's newfound obsession with "spiritual serenity," as she called it, but maybe there was actually something to it.

Though she hated to admit it, she liked that her mother was having dreams about her and appreciated her caring enough to call and tell her about it. Julia wouldn't actually dream about people, but she would randomly have a friend's name pop into her mind like the dust blown off an attic treasure. It always left her wondering why a long-lost friend or relative would suddenly come into her consciousness. Never would she call that person or text them to say she was thinking about them. That would seem too weird. But here was her mother, doing exactly that.

She made a mental note to consider contacting the next person whose dust was blown off in her mind. Maybe they would appreciate it, too. Well, she would think about it at least.

"I have news about Savvy," her mother said.

Realizing this conversation wasn't over, Julia got out of bed so that David could sleep in peace. She pulled on her gym shorts that lay crumpled at the side of the bed. She had become accustomed to wearing one of David's t-shirts with a pair of gym shorts in the evening, then pulled off the shorts just before sliding between the sheets. He did the same thing, except shimmied down to his tighty whities. There was nothing sexy about how they went to sleep except that it communicated their comfort with one another. And to Julia, everything was sexy about that.

She tip-toed into the kitchen and grabbed the keys to her car. Their favorite donut shop would be open and its drive thru window meant she could pop by without anyone noticing she was braless and her hair was disheveled.

"Oh, yeah," Julia said, invigorated by the idea of fresh donuts and coffee. "What's the scoop?"

"Well, it turns out she's dating a new man, a waiter at some five-star restaurant. She says he's the best-looking man she's ever seen."

"She said that about her last boyfriend. Remember the tattoo artist from Kansas?"

Savannah, or Savvy as they often called her, was Julia's sister, two years younger and ten years less mature. She had a knack for getting herself into trouble—and for getting out unscathed. When she was pulled over for a possible drunk driving, Savannah had told the officer she wasn't drinking but had been crying uncontrollably over a lost dog. Her car had swerved when she looked out the window screaming the dog's name.

Everyone in the family knew that Savannah didn't have a dog, but the officer was so moved by her antics that he helped look for the imaginary mutt for an hour. By the end of their search, the officer had asked her on a date. That's what a size two waist and a size D bust will do for a girl. Her looks were always Savannah's "get out of jail free card." And in this one case, it had been literal.

Of course, Savvy could only go on three dates with the policeman before announcing that his overly large hands creeped her out. She always found the most obscure and, usually, shallow reason to end a relationship.

"She swears this one is different," her mom said. "They've been on two dates and next weekend he's taking her to meet his parents in Texas." Her mom's voice rose with excitement. "Maybe this is the one."

"When do we get to meet this fancy waiter?" Julia asked. "And what kind of grown man works at a restaurant as a waiter? Shouldn't we call him a boy?" She was snarky about her sister and her unending escapades. Julia fell for David because he was like her, with a solid emotional foundation, ambitions to achieve great things, and the ability to work diligently toward those ambitious goals. She couldn't understand Savvy's lack of forethought about the future. Julia wanted to have a plan and liked roots. Savvy wafted like a leaf free-falling through air, blown by a wistful wind without direction or purpose.

They had never been close growing up. Where Julia was into soccer, Savvy was into dance. Where Julia excelled in academics, Savvy excelled in art. It wasn't that they necessarily fought; it was that neither Julia or Savvy was burdened by her sister's existence. Thanks to Beaty, their home life had been a manic-depressive roller coaster. In response, Julia had taken to concentrating on making something of herself. Little sister did as she wanted.

When Savvy came home at eighteen years old with a tattoo

of a key on her shoulder and announced her decision to move to the west coast, it seemed reckless and irresponsible to Julia.

"Cool, right," Savvy said about the tattoo.

"A key?" Julia said. "Was it on the wall between the butterfly and the Chinese letters?"

"You just don't get me," Savvy said. And with that she went to pack her things. The next day she left for California.

Now, they mostly kept track of one another through their parents and an occasional "happy birthday" text.

It wasn't Julia's intention to look down on her sister's new boyfriend. She was supposed to be big sisterly. But after years of watching Savvy repeat the pattern, Julia was, frankly, annoyed by her antics.

"Wow, you are in a mood this morning," her mom said. "Did I hear a horn, where are you?"

"Sorry, I'm not in a mood," she said. "I'm on my way to the drive-up donut shop. Almost there."

"That stuff will kill you. You know that don't you. Plus it'll keep that extra ten pounds on you."

"Keep it on me!" Julia blurted out. If she had been drinking a soda it would have come spewing out of her nose. She may not have been in a mood before, but she was damn sure in one now.

Of course, she knew she had some weight to lose, but no one says that out loud. And who did her mother think she was, calling at seven in the morning to wake her up and tell her she was fat?

"Oh, you know what I mean, Honey," her mom said. Julia could picture Beaty waving a hand dismissively. "I want you to be at peace with your body. That's all."

"I don't even know what that means, and I don't care," she said, hurt. "I have to order now Mom. I'll call you later." She hung up the phone.

Ten pounds, my ass, she thought.

If Julia was being honest with herself, it was probably more like twenty-five. But that wasn't the point. A mother shouldn't say things to intentionally hurt her daughter. Julia promised if this baby ended up being a little girl, she would never discourage her by commenting about her weight. There were so many things Julia would do right with this baby.

She took the bag of donuts from the teenager at the window and decided it was the sweet things of life she would concentrate on.

"Le Dolce Vita" as they say: The Sweet Life.

CHAPTER 7

When David gave her the news that he'd be working late, Julia rolled her eyes. He usually spent a night or two each week in the office after hours.

She hated for him to work so much. She knew the job was his passion and loved seeing him proud of his success. But she also knew he disliked some of the people in the office, and the company he worked for was becoming overly bureaucratic. So why did work have to come at the expense of their time together?

Usually, she'd run a few extra errands, grab a drink with Sarah, or, as she did tonight, slip into the mall for indulgences she didn't even know she had. She stopped in front of Victoria's Secret, a place she always thought wanted too much money for too little fabric—not to mention it was all so adolescent. But the idea that David liked the new "fun" Julia propelled her into the store.

Julia picked up her phone and called Sarah. "I'm going in," she said.

"Where?"

"Victoria's Secret."

"Really," Sarah said. "You hate that place."

"I still hate this place. Where sexy is trashy," Julia said. "Who thinks that's a good idea?"

"You don't wear g-strings, do you?"

Usually she didn't. But these last weeks had made her

uncharacteristically unashamed, and eager for a g-string or two. She wanted to ride this wave of sexual discovery and freedom with David as long as she could.

Head held high, she checked her preconceived snobbery at the door and marched into the heavily scented store to look around. She grazed her fingers over the panties in a display that read "3 for $30." She walked over to the wall of bras in every shape, size, and electric color imaginable. Near the back of the store a suggestive black number caught her eye. The push-up bra was trimmed with lace at the top to accentuate the repositioned fullness. Though dark, the material that cascaded from the bra was translucent, hinting at coverage but really providing little to cover the stomach and bottom. A tiny black thong was draped over the hanger.

Julia took the slinky thing into the dressing room with no intention of trying it on. Would anyone actually test drive an outfit like this, she wondered. Once the door was closed behind her, she took out her phone, snapped a photo of the lingerie, and sent it to David with the caption, "Thoughts?"

She hoped this little seduction would entice her husband home from the office.

He replied instantly. "Buy it. I don't care what it costs!"

Her heart beat faster and her cheeks flushed. She realized that she felt sexy and desired and loved. She enjoyed toying with her husband like this and delighted in being wanted by him. It was reminiscent of their first few months of marriage, and she savored their closeness.

Three weeks of blissfully sexy encounters had followed their decision to start trying. Their nights used to consist of wine with dinner and then some time in front of the television. When the mood would strike, they would make love. Now, dinner was followed by kitchen dancing, which led to wistful looks, which led to kissing, which led to the bedroom. It was exciting and creative. It was athletic and playful. She prayed that long into their life, this desire would remain.

"Did you find everything you were looking for?" the

woman at the register asked, lipstick too pink, breasts too fake. She was too young for the look, but she had a great smile that helped Julia's intimidation dissipate.

"I think so," Julia said, more sheepishly than she had wanted as she handed over the little black ensemble.

"Our panties are on sale, too," she continued.

Oh, right, g-strings. She had talked herself into those things earlier. "Go ahead and ring me up for four. I'll grab them real quick," Julia said.

"Excellent," the woman said. "That will be $100.12."

Twelve. There had only been twelve little pills remaining in her birth control package. Twelve. If three weeks had passed then . . .

A giddy rush of excitement bubbled into a smile. Could she be pregnant already? How would she tell David? He would be over the moon when he found out. She started planning the whole scene.

When he came home, she'd have candles lit and soft music playing. She'd be wearing her new lingerie and kiss him seductively on that soft spot on his neck. She'd nibble his ear the way he loved and whisper, "I'm pregnant." He would pick her up, twirl her around. No longer the world revolving around the sun but the sun revolving around their love.

First a stop at the drug store for a test kit and then home to prepare.

She walked down the aisle with the feminine hygiene products. She never dreamed there would be so many options, all sitting there unashamed. She reached for the generic brand, opting for low cost over high marketing. How much should a person really pay to pee on a stick?

Turning to go, she discovered a few other treasures along the aisle: personal lubricant, massage oil, personal massagers. Had all these goodies been here last month when she came for her multivitamins and printed photos? She really needed to pay more attention.

At the register she felt a rising need to explain her purchase, to tell the complete stranger at the register, "Yeah, my husband and I have just started trying to have a baby, and, what do you know, I'm late. So here I am buying a pregnancy test!" But she didn't. Thank God. She bit her lip and handed over the cardboard box and a Kit Kat.

The overwhelming anticipation of telling her news began to boil within her. Her smile, so large it began to hurt her cheeks, would not subside.

She couldn't wait to tell Sarah. She could only imagine the show she'd put on. Julia would take her to lunch at Ringo's Bar and Grill. Over their Fancy Salad and sweet tea she'd hand her best friend a gift. When Sarah opened it and saw the tiny socks, she'd instantly know. She pictured Sarah standing on her chair and announcing to the entire restaurant, "My best friend, Julia Ellis, is going to have a baby." And Ringo's patrons would cheer as Julia waved like a pageant queen.

Oh, how she couldn't wait for the day to come.

Pulling into the garage, Julia knew how perfect it would all be. She'd just had a birthday, so the baby would be born while she was still twenty-seven. It would be a boy, probably. Then in two years they'd give him a baby sister. It would all happen before her thirtieth birthday. Of course sometimes in these visions the baby was a girl. Oh, she'd let fate chart that point, she'd handle the rest.

Grabbing the pink- and white-striped Victoria's Secret bag and the drug store sack, she ran inside the house. Her pants were unzipped before she got to the bathroom. Sitting down on the toilet, she read the directions to the pregnancy test. Who knew peeing on a stick required an instruction insert as long as your sleeve?

Frustrated with the details, Julia ripped open the package. She hadn't intended to buy a three-pack, but if it came out positive, she'd be happy to see the pink plus sign over and over again.

She'd read the information in depth while waiting the two to five minutes for results. She wiped, and there it was, a spot of red. The burst to her bubble. Her period.

"No, no, no, this can't be," she said. "Damn it."

Her heart felt heavy. How could her period come when she had things so well planned? Of course, this was only their first few weeks of trying. David said it would probably take a month or two to get the birth control pill out of her system. But still, she really wanted this.

Disappointment annoyed her, like a swarm of gnats, easy enough to brush away.

Julia sat down on her bed, flicked on the television and ate her Kit Kat. At least the trip to the drug store was good for that.

David came home to find her lying on the bed, defeated.

"It's that time of the month again," she told him.

"I was afraid of that," he said. "Your 'little visitor' and dinner at your mother's house once a month usually coincide. I've always thought that was funny."

"Are you kidding?" Julia said smiling. "How did you figure that out?"

"They are the two things I look forward to least each month," he said, and gave her the half-head tilted smile that showed his playful side. She knew her mom made him a little crazy, but David loved her parents, especially her dad.

Julia sat upright, picked up the pillow she had been lying on and threw it at him. "And to think, I bought you something special today. For that, you will have to wait a whole week."

"Am I grounded?" he asked.

"Yes," she said. "You have one week to figure out how to make it up to me."

CHAPTER 8

Friday evening the couple knocked on the door of Julia's childhood home. When her dad opened the door, the smell of curry greeted them.

"There's my girl," he said and pulled Julia into a hug.

She loved it when it was her father who opened the door. It reminded her of her childhood when he'd come home from work. The door would open and his warm presence would fill the house like the smell of baking cookies. He'd always say something like, "Where are my girls?" And would find Beaty, Julia, and Savvy ready for a kiss.

When the girls were young, they'd wait eagerly for him to get home so that they could sit down to supper. They competed for his attention and acceptance. As the sisters grew, dinner started later and their conversations grew more mature. Somehow, Julia's dad had always been a beacon of stability in a house of hormones.

"Beaty's experimenting tonight," her father said, " and I'm so glad you are here. If one of us goes down we have back up."

"But won't we all be eating the same thing?" David asked, shaking his hand.

"Good point," Dad said. "We need a designated eater. Who's in?"

All three raised a hand and said "me" at the same time, then fell into laughter.

As they made their way toward the kitchen, , Julia fell

behind and watched her father put his hand on David's shoulder as he announced, "Beaty, look who I found on the front porch."

That gesture had always been part of the kindness that made James Meyers' character, like the way he loved to watch golf on television, hated guns, and winked at people with encouragement. He was the sort of man who loved through touch, letting those around him know it wasn't just their proximity that made them near. In James's dental practice, these qualities of comfort were especially welcome.

Julia had compared every man she dated to her father, wanting to find someone as much like him as possible. When David picked her up for their first official date and winked at her in the same reassuring way her father did, she knew he was a contender.

"Namaste, my darlings," Beaty said flamboyantly. "How are we this evening?"

"You look . . ." David said, pausing to find the right way to describe her attire, ". . . festive."

Beaty was wearing a traditional Indian sari, yards and yards of beautiful silk fabric in red and gold draped across one shoulder. Her hair was pulled back into a tight bun at the nape of her neck and she had a bindi in the middle of her forehead.

"Thank you, David," she said, kissing him on the cheek. "If you're going to cook Indian food, you had better go all the way."

"Wow, Mom," Julia said, entering the kitchen and glimpsing her mother. "That's actually pretty fantastic."

"I know!" she said, calling her truth as she saw it. "Now, that salad is not going to make itself."

Julia fell into the comfortable actions that transpired at every monthly dinner. She cut the tomatoes, cucumbers, and avocado and tossed them into the salad greens. Tonight, something new, her mother played energetic Indian music on her iPhone and moved her head rhythmically to the sound.

"You know, if I had known how concealing these saris are

I might have just stayed fat. The universe was smart not to introduce us till now."

"The universe introduced you?" Julia said with humor in her voice.

"The universe introduces us to all kinds of things, my darling. The universe introduced me to AA, don't you think?" Beaty said, seriously

The comment about Alcoholics Anonymous surprised Julia. She had never thought of her mother as an alcoholic. Beaty had started attending meetings when Julia was in her first year of college and, though she was still sober, had stopped going after two years. Savvy was still in high school when Beat announced her sobriety, and it was her sister who called to tell her the news.

"I think I saw more of it than you did," Savvy had said. "The drinking is what made her so uneven, why she would be so fun and loose one second and so angry the next."

For Julia it had been like the picture of her childhood had sharpened and everything in her past came into focus. She and her mother had always been so different, and as the distance between them opened, the reasons had grown more obvious.

Julia had never liked talking about AA. Several years ago, Beaty had asked Julia for coffee, a rarity, and had told her about the steps involved with getting sober. Beaty explained that in order to forgive herself she had to ask forgiveness from others. So her mother went down a long list of apologies she had and asked for Julia's forgiveness. It was given.

Listening to her mother's perspective on Julia's childhood had been a gritty and painful thing. She appreciated the sentiment but never wanted to revisit that moment again, especially now over dinner preparations and Indian music.

No doubt sensing Julia's hesitation, Beaty turned on a dime. "I told you about my dream. So you tell me. What was the sexy universe introducing with that one?. Julia wasn't ready to travel down this path either or walk back through the shards of her broken plans, especially while she dealing with the bloating, fatigue, and headache that came with her period.

"How's Savvy?"

"Funny you should ask. She called just a little bit ago and told me she wants to come to monthly dinner next month."

"She didn't say she is coming; she said she wants to," Julia admonished. "You know better than to expect her. There's no planning with Savvy; she just appears on your doorstep."

"Maybe she's finally finding her way," Beaty said, in an all-knowing voice more befitting a wise, wrinkled yogi than herself. Obviously she had not heard a word Julia had said.

Julia set the table as she was taught: fork on the left, knife and spoon on the right. Each piece of silverware perfectly square to the table's edge. Though the dish did not require each utensil, her mother had drilled into her the importance of proper etiquette. To this day, Julia never passed the salt without the pepper.

She watched her husband and father together through dinner—a lumpy, pale, orange-colored sauce over rice, and surprisingly good. Julia had always thought of her dad as just her dad. Not as a husband and the father of someone's children. Sure, it was semantics. But knowing that one day David would be in her father's position made her look at her own dad with new, more respectful eyes.

She wondered if her dad had posed the same question to her mom about starting a family? Or had it been her mother's idea to expand the Meyers clan?

When dinner was finished, everyone helped clear the table. The men retired to the back porch to drink a Bud Light while the women did the dishes. When her mom had first gone to meetings, there was not alcohol allowed in the house under any circumstance. But as Beaty learned her own limits, beer and wine were allowed in. Vodka had been her vice; the others had never tempted her.

This separation of males and females was an archaic display of roles that usually set Julia's skin on fire. But tonight she didn't mind, she wanted time alone with her mom.

"Life seems so easy for you and dad," Julia said with her hands in the warm, soapy water. "As long as I can remember, you'd cook and clean and he'd be in the backyard relaxing. It just doesn't seem to fit the rest of you."

"Honey, your father is the 'rest of me,'" Beaty said. "We found this pace long ago. But no. Oh, no. It hasn't always been easy."

Her father loved the traditional family structure but had married an eccentric woman who tried her best to blur the lines. Somewhere in the melding of their lives, she had fallen into the square of kitchen duty and found a way to add flair within that shape. A comfortable compromise, its importance need not be underestimated.

"Why do you ask?" her mother said, taking a dish from Julia and drying it.

"Just curious, I guess."

"Are things okay with you and David?"

"Yeah, they're great. Really great, actually," Julia said.

They washed in silence for a while. Scraping the left over curry into the drain on the left side of the sink, submerging the plate into the water in the right, scrubbing it clean, rinsing it, drying and replacing it in the cupboard. The sounds of each step mingling with the music, creating the rhythm of real life.

The years of Julia being out of the house had made her relationship with her mother stronger. Through her late teenage years, just before leaving for college, they had fought almost daily. Julia wanting a few dollars to go to the movies and more freedom. Her mother demanded an early curfew and a summer job.

Ten years ago, this very dish-cleaning scene had turned into one of their biggest battles. Julia asked to borrow the car for the night, and Beaty said no, though she had often let her do it before. Then Savvy came in and told their mother that Julia had taken five dollars from their dad's wallet—the tattletale. The eruption was epic. Julia remembered a plate, broken in anger and aggression, lying on the floor in pieces.

Looking back, Julia knew her mom had been drinking and was unstable, but the shame Julia felt when the plate shattered was still engraved in her mind. It had been the only time Julia ever stole.

As the years passed, Julia grew sensible like her father, and Savvy modeled their mother, the rebellious one. Now it seemed her mother had grown even more flamboyant. What middle-American woman in her fifties wears a sari to supper?

"One of our biggest fights was about you, Honey," Beaty said as the women finished the dishes.

"Me?" Julia asked pouring herself a glass of wine.

"Yep. I hope you don't take this wrong, but we didn't plan for you," she said.

Julia furrowed her brow in question. She had never heard this before.

"We didn't think we were ready for children, but the pill wasn't something everyone used in those days. We found out you were on your way a month after our honeymoon. I blamed James for not being responsible with his sperm, and he blamed me for not taking proper precautions. We were so angry with each other that we didn't speak for almost a week. We slammed dishes and closed doors too loudly. We let our anger be a physical presence in the room. It got so bad that I stayed with your grandfather for a few nights."

Beaty sipped her ice water, putting herself back in that moment.

"He was so good to me, your grandfather. He never asked me what was going on. Never asked about James. He just let me be."

"How did you get over it?"

Julia had a million questions but started simple.

"One night your grandfather came into my old room and sat on the edge of the bed. It was late, but I had been up crying. Hormones are terrible when you're pregnant and worse when you've been fighting with your new husband. He put his hands on mine and told me he wished my mother was here to help.

He apologized that she'd run off, and he said something about it being so important for family to be there for one another."

It had been so long since anyone had brought up Beaty's mom that Julia had almost forgotten about her. In fact, her grandmother was so distant that Julia didn't even know her name. Beaty had been nine years old when her mother left. Julia was told that her grandmother had made bad choices and leaving the family had been the one good thing she did for her daughter.

As Julia grew up, the specifics of these "bad choices" expanded in her mind like freezing water. In her childhood, she assumed they had been telling lies, writing on the wall, or saying a curse word. In her teens, she longed for details. She wondered if her grandmother had been with other men or had fallen into drugs. During college, Julia assumed Beaty's mom had been an alcoholic since the genetic link is so strong. Now, however, she didn't need to know to understand the lessons of her mysterious grandmother's mistakes.

Perhaps a legacy from her mother, Beaty had always felt the impulse to run free like a mustang. But her father helped her tame that vivacious spirit. Years ago, Beaty too must have had a choice—wild and dangerous or safe in the stable.

Julia's legacy was a vow never to make "bad choices" that would ruin her family.

Julia assumed her mother must have grown into that same understanding and made a similar vow. Julia hoped her wild younger sister would do the same. Beaty was determined to keep her family close to her heart if not close to home. It was the reason for their monthly dinner.

Julia studied her mother—her sari alive with color and light, her kitchen immaculate. Fresh lipstick fought a cosmetic battle against the age beginning to show in the darkened puffy areas under her eyes. The polarity of her personality traits was like a blend of cigarette smoke and perfume, distinct and contrasting yet blending in a single familiar aroma.

"What did you do?" Julia asked.

"I realized we'd be a family instead of a couple," Beaty said with the shimmer of tears in her eyes. "It was a beautiful understanding. Your father and I forgave each other."

"So you weren't expecting a baby and it just happened?"

"Yes," her mother said. "And now it's your turn."

"We'll see," Julia said and hugged her mother.

On the drive home, Julia's heart was warm. She felt relaxed at learning how easily her mother had gotten pregnant. While she had her father's personality, she had her mother's body, and maybe its performance would be similar too.

She reached for David's hand and squeezed. This is going to be great, she thought.

CHAPTER 9

The phone was in Julia's hand, the number had been dialed, but she couldn't bring herself to hit SEND. They'll think I'm stupid, she thought.

As her body had recovered from the effects of the birth control pills, her period had alternated on and off and on for almost four weeks, like some annoying tennis match. As soon as she thought it was finally over, back it came heavier than before. She didn't want to go to the doctor and tell him that she hated her period. What woman didn't hate her period? But she had started to grow concerned and wanted the comfort only a medical professional could provide.

After the second week of her period, she did a bit of research on the Internet, despite knowing it could be dangerously misleading. She worked in the medical field and often saw people misdiagnosing and mistreating their supposedly fatal illnesses. Online a person can find all kinds of terrible disorders and diseases to match a symptom or two.

The most realistic thing she read was in a chat room where a woman said her period was all over the place after she stopped the pill. The woman's general practitioner had prescribed a medication called Clomid, which regulated her period and encouraged conception.

Among the chat room responses someone recommended charting your flow—it's length of time, symptoms, spotting, everything. Julia learned there are even apps available for her phone to calculate her cycle and symptoms.

Problem was, she couldn't imagine doing such a thing. She'd be mortified if David saw her chart. What if he was so disgusted by the truth about a woman's body, her body, that he'd never want to touch her again. That he could never again find her sexy. That black nightie would stay in the closet, tethered to its price tag, unused forever. She wasn't willing to risk it.

Now, however, almost a month had passed with no relief.

She took a deep breath and pressed SEND.

"Dr. Lamont's office," said a woman's voice. "How may I help you?"

"Um, hi," Julia said, not sure where to start. "I have a question for the nurse, is that okay?"

"Of course," said the woman. "I'm one of Dr. Lamont's nurses, how can I help you?"

"Oh really, wow. I thought I'd get a recording or something." Why was she so nervous?

"It's your lucky day," the woman said. "How can I help?"

"Well, I, um . . . I have been having my period for a really long time and I um . . . just want to make sure that is okay?" She paced the kitchen. Why was she being so childish?

"When did you begin to menstruate?" asked the woman, casually, as if asking the time of day.

"Right," Julia said. "Like four weeks ago." I sound like a Valley Girl, she thought to herself. What an idiot.

"Well, that doesn't sound like much fun. To pull your chart I'll need your name and birthday."

Julia gave the information, grateful she didn't botch that too.

"Let me put you on hold for a moment."

"Thanks," Julia said.

The hold music, some sickly-sweet orchestra tune, annoyed her instantly. She had never felt at ease with this kind of music because it was intended to do exactly that. How could a person possibly relax when they were being told do so? It was like telling someone not to smile—it's the first thing they'll do. The least they could do would be to play classic rock so you could sing along instead of counting the seconds like a metronome.

"Mrs. Ellis?" asked the nurse, surprising Julia from her thoughts.

"Yes, I'm here."

"I see from your chart that you haven't been in to see us for almost three years."

Here comes the guilt trip. Maybe subconsciously that was why she was nervous. She'd had no reason to go in for an annual. In fact, she didn't even have a regular doctor. She just didn't get sick. She was young and healthy, and she didn't need someone violating her private parts to prove her vitality.

"Has it really been that long?" Julia asked, faking shock.

"Dr. Lamont will want to see you to discuss your prolonged period. How about two weeks from tomorrow at two o'clock. Can you make that?"

"Sure," she said, thinking that if this period lasted that long she might die. "See you then."

When Julia hung up, she called Sarah and arranged lunch. If Sarah was good for one thing, it was making her laugh.

At lunch, when Julia mentioned she was going to the OB/GYN, Sarah shared the most hilarious cautionary tale.

"It was female lore," Sarah said, "that a woman had to visit the gyno and was super nervous about her appointment. Not only did this woman hate the pain of the Pap but she hated exposing herself to the cutest doctor to ever graduate medical school. So, after dropping her daughters off at school, she rushed home to do a quick freshen up. She found a washcloth next to the sink and wiped down, changed into cuter panties and ran out the door.

"The small talk was over and the doctor had her feet in the stirrups when he said, 'This is a first.'"

Julia looked at Sarah worried, wondering where this story was going.

"The woman sat up and looked at the doctor over the sheet. 'What's wrong,' she said.

"'I've never seen quite so much glitter before,' the doctor said.

"It turned out, her daughter had used the washcloth that morning to clean up an arts and crafts spill."

Sarah hit the table in a whoop of laughter.

When Julia finally stopped giggling she said, "I would take glitter over this long period any day."

"Really," Sarah said. "The red river over embarrassment. How long has it been?"

Julia told her and then said, "It's so frustrating to have this big family plan and no way to make it happen."

"Speaking of making it happen," Sarah said, "I got you something."

"More gifts? If I knew I was going to be getting all these gifts, I would have started this process a long time ago."

"This is just a loaner, my friend. You may not have this forever. I want it back."

"I'm intrigued."

"Come on. It's in my car."

The women left the restaurant and walked to Sarah's car. Sarah held the gift behind her back, making Julia promise she'd read it and then give it back immediately. Julia agreed to the terms, and Sarah held out a gold-wrapped book like the crowning jewel of the Queen's collection. Julia opened it—Fifty Shades of Grey.

"This will liberate you," Sarah said with a smile. "Now call me after chapter nine. You won't be able to put it down before then."

CHAPTER 10

Julia had a theory that the perfect remedy for a head cold was to call the doctor. Not because of any prescription the doctor would write, but because by the time the doctor could actually see you, your cough would have magically subsided and your fever remarkably disappeared, leading the doctor to think you were a hypochondriac.

The same proved to be true with her period. Had she thought about it sooner, she would have called Dr. Lamont ages ago. After an entire week without her Aunt Flow, her least favorite relative, she phoned the OB/GYN office to cancel.

The nurse she had spoken to last time told her the cancellation was no problem but did recommend she come in for her annual. Together, they scheduled a date five months into the future.

"I'll go ahead and make a note in your chart that you've stopped taking the birth control pill Dr. Lamont prescribed for you in order to attempt conception," the nurse said.

"Okay," Julia said, taken aback once again by the direct nature of clinical talk.

"Good luck, Mrs. Ellis," the nurse said. Julia could almost picture her winking.

Hanging up, Julia said a silent prayer of hope that in five months she'd be seeing her gynecologist for an ultrasound and not a Pap.

Giving Julia Fifty Shades after their lunch, Sarah had

specifically told her not to open it till her period was gone. "No sense getting all worked up and not be able to scratch the itch," she had said.

Now free of restrictions, Julia opened the first page with reluctance. She honestly found the writing poor and the story lacking depth, though she would never tell Sarah this. She quickly grew tired of reading about Christian Grey's unreadable face. You're an author for goodness' sake, read his face a little, she thought. But the suggestive scenes were written with vivid color. Julia pictured the author as a stripper turned housewife and writer. Maybe she could only properly write the detailed seductions because that is what she knew best. Julia promised herself she wouldn't critique the words but enjoy their intent.

And it worked. Her affair with David started with the black nightie, which had been neatly folded, wrapped in tissue paper, and sitting in a pink bag for well over a month, and ended in two sweaty, satisfied bodies intertwined as one. She had allowed herself to be free and to enjoy her husband's touch, setting aside the thought of trying to conceive. But now as they lay together she realized that David hadn't brought it up since the start of her period so many weeks ago. Had he forgotten, or changed his mind?

"Okay, so here's the thing," Julia said to Sarah over their salads at Ringo's. "I've read your book. And the next one. And the next one . . . and they work!" Julia pretended to fan herself as if trying to cool down.

There was no one in the world she could tell this to except Sarah. Julia had grown up in a house of women, but closed doors were mandatory for all things feminine. These days, her mother was this tree-hugging free spirit who'd probably welcome nudity and talk about the birds and the bees. But growing up, Julia had been taught to be more prudish, and changing that attitude wouldn't be all that easy.

Sarah was comfortable with her body in a way that Julia envied. Once when they had been bathing suit shopping, Sarah joined her in the dressing room. Julia had kept her underwear on and turned her back as she slid the one piece over her bust. Sarah had stripped down to nothing, oblivious to the shock her nudity had on her friend. Sarah exposed her entire body like it was nothing more than taking off her shoes and going barefoot.

Julia couldn't blame her. She had a beautiful, fit body. Her stomach showed no sign of her past pregnancy, and her limbs were lean and long. Julia hated to have looked, but her friend really was stunning.

Not only was Sarah unafraid to be naked, she also loved to talk about sex. Julia knew more about what Sarah liked in the bedroom than what David liked. While he quietly moaned when she did something right, Sarah shared details that would make a man's toes curl.

"Spill it, my friend. You know how I adore the fun stuff," Sarah said.

Julia took a bite of lettuce and glanced around the restaurant. Mostly it was people in business attire discussing work, and there were a couple of women in the corner booth trying to have a conversation while tending to their toddlers, cutting their food into tiny pieces and helping hold their cups.

"It's fun, but that's not it," Julia said, letting her head drop a bit. "It's that it's not working."

"What's not working?"

"The sex," she said, louder than intended. "We have sex all the time, and it is fun and fresh, but it's been four months and we still aren't pregnant."

Sarah was silent, which Julia took to indicate she should continue.

"I see babies everywhere now. They're always at the Health Department. They're at every grocery store and park. They're right over there in the corner booth. It breaks my heart. I'm going to have to start living in a bar so I'm not constantly reminded how NOT pregnant I am."

Sarah sat quietly, letting Julia talk.

"You know, at first I was on the fence about becoming a mother, but the more time has passed the more I want it. It's all I think about. It's starting to become an obsession. Do you think I am crazy? I mean it's been four months." She exaggerated the number four, hoping Sarah would feel her anxiety.

That's when the tears started to fall. They came from nowhere, which had been happening lately. She found herself crying in the shower after David left for work. She didn't want to freak him out, but she was beginning to worry about their ability to get pregnant and what that would mean for their future.

Without the pill to regulate her, Julia had all these crazy hormones making her overly emotional, so much so that a commercial on the radio offering help for drug abuse actually made her cry.

"Oh, honey," Sarah finally said. "I wanted this to be a happy lunch. I didn't realize you were so upset."

"Me either, actually," Julia said, blotting her eyes with her napkin while trying not to smudge her mascara. "I just don't want to be like those chicks on TV. You know, the ones on that MTV reality show. I mean, what if this doesn't work. You've seen what those women go through. What if I'm just like them? What if we can't have kids? What if David has some medical problem. What if I do? I mean, what if he leaves me because we can't have kids? You hear about that, right?"

"Okay, you are not on True Life. And really, we need to introduce you to more mature programming. It has only been four months," Sarah said, and then fell silent.

Julia knew the woman across the table from her like she knew every episode of Friends, with deep love and by heart. She could tell from the silence that something was going on. Sarah would usually have some snappy remark that would make her laugh and shed some kind of remarkably uplifting light on the situation. Instead she was sitting in the booth moving the tomatoes around the dressing in her salad with her fork.

An uneasy feeling grew in Julia's chest. It started as a pinprick and slowly radiated out like spokes of a bicycle wheel, heating her insides. The feeling grew until a foul taste filled her mouth and dried her tongue. Realizing she was holding her breath, she released.

"What do you have to tell me?" Julia asked as she flattened her eyes.

"Now is not the time," Sarah said.

"You're pregnant, aren't you?" Julia said.

Sarah set down her fork and looked Julia in the eye. "Yes, I am," Sarah said, leaving no room in her voice for apology or joy. "We'd been toying around with the idea for a while now. With Joshua being three and with you trying too, we thought now would be the perfect time. I got off the pill last month."

Julia felt like she had been stabbed as the pain in her chest continued to expand.

"You know how fertile I am," Sarah offered as a consolation, trying to lighten the darkness that had fallen on Julia.

She took a drink of water to regroup. This is Sarah's big news, not your disaster, she told herself. You need to pull it together.

As she took the glass from her lips, Julia smiled. Sarah had the glow. How had she missed it? She had also ordered water instead of sweet tea. The signs were all around, and Julia had allowed herself to be blindsided.

Julia stood up from the booth and reached for her friend. "Well get up here and hug me already. This is wonderful news."

Julia turned to the restaurant and announced, "This is my friend Sarah, and she is going to have a baby!"

A plate of chocolate cake and the bill were placed on the table. "Congratulations," the waitress said to Sarah. "The cake is on the house."

The women had little time to talk as they synchronized their bites of the shared desert. When the last of the cake was gone, Sarah put her credit card on the bill.

Julia removed Sarah's card and put hers in its place. "I've

got this. Please. It's my treat," she said.

Sarah squeezed tighter than usual as the women hugged goodbye. Julia knew this was an act of kindness, maybe even apology. But Julia didn't want any of it. She did the best she could to lightly tap the back of her friend and then escape to the solitude of her car.

That was not how this was supposed to go, she thought to herself as she pulled away from the restaurant.

Julia picked up her phone, "David, it's me. Grab a box of wine on your way home. Sarah's pregnant."

CHAPTER 11

The rest of Julia's day moved like molasses. She busied herself with tasks that required little thought and looked forward to the haven her home would provide. At five o'clock she grabbed her purse and took her leave.

When she pulled into the garage at home, she turned off the car and rested her head against the steering wheel. Without looking she pressed the button on the console to close the garage door.

In the dark of the garage she let sadness melt into her, transforming from an distinct emotion to a part of the whole, blending into her essence. It had taken Sarah only one month to get pregnant. Her mother hadn't even wanted to get pregnant and it happened. And now here Julia was failing yet again.

She failed at losing weight. And now this. Just one more big failure.

She cried on the steering wheel until relief came. When the tears finally stopped, abruptly like a water hose had been pinched, she went inside.

She lit the grill and seasoned the pork chops that she had taken from the fridge. She sliced vegetables and started a pot of rice. She wanted none of it.

At six o'clock David walked in the door carrying a bouquet of flowers he obviously picked up from the grocery store—ridiculously dyed long-stem daisies so vibrant that nature herself would never have made such an obnoxious flower.

"Thanks," she said and continued to stare at the boiling rice.

"Wait here," he said after kissing her on the cheek. "I have a few more things in the car."

He came back carrying a handful of bags and a box of red wine.

"What is all of this?" Julia asked, not masking the annoyance in her voice. "I just went to the grocery store yesterday."

"Jules, I know this Sarah thing sucks for you, so we are celebrating your un-pregnancy."

The sinking feeling returned to her chest, heavy and unwelcome. Her shoulders sagged and she felt tears nearing the surface.

She never understood men. It was like they wanted to slip into a mess with a fast fix and then wipe their hands on their shirt with satisfaction. It was all problem meets solution. Period. No emotion involved, no "what ifs?" or "how comes?. Usually she'd talk to Sarah when something hurt her this deeply. They'd sit on the floor with a box of Kleenex and a chai latte until, three hours later, they decided the world would continue to spin. But, of course, she couldn't call Sarah this time.

"Wait, wait," David said. "Before you think I ruined this, hear me out. We've been so caught up in getting pregnant, we've forgotten to be married. We forgot to celebrate the life we have now. So . . ."

He waved his hands at the grocery bags displaying them like Vanna White on Wheel of Fortune.

From one bag he took out cheese, lunchmeat, a Kit Kat bar, hair dye, and a package of cigarettes. From another bag he produced Styrofoam boxes with take-out from their favorite sushi restaurant.

"Voila," he said, as if everything should now be crystal clear.

"Voila what?" Julia asked, unable to keep her eyes off the pack of cigarettes. Neither of them had smoked since giving it the old college try. Back in the day they both claimed to smoke when drinking, but it was never a full truth. Really they just smoked to fit in, to be where their friends were. The smell on her clothes the following morning always left Julia more nauseated than the hangover. Now, however, she longed for a drag.

"These are all the things YOU can do that Sarah can't."

He held up the cheese. "Unpasteurized cheese is a pregnancy sin, and apparently so is lunch meat. So we will have that for an appetizer while we guzzle this box of wine. Then we will eat the sushi . . ."

"How do you know all of this?" Julia interrupted before he could finish.

"Brian complained about it all the time when Eve was pregnant. If she wasn't allowed to eat something, she didn't let him eat it either," he said. Brian had been David's best man and was recently a new father. It was obvious who wore the pants in their family.

The last time the couples spent time together, Julia had asked David, "How does Brian seem?. And David just said "fine."

She was looking for details about how he was doing since he lost his job and how they were dealing with the new baby. When she probed for more, David said, "Brian said it sucks, but the baby's good." And that was it.

Julia always pictured two-word-sentence exchanges between the friends, but apparently there had been a deeper conversation that she was not privy to.

"I called Ho at the sushi place," David continued, "and told him to make us two of whatever was on special and toss in some salmon sashimi. When our bellies are full, we're going to eat that Kit Kat bar in the hot tub while smoking a cigarette!"

She laughed at his enthusiasm and the display laid before her. "And the pink hair dye?"

"Is it really pink?" he blurted a laugh and grabbed for the box. "I was a little embarrassed standing in that aisle so I just grabbed the box on the corner and high-tailed it out of there. We can do it if you want!"

"Thank you," she said, grabbing the collar of his shirt pulling him to her lips. Kissing him feverishly, she walked backwards, leading him to the bedroom.

Two hours later, they were satisfied both in body and stomach, sitting in the hot tub trying to blow smoke rings into the night sky.

"Are Kit Kat bars really on the shunned list?" Julia asked.

"Something about not eating empty calories because of a smaller stomach. I don't know."

"Sounds like bullshit to me," she said, taking a bite.

The summer air mixed with the steam rising from the tub. They usually ignored the hot tub in the warm months, but she relished the relaxing feeling that surrounded her tonight. She leaned into the crook of his arm, and they looked up at the unfathomable expanse above them. The sound of water jets and bubbles bursting helped Julia escape.

Stars had always been a steadying calm for her. The lights from the heavens reminding her there was more than she could see, more than she knew.

And why didn't she know more? Why had she chosen to love these stars without getting to know them? She could point to the Big Dipper but couldn't always find the little one. She knew some of those stars could be planets but didn't know which. She noticed that a few seemed to sparkle boldly while others maintained a steady glow. She assumed these steady lights were the planets, but it was only a guess.

She loved to find one star, bright against the dark sky, and concentrate all her attention on that small point. She loved the way the other stars slowly dissolved from her field of vision leaving just the one to perform its dance—a flickering melody of red and blue and white. Julia thought they looked like the lights atop a police car interrupting the perfect blackness. Only these were minuscule, requiring patience and concentration to discover—a difference worth thought.

Julia loved the contemplation of stars. Their existence left her with two distinct options. Either feel drawn in as a crucial part of the great creation, wholly important as a contributing member of the process of life and growth and death, knowing as fact that God created all things, including her, thereby giving her purpose.

Or, Julia thought, feel simply insignificant, a grain of sand on a beach, one tiny trivial piece whose existence is neither important nor substantial.

While the latter option may be a more bleak perspective, it allowed Julia relief from the pressure she put on herself. The importance of errands and the all-consuming conversations about work dissolved as she contemplated the purpose and relevance of life.

Julia thought she could never experience both emotions at the same time. She lived her life as if the world's ability to function depended on her achievements. But here in the hot tub, she was able to set her compass on a new direction, even if only temporarily.

And the moon. Oh, that beautiful moon, a celestial symbol of reliable change. What a contradiction. Why had she never purchased a simple telescope? Why had she not bought a book or Googled the most basic information?

Comfort in the unknown, Julia thought to herself, and settled more deeply into David's arm.

The way she felt about the stars above was the way she felt about a lot of things in her life. She loved art but couldn't intelligently discuss anything about style or artists. She loved to travel but didn't know much about different cultures or even how to really read maps. She wanted to know a foreign language but had never purchased Rosetta Stone. And she wanted to be a runner.

Sarah was a runner. She had a beautiful body and a vivacious way that Julia had always admired. Those things must be in part due to running. Of all the proverbial stars she could grab, this one might be attainable in the short term.

"What if I started running?" Julia said, breaking the silent darkness.

"Right now?" David said. "Where are you going?"

"I'm serious," she said, smacking him playfully on the chest. "Maybe I could be a runner. They have apps for everything."

"You mean like a 5k," David asked

"I guess," Julia said. "How far is that?"

"The perfect distance to get started," David said. "Go for it."

And she would. When they got out of the tub she would 'go for it.' She'd find an app and start the day after tomorrow . . . when the wine headache she was sure to have had faded away.

CHAPTER 12

And she was right, the wine took a toll. Sarah was still pregnant, she wasn't, and now she had a hangover to battle. Wine in a box may not have been the best solution to tears, but the time under the stars had proven therapeutic.

Before work, Julia stopped by Flavors. Savoring the smell of coffee, she nodded to the gray-haired man in the pageboy hat and noticed Yvette among a group at a table near him.

"Yvette," Julia said, approaching the women. "How are you?"

Yvette was in a summer dress, still carrying the baby weight, but it had only been three months since Charleston was born. A formal sounding name, it was chosen because Yvette had a love for everything South Carolina. The poor kid could have been named Columbia or Greenville. Or worse yet, he could have been called Cocky after the University of South Carolina gamecock mascot. Yvette had gone to school there on a partial music scholarship. Her parents agreed to pay the remainder of her tuition only after forcing Yvette to promise she'd return home after receiving her degree.

Yvette had kept her promise but not before marrying a South Carolina man and convincing him to move with her. He was . youth pastor with the southern accent to pull off the phrase "all ya'll." Yvette was the church's music director.

Charleston sat beside the table in a blue gingham carrier, oblivious to the talking people, the scream of the milk steamer, and the grind of the beans.

Julia took a quick look at the boy but didn't allow her eyes to linger. She wouldn't do that to herself today.

"Jules, I was just talking about you," Yvette said. "Girls, this is Julia Ellis, the one I was talking about."

Feigning shock, but actually a little uneasy at the introduction, she deflected. "You were telling them about how much I look like Heidi Klum?"

The ladies laughed and one gestured to an available chair, which Julia took.

"These are my Bible Study friends," Yvette said. "We started a study two weeks ago, and I was just telling them how much I wish you'd join us."

Bible Study and Julia Ellis did not go hand-in-hand. She and David would show up for church from time to time, but a Bible Study was more religion than she wanted to sign up for.

"That is so nice of you," Julia said. "Maybe next time."

She visited with the women for a while and then excused herself for work.

Yvette walked her out. "I haven't seen you in a while. How have you been? I miss you."

"I miss you too," Julia said. Yvette was a good friend with a kind heart, and Julia really needed to reach out to her more. But she wasn't sure she had the emotional strength to be around a swooning new mom.

"Last week we discussed the most amazing story, and for some reason the whole way home I couldn't stop thinking about you," Yvette said. "Does that ever happen to you?"

Julia flashed back to the morning her mother called her. Maybe people really did think of others and act on it. "Sometimes. What was the story?"

"It was Matthew 20," she said as if everyone knew the story. When Julia gave her a blank look, Yvette said, "Look it up when you get a chance."

"Okay, I will," Julia promised, knowing the chances were slim. "Call me and we'll have lunch next week."

They hugged their goodbyes, and Julia looked down at Charleston. Julia tilted her head and her heart filled with an envious love.

Work passed with ease—an uneventful Friday was usually a good thing. But today, the scripture Matthew 20 wouldn't leave her mind.

At the end of the workday, Julia reluctantly opened Google and typed the scripture into the query. She clicked on the link to BibleGateway, found the "easy-to-read version," and clicked on it.

The passage's title, "Jesus Uses a Story About Farm Workers," had Julia second-guessing her decision to read. To Julia, the Bible held all kind of hidden truths, but she didn't know how to uncover most of them. There were stories to live by and stories to grow within, but she needed wisdom and training from the pastor to give the words meaning and life. Honestly, all the effort hadn't seemed worth it. Trying to read the Bible usually left her feeling ignorant and shallow, so she did her best to avoid it whenever possible.

Against her better judgment, Julia read:

God's kingdom is like a man who owned some land. One morning, the man went out very early to hire some people to work in his vineyard. He agreed to pay the workers one silver coin for working that day. Then he sent them into the vineyard to work. About nine o'clock the man went to the marketplace and saw some other people standing there. They were doing nothing. So he said to them, "If you go and work in my field, I will pay you what your work is worth." So they went to work in the vineyard. The man went out again about twelve o'clock and again at three o'clock. Both times he hired some others to work in his vineyard. About five o'clock the man went to the marketplace again. He saw some other people standing there. He asked them, "Why did you stand here all day doing nothing?. They said, "No one gave us a job." The man said to them, "Then you can go and work in my vineyard." At the end of the day, the owner of the field said to the boss of all the workers, "Call the workers and pay them all. Start by paying the last people I hired. Then pay all of them, ending with the ones I hired first. The workers who were hired at five o'clock came to get their pay. Each worker got one silver coin. Then the workers who were hired first came to get their pay. They thought they would be paid more than the others. But each one of them also received one silver coin. When they got their silver coin, they complained to the man who owned the land. They said, "Those people were hired last and worked only one hour. But you paid them the same as us. And we worked hard all day in the hot sun." But the man who owned the field said to one of them, "Friend, I am being fair with you. You agreed to work for one silver coin. Right. So take your pay and go. I want to give the man who was hired last the same pay I gave you. I can do what I want with my own money. Why would you be jealous because I am generous?"

"Why would you be jealous because I am generous?" Julia repeated out loud. "Jealous because I am generous."

The pain in her chest felt like a heart attack. No wonder Yvette had thought of her. These were the words she needed to hear. The universe was closing in all around her, but she couldn't decide if it wanted to enfold her into its breast in a protective embrace or smother the life out of her. First, her mother called with the "feeling," and now Yvette did the same. Was she being cradled by a knowing and understanding God or crushed by the weight of people knowing too much and trying to help.

The perspective was Julia's choice. Right now, she wasn't sure which she'd choose.

She wasn't sure of much, but she was positive she needed a deep breath. She got in her car and cranked up the '90s on 9 channel on her XM radio. Nothing cleared a girl's head like the sound of old-school music.

The August day was hot, and something pulled her to the lake. She drove down the tree-shadowed lane until a dock appeared and she pulled over. Leaving the car running and the radio singing TLC's "No, I don't want your number. No, I don't want to give you mine . . ." she opened the door and stepped out, shading her eyes.

When her foot hit the ground, it wasn't gravel beneath her feet but fireworks. They must have been set off for Fourth of July and never cleaned up.

Julia bent down and picked up the small black tube. She could just make out the image of the angry cat. A black cat. Her least favorite of all the fireworks. What was the point of a loud explosion with nothing visually exciting? Intended not to be enjoyed but to scare someone into covering his ears. It had always seemed like a cruel way to celebrate.

She thought of Sarah and knew what she needed to do.

Julia knocked on the door of her best friend's house with a gift in hand. Joshua answered the door, and when he recognized Julia his smile grew. He hugged her legs saying, "Aunt Jules, I'm gonna be a big brother."

"Is that right?" she said bending down to rub the three year old's little back.

"Yep, and I have a new dinosaur to prove it," he said, taking her by the hand and leading her into the house. "Mom, Aunt Jules came over to play with me," he yelled toward the kitchen.

"Give me a second with your mom, and I'll be right there to see your dinosaur. Okay?" Julia said.

"Okay," he said, looking toward the ground. His demeanor changed suddenly, "I'll go tell them not to eat you when you come in." And he ran down the hallway out of sight.

Julia found her friend in the kitchen and hugged her tightly. Taking a deep breath within their embrace, Julia forgave herself for her jealousy toward her dear friend. I have been jealous because He has been generous.

"I brought you something," Julia said. Many years ago she had read the book The Five Love Languages. The book taught her it was best to love people in a language they could understand. While Julia thought her "love language" was "quality time," and knew her dad's was "physical touch," Sarah's language was definitely "gifts."

Pulling the tissue paper from the small gift bag, Sarah unwrapped the black cat. She looked at Julia not understanding. "There's more," Julia said, encouraging her friend to dig through the rest of the gift bag.

Sarah revealed a pair tiny blue socks.

"When you announced you were pregnant yesterday," she said, "I blew up." Julia held up the firework. "I am so, so, so happy that you are going to have a baby. If this one is anything like Joshua, you will be so lucky."

Sarah wiped a tear and hugged her friend again. "I love you."

"I love you, too," Julia said. "Now, let's go play dinosaurs."

When Joshua let his mother and "aunt" to leave his dinosaur domain, they sat at the kitchen table drinking a glass of water waiting for their husbands to join them.

Sarah had stopped making dinner and called John, her husband, to pick up something for the Ellis clan too. An impromptu dinner party was just what they all needed to steady the waters churned up by Sarah's pregnancy.

CHAPTER 13

Sarah was surprised to learn that David and Julia weren't doing anything to try to get pregnant, other than having sex. "There is so much more than just sex involved," she said.

"I was just hoping it would happen naturally," Julia admitted.

"It still can, you just have to decide what 'naturally' means to you," Sarah said.

"What does that mean?" In Julia's mind "naturally" had no grayscale. It was the simple act of a man and woman coming together, end of story.

"When I went off the pill, I took Robitussin every day. It's supposed to thin your mucus," Sarah said and Julia made a face of surprise mixed with disgust. "Don't make that face. I also stopped drinking caffeine and switched John from boxer briefs to boxers. I also put a pillow under my butt after every time we had sex."

"Huh," Julia said, mentally taking copious notes but not letting on how desperately she wanted to know more. She should have done more research on this. She should have started all this stuff the second David proposed making a family. Like with the stars, she had been comfortable in her ignorance to the point of being negligent.

When Julia and David got home that evening, Julia bought an app for running. She liked the plan in the app store that read "30 minutes a day, 3 days a week, 9 weeks equals 5K ready." She liked formulas, they were predictable. She was sure she could do this.

Then, sitting down at her computer, she typed in "help getting pregnant." She couldn't believe all the links that popped up—"8 ways to boost your fertility," "get pregnant faster," "12 ideas to help you get pregnant now," "how to get pregnant by the Mayo Clinic," and on and on and on. Everyone had a remedy, a quick fix. She rolled her eyes at herself for not doing this earlier and for falling for the same kind of marketing she had when she bought the running app. Julia knew she couldn't improve herself with a quick formula, but she was damn sure going to try.

Frozen by information overload, she was unable to click on a single link. She stared at the number at the top of the page—"Results 280,000,000." After her first run tomorrow, she would jump into this. She'd make a pro and con Word document with all the best things to do and everything she should stop doing. She would checklist her way to pregnancy, just as she had checklisted her way through college and into her job.

Yes, David had made fun of all this last night, but if she was going to have a family, she was going to pull her head out of the sand and get proactive.

Waking up early with David the following morning, she laced up her sneakers and popped in her headphones. If she was going to run, she was going to do it with some loud rock music that would drown out the sound of her heavy breathing, the reminder of her painful exertion.

The run-some, walk-some program the app outlined made Julia feel like this was not the insurmountable task she had thought it would be. She remembered back to her freshman year of college. She had called her mom in tears, unsure she could handle the stress and the load that the university was putting on her. Beaty asked the most ridiculous question, "Honey, how do you eat an elephant?"

Oh Lord, she's drunk, Julia thought, enraged. I'm coming to her for encouragement, and all she does is tell stupid joke. Julia gave in, "I don't know, Mom. How?"

"One bite at a time."

Maybe Julia could conquer this running challenge just as she had conquered college, one bite at a time.

Wiping the sweat from her forehead with the kitchen towel, she noticed the box of pink hair dye still on the counter from the celebration days earlier. Marching into the bathroom, she chose a section of hair behind her left ear thinking it could stay hidden when she was at work. Following the directions on the box she colored the strands, feeling empowered by her new choices.

Julia had rearranged herself these last few weeks. She discovered decaf tea and scaled back the wine, hated waking up early but kept running, included diet beans, olive oil and spinach in her diet to help her ovulation, and added whole wheat bread to help with insulin levels. David still refused to wear boxer shorts, claiming that they bunched in his slacks and made him look like he had a bulge in his pants.

She prayed this would be the month the beautiful pink plus sign would appear on her pregnancy test—the last of her original three-pack. When she had bought the test six months ago, she at first didn't realize they came three to a pack. Multiple tests in one package had seemed bizarre back then, but if this test proved positive, she'd go and get another three-pack for as much reassurance as she could get. Hell, it if was positive she'd probably save the first one to hang on the Christmas tree. Wonder what David's mother would think of that, she thought with a light heart.

Julia planned to use the final test in three days. And the third day couldn't come fast enough.

So as not to jinx the pregnancy, she'd buy an ovulation kit in the meantime. Every how to site she looked up talked about the importance of understanding your ovulation. What was once simple chemistry between man and woman had now become hormone science.

She had a hunch that this was going to be the month. Her emotions had been all over the place. She snapped at David for not changing the batteries on the television remote. She could have done it herself, but she had specifically asked him. When two days went by and the remote was still useless, she lost it. The conversation ended with Julia slamming the door. Her apology was as sad as her anger had been deep. Surely this kaleidoscope of emotions was a sign of pregnancy.

At the grocery store, she fiddled with the pink streak in her hair as she stood in front of the feminine hygiene products aisle once again. The streak did its job, reminding her that she was going to kick this pregnancy situation with a bit of muscle and will power.

Julia wanted to call Sarah. She wanted her best friend to talk her though this, to make her laugh, to give her encouragement. But she didn't want to remind herself of Sarah's luck and her own misfortune. If their friendship was going to survive this divide, Julia would have to act as if nothing had changed. Julia dialed Sarah's number.

"Hey, I'm in the feminine hygiene section," Julia whispered into her phone. She didn't want the other shoppers to overhear.

"What a freakin' dumb name for a section," Sarah said. "It should be called the twat spot."

The girls laughed and Julia knew she made the right call.

"I know, right. I'm buying an ovulation kit. How lame is that?"

"Not lame, " Sarah said. "Want me to Google the best one."

"No, I got this."

While reading a Southern Living magazine a few days earlier, Julia had ripped out an advertisement for an ovulation kit. The photograph was a close-up of a woman's well manicured hand cradling the feet of an infant. The tiny toes, perfect and delicate, made Julia's breast ache. There was a simplicity to the ad that she appreciated, and so she decided it would be that ovulation kit she would splurge for instead of the generic brand.

"But I'm a little pissed off," Julia continued. "I wanted to find these things next to the shampoo or the dark chocolate or something. This aisle is killing me."

"I get ya," Sarah said. "Good luck. I gotta get to this meeting."

And there it was, the thing Julia feared. Of course Sarah didn't get her. How could she? She was busy growing a person in her belly and Julia was in this terrible aisle. The fact of their difference was a physical ache.

Truth was, the placement of these ovulation tests, next to the tampons and pads, was offensive no matter how you looked at it. It was as if the feminine hygiene products were saying, "we all know you are going to have your period, so just buy us too. We are only being convenient, that's all."

Just below the ovulation tests sat forty-five kinds of condoms in every color, style, and pleasure-inducing variation. The buyer could choose to be embarrassment in front of the cashier by handing over an extra-small condom or she could choose not to experience the embarrassment and risk the life-altering possibility of pregnancy. It all somehow felt offensive.

Julia wanted to find the marketing genius who planned these product placements and punch him in the stomach. And it had to be a man because no woman alive could be so inconsiderate.

On the way to the checkout counter she passed a refrigerated stand of fresh flowers. Stopping, she admired an arrangement of white lilies. A beautiful flower, especially magnificent next to the manmade neon-colored daises. Of all the options in the case, why had David ever chosen those?

She did have to give it to the flower, the darn things wouldn't die. They'd been sitting in a vase on the kitchen table for weeks with barely a wilt and absolutely no change in color. Only the good die young, she thought to herself. She smiled at David's decision, in love with even the poor flower choice.

Then she noticed the bouquets of tiny, delicate roses. A

light pink hue tipped the white flower, like an angel's kiss. She picked up the plastic-wrapped bunch and brought them to her nose—the aroma a sweet blessing, the whole bouquet so fragile she almost cried.

Almost crying. That was happening a lot lately too. At the sight of small children holding their mother's hand, at the idea of sending a child off to college, at the first glistening, feathery snowflakes of the season, at the tiny, naked baby bottom in the diaper commercial on television. All these things mocked the life she was leading now.

She made her purchase, without the flowers, and began the drive home when she felt it. The moisture between her legs, warm and sticky. "No, please no," she said as she pressed harder on the accelerator.

"What are you doing on the sink?" David asked, finding her in the master bathroom when he got home from work. Her knees were pulled up to her chin, her head bowed, hiding her face.

"Sulking," Julia said, wiping the tears from her cheeks.

"What now?" David said opening his arms for a hug.

She slapped his hand away and squinted her puffy eyes through the tears. Angrily she replied, "What is that supposed to mean? That I am always sulking? That something is always wrong? Is that how you see me?"

"Honey, no," David backpedaled. "This is me being sympathetic."

"You suck at it," Julia said, not allowing her temper to cool before continuing her rant. "I have tried everything this month, and we get nothing but a big old mess of red."

David scrunched his nose in disgust, disliking the details as she knew he would.

"Don't make that face. You liked my body enough last night—and today it grosses you out? It's been six months of trying to get pregnant, and what do we get?"

"Lots of fun sex."

Seeing his smile, she forced herself to thaw. She wasn't fighting him, she was fighting nature. "True," she said. "But we don't get a baby."

Saying those words out loud gave them substance. Shared by another's ears, they became real and tangible, a thousand times more painful. Julia went to David's arms, finally accepting the hug he had offered.

As her body trembled with grief, he held her tight and let her cry.

"Has it really been six months?" David asked.

Julia couldn't believe he didn't realize how much time had passed. She made a conscious choice not to get angry with him for it, but with her emotions so chaotic she didn't know how long that would last.

"Jules, sometimes it just takes a while. You need to lighten up a little about the whole thing. It will happen when the time is right. Stress doesn't help."

"Don't stress" was the worst thing a person could say to her. With all her might she resisted the urge to punch him in the face.

But Julia had to pull herself together. Tonight was their monthly dinner with her mom and dad. At least she could drink a tall glass of wine at her mother's house, and in fact she was eager for the comforts her childhood home would provide.

"Do you know the news yet?" Beaty said, as an overjoyed greeting when Julia and David walked into the house.

"Hello to you too, Mom."

"Seriously, did James tell you?"

"No, we haven't' even seen Dad yet," Julia said.

"Great. Great. Great. So, are you ready?" Beaty asked. "Savvy is moving back to town." She clapped her hands together, unable to control her excitement.

This was news Julia never expected to hear. Savvy had left this town the moment she was legally able. No one expected her to move home.

"Let me guess, she's broke or in an abusive relationship or robbed a bank and needs a hideout," Julia said.

"No," Beaty said, "nothing like that. She said she just misses home. She already has an apartment picked out and will be here in a month or so."

On their drive home, David asked Julia why she was so against Savvy moving home.

"Something's not right David," Julia said. "Trust me, she wouldn't come back for nostalgia."

CHAPTER 14

The arbitrary date set months ago with Dr. Lamont appeared on Julia's weekly calendar. She felt like a boxer in a losing match, receiving blow after painful blow.

The waiting room, intentionally decorated in soothing tones of maroon and gray, contained six people. A kind-looking woman who Julia assumed was in her mid-60s tackled the crossword in a thick, large-print workbook. Three exceptionally pregnant women, two with husbands, sat patiently in the uncomfortable waiting room chairs. And now her, no doubt the only woman here trying to conceive.

Diverting her eyes, she tried not to look at the pregnant women. Their bellies full of life, their skin aglow. With one look at their ankles, she knew pregnancy would be uncomfortable. She knew it would be emotional. But she wanted what they had so desperately it had become an ache, increasing with intensity with each passing day. What had these women done right? Why had they been chosen to carry a baby while she had not?

"Why are you jealous because I am generous?" The thought came barreling down on her like the white hot lights of a locomotive at night.

When her name was called by a nurse with a clipboard, she stood more quickly than she would have liked. She would have followed the nurse anywhere just to get out of that room.

Dr. Lamont was as professional as possible. Thank God

he wasn't handsome like in Sarah's glitter story. The thought of the cautionary tale allowed Julia a small reprieve from the waiting room-induced depression, but not much. He was mid-50s, a bit overweight, with a well-manicured beard. He actually looked more like a lumberjack in expensive shoes than a gynecologist.

She lay on her back while he examined her breasts. Julia stared at the poster on the ceiling, not seeing it. Whose job was it to select those posters. Was there some kind of website that sold ceiling posters approved by an overfunded government agency? Or did the person charged with decorating just run through the nearest Walmart and see a cutsie image and think "yes, that is what a woman wants to stare at while having a stranger stick metal tools in her private places?"

She put her feet in the stirrups and pushed her bottom to the edge of the table at the doctor's request. He had to ask her twice to relax her knees and let them fall back as he did the tests. She closed her eyes and breathed deeply, forcing herself to relax, thankful the instrumental music she heard during her original telephone call wasn't playing in here too.

"I see from your chart that you are trying to conceive," Dr. Lamont said.

"Yes," Julia said, as he inserted his uncomfortable instruments. "No luck yet."

"It can take a while," he said.

"Uh huh," she groaned.

Julia had prepared a list of questions. How long will it take to get pregnant? Should I be on Clomid, like the woman in the chat room? When should I worry? Is one position better for getting pregnant than another? For best results, how long should I lay still after sex? But none of these questions came to her.

He told her that her spotting mixed with heavy flow from a few months ago sounded like her body getting use to being off the pill and "flushing the excess."

"The pill is designed to keep menstruation regular and

predictable. For women who thrive on schedules this is a nice benefit. So when we get off the pill and your period comes later than expected, we think something is wrong, when really it's just your body producing on its natural cycle."

She should have wanted to know more. She should have wanted to beg for a lesson in the female reproductive process. Instead all she could concentrate on was how Dr. Lamont said "we." He didn't know firsthand what it was like to get off the pill. He wasn't waiting around with a stash of tampons in case he started his period. Why would he say "we"?

Why couldn't she concentrate?

"If you don't hear from us," he said, "then all is fine with your Pap." Then he wished her the best of luck and mentioned he'd be honored to care for her during her pregnancy and delivery.

He had so much confidence when he spoke that last sentence. If her doctor had faith in her body's ability, why should she be questioning herself? Six months was nothing in the grand scheme of things. Her body was still just adjusting to its life without prescribed hormones, nothing more.

In her car after the appointment, Julia turned the XM radio to '80s on 8 and sang along to Def Leopard's "Pour Some Sugar on Me." The dramatic release of scream-singing to loud music in the privacy her car was unlike any other.

She was thankful to have left the doctor feeling more confidence. It allowed her the chance to shop for Adam and Gracie's birthday without tears. David wanted to go to his nephew and niece's joint birthday party that weekend, but he would have no idea what to get them.

The job of shopping for gifts and cards fell to Julia, regardless of the holiday. It was a task she actually loved—the opportunity to walk into a shop, look at it through the eyes of someone she loved, and select a gift they'd enjoy felt like a precious opportunity. A toy store or anything baby-related, however, had proven to be an emotional minefield lately.

Adam and Gracie had been born two years and three days

apart, and a joint family party had always been an easy and wonderful way to cheer on the passing of time. Since Adam was turning six, Julia bought him a few boxes of Legos. The largest box contained a fire-extinguishing airplane and a fire truck. The two smaller Lego sets had something to do with ninjas. Over 1,000 pieces in all. Julia could picture Adam spreading out on the floor and creating these feats of engineering with David and Pops, their great-grandpa, who had always loved building things.

For Gracie, Julia purchased a play kitchen set and a high chair. She could just see her sweet little niece cooking up something fantastically magical for her baby dolls.

Stacy, David's sister, had set the party for noon so the three-hour drive wouldn't be too difficult for Julia and David—long, but not unmanageable. It provided the distance that Julia needed but also allowed the family to gather at special events like this.

The kids were ecstatic with their gifts. Apparently those ninja things were all the rave, and Adam had felt like he was the only kid on the planet without them. Gracie ripped open the kit of plastic food so hard that pieces shot into the air in all directions. The family laughed at their displays—so childlike, so wholesome.

"I can't believe they're so big already," Julia said to Stacy. The sisters-in-law had always gotten along well enough, but no more than that. They never sought one another for advice or friendship. Stacy, unlike David, was a little dry and bland, like toast before it is buttered.

"I know," she said. "It happens overnight." Stacy was a good mom. The love she felt for her children was unmistakable, and a pinch of envy struck Julia again.

"I am so glad the kids like their gifts," Julia said, trying to make conversation. "I had fun shopping for them."

"They seem to like them," Stacy said. Julia noticed the clipped speech but disregarded it—her sister-in-law was difficult.

"I probably got a little carried away with the Legos, but I loved those things when I was a kid. Did you have Legos growing up?"

"No."

"Oh, really," Julia said, feeling like she was always doing the heavy lifting. "I thought they were a requirement in all households."

The ladies patiently smiled at one another.

"Honestly, Julia, I really don't like having Legos in the house. And the kitchen set is going to be tough, too."

Julia was shocked. Whoa, what? Not only was Stacy sharing something voluntarily, but it was negative and aggressive.

"Um... Oh," Julia stammered. What could she say? "I had no idea, I'm so sorry." She needed to be as delicate as possible. Any ruffling of feathers in a family as close as this could cause major distress for everyone. "Can I ask why?"

"I know you don't have kids, so you can't really understand, but you just gave my kids over a thousand tiny pieces of plastic that I'll be cleaning up. At this age, I am always picking up after them or arguing with them about doing it themselves."

Julia couldn't speak. The words, "you don't have kids, so you can't really understand," slammed into her stomach, knocking the wind from her. The pain punched hard.

"I didn't mean to upset you," Stacy said. "But maybe next time we can coordinate on gifts."

With a forced smile Julia said, "Of course."

From across the yard she caught David's eye. Her pale face and stunned look had him at her side in a moment.

"Hey, Jules," he said rescuing her. "Let's grab a beer."

Julia escaped into the house with David and allowed the words to set up camp in her heart, planning to stay a while.

She didn't tell David what Stacy had said and explained the physical response as "just needing a moment."

With all the moments she had been having lately, David had gotten good at not pushing for answers.

CHAPTER 15

Julia's cell phone rang at eleven o'clock on Monday morning. She had spent the first part of the morning looking over the schedule of events at the Health Department and ensuring that everyone was prepared for the week ahead. She had a few calls to return and had been checking her email when she saw the call was from Dr. Lamont's office. Had she forgotten something on Friday?

"Hello, this is Julia," she said.

"Mrs. Ellis, this is Beth from Dr. Lamont's office. Have I caught you at a bad time?"

"No, ma'am. How can I help you?"

"We got the results from your Pap this morning, and Dr. Lamont has seen some abnormalities. He has already consulted with Dr. Pinnison. Are you familiar with him?"

Julia's mouth dried, and she could feel pin pricks on her skin as if danger were near. "No," she said, her voice hollow.

"He is a great doctor. He would like to see you at four this afternoon. If that works for you, please call his office to confirm or make another appointment."

"What kind of abnormalities?" she asked, not sure if she really wanted to know.

"I'm sorry. I don't have that answer. I am just the appointment coordinator, and I don't have access to the files. But again, Dr. Pinnison is really wonderful."

Julia took down the number, and said goodbye.

She stood up from her chair and closed the door to her office. Leaning against the door, she closed her eyes, steadying herself, the intuition of danger having dizzying effects.

Normally, she'd call David, but she knew he was giving a presentation all morning and would be either speaking or in meetings from noon until four. She couldn't bother him. She didn't want to call Sarah, not when there was nothing to report. She wouldn't call her mother, who would freak out with overreaction.

Surely there was nothing to worry about. Surely this had to do with getting off the pill and her wacky period. But why had the doctor consulted with someone else, and why did they have to see her so quickly?

Dark clouds building, she picked up the phone and dialed the number. Of course she would make herself available at four o'clock. No one gets news about an abnormality and reschedules for a more convenient time.

The phone rang twice. "Doctors Pinnison and Belvedere Oncology. How may I help you?"

Oncology?!

She hung up the phone.

Oncology? That's a cancer doctor, right? Oncology?

Deep breaths. One in. One out. One in. One out. Oncology.

She called the number again, acid churning in her stomach eating away any confidence or composure that was remaining. "This is Julia Ellis . . ." She didn't know what to say. Do I have cancer? Am I going to die? Why are you so chipper when I am freaking out?

"Oh, Mrs. Ellis. I just got off the phone with Dr. Lamont's office. Will we be seeing you at four today?"

"Yes," she breathed.

"Excellent," the woman said.

There was a pause, and Julia knew she was supposed to speak. Fear was beginning to collapse in on her.

"Do I need to do anything?. Her voice shook. Julia felt ridiculous asking the question, but she had never seen an oncologist before. Should she fast? Should she pull her husband out of his meetings and bring him along? Should she call a lawyer and write a will?

"Oh no. It's just a consultation and an exam. Dr. Lamont has already faxed all your files so you don't have to do a thing."

Except worry, Julia thought. She wanted to DO something. How could she possibly wait five hours with nothing to do except create worst-case scenarios in her mind?

Julia watched the clock compulsively. Every ten minutes she checked her phone to make sure time was still passing. Somewhere in her convoluted thoughts she expected someone from the medical offices to call and say they had mixed up files and that her Pap was fine. She didn't need to see the oncologist. The person would laugh and apologize for the mishap. Please, someone call me with that news, she thought.

She watched the clock... 3:28... 3:29... 3:30. She grabbed her purse and walked out of her office. She told Becky at the front desk that she'd be at the hospital for the remainder of the day. Back tomorrow morning.

It wasn't entirely a lie. Dr. Pinnison's office was located in the medical practice wing of the hospital, a fact that did not make her comfortable. And she often went between the Health Department and the hospital for work, so no one would be suspicious about her leaving that afternoon.

Heading to her car, Julia reached in her purse for her keys and pulled out a piece of paper—and paused at the irony. She had recently read The Time Keeper by Mitch Albom and was stuck by the recurrence of the phrase, "It is never too late or too early. It is when it is supposed to be."

When she had first read the quote, it seemed powerful and poignant. The tiny hairs on her arms had stood on end as if she needed to be reminded of the importance of time's timing. Like a reminder that, ultimately, she was not in charge. It was a truth she wanted to keep with her. She had reached for a piece of scrap paper to jot it down, not sure how she'd use the quote but sure it was going to be important to her someday. She must have then put the paper in her purse.

Julia took a deep breath, contemplating the quote. Today, she thought, it all sounded like bullshit. Getting in her car, she crumpled the paper in a ball and threw it on the passenger seat.

The waiting room at Doctors Pinnison and Belevdere Oncology was completely empty except for the magazines intended to keep the patient occupied. Julia walked to the reception area and gave her name.

"Glad to see you," the woman said. "I'm Rebecca. We spoke on the phone."

Julia smiled an uneasy smile.

"I knew your name was familiar. I'm friends with Yvette. W met at the Flavors Coffee Shop a few months ago."

Julia looked at the woman more closely. She was pretty with her dark, almost black pixie cut and her skin a glowing olive color, but Julia didn't recognize her. That day at the coffee shop she had been so intent at not looking at Yvette's new baby boy that she had all but ignored the women she was introduced to. Julia felt a pang of guilt at her self-centered behavior.

As Rebecca smiled, waiting for recognition to kick in, Julia noticed that her upper lip went too high, showing more of her gums than necessary. Fortunately, her teeth were white and straight. Since Julia's dad was a dentist, it was always a person's smile she assessed first. Rebecca's face was square and a bit small, but it was full of a kindness that Julia sensed was honest and true. She wore low-hanging earrings that Julia thought to be a bold statement with her short hair.

"Good to see you," Julia said. She was having friendly chitchat in an oncology office, how could this be? Surely soon she'd wake up from this nightmare.

"Meet me over there," Rebecca motioned to the door against the wall. "I'll take you to Dr. Pinnison."

Julia felt light-headed. She was inside an oncology office, with an appointment, being walked to the doctor. She began to have tunnel vision and tasted metal.

Julia was not overly physical. She didn't hug new acquaintances the way Sarah did. She didn't grab a girlfriend's arm when walking down the street shopping together. But still she was grateful when Rebecca wrapped her arm around hers and led her to the room. She may not have been able to walk the fifteen steps alone.

Rebecca opened the door and motioned to Julia to take a seat in an office that looked more suited for a CEO then an MD. A large mahogany desk sat in the middle of the room like a statement of power. Organized piles of papers covered the top. A laptop sat to one side. Behind the desk was a matching credenza filled with books, photographs, and trinkets that meant nothing to Julia but told a story to their owner of a time worth remembering.

On the wall above the credenza hung one beautifully framed diploma after another. Awards for service and acknowledgements from professional organizations were set on the wall at perfect right angles, evenly spaced. There were so many acronyms following Dr. Pinnison's name that Julia wondered if maybe they were made up. The wall next to the door held an image of the Arkansas Razorback mascot. Julia wasn't sure if a doctor from Arkansas was a good thing—surely there was a joke in there. But the diploma from Harvard counterbalanced her anxiety.

She sat on one of the plush chairs opposite the desk. Feeling uneasy with her back to the door, she did her best to angle her body to see the doctor when he came in. The call to be here had been surprise enough.

She continued looking around trying to learn about this doctor and trying not to think about where she was and why. Not until this day had she ever experienced such dramatic slowness of time.

Along with the papers and computer, the desk held one of those contraptions that dangled five balls from wire strings. She pulled one ball to the right, away from the others, and let go. It hit the second ball, sending the last one off to the left and then back again—the sound a steady metallic clack, clack, clacking.

It replicated the beating of her heart—loud and repetitive. She listened for a while before realizing the methodical clacks were eventually going to slow and then stop. She couldn't draw this parallel to her own heart and then allow the balls to fall silent on their own. Would her heart eventually do the same? She was in an oncology office for God's sake.

After seven more clacks, Julia stopped the balls.

"Mrs. Ellis," came a voice behind her.

Julia started and jumped to her feet, knowing she had been caught.

"I hope I didn't keep you waiting," he said and extended his hand. "I'm Matt Pinnison."

The thick Arkansas accent was not the first thing she noticed about Dr. Pinnison. If he had told her his twin was Matthew McConaughey she would have absolutely believed him. Real doctors were supposed to be old, grey-haired men with mild manners or like her lumberjack gynecologist. Not like a model for the cologne Obsession.

He took her hand in both of his and shook it with warmth and familiarity.

She instantly stopped thinking "cancer" and started thinking "glitter."

"I kept myself busy with your balls," she said, and melted into herself with embarrassment. "Um. The time-keeping things on your desk," she pointed to the contraption to clarify.

"I hate those things. My sister gave that to me, and she is in town this week. I put them out in case she stops by."

Julia smiled. "Oh thank God. I hate them too."

"Please have a seat," and he motioned to the chair she had been occupying. Instead of sitting behind the desk he sat next to her. "Has your husband come with you today?"

Panic resurfaced and "cancer" repossessed her mind. "Do I need him?" A tear she didn't expect wetted her cheek.

He handed her a tissue, "This is a starting point, nothing to worry about. Oftentimes it's nice to speak to a couple because you two will hear things differently. I'll tell you what I'll do. When we're done, I'll write down everything we said so that you can discuss it with him tonight."

Oh My God. Oh My God. Oh My God, Julia thought. This is worse than I thought. An oncologist wants my husband here.

God? Why hadn't she thought to call on God? She considered calling her husband and her best friend—and decided not to call her mother. But God had never come into her conscious. Shouldn't that have been the first place she turned? She obviously needed to more church because she was feverishly and frequently calling on Him in this moment.

"Ready?" he said with the patient strength of a teacher. "Your Pap showed abnormal cells. This doesn't necessarily mean you have cancer. A biopsy will tell us what's going on in there. We'll do a pelvic exam today so that I know what we're looking at."

"Uh huh."

"I know meeting an oncologist can be scary," he said. "That's why I like to visit in my office first, so we get to know one another and I can answer any questions you might have."

"I don't even know what to ask," Julia said. This trembling truth would have been embarrassing if she wasn't entirely struck with terror.

As he talked, Julia wished she had let the little metal balls to continue their repetition. She needed something else to concentrate on. Dr. Pinnison, with all his handsome looks, could have been speaking another language. She didn't understand a word and yet continued to nod her head in affirmation. The war drums of fear were beating throughout her body.

Eventually he led her down the hall and into an examination room. He asked her to undress from the waist down. "I'll be back in a few minutes with the nurse."

She did as she was told, neatly folding her underwear and

placing them into the middle of her folded pants. She set it all atop her shoes and then pulled the drape to hide her clothes, completely aware that she was taking care of the things that didn't matter. Sitting on the exam table, she draped the paper cape over her legs and continued to chew on a plea for health.

When Dr. Pinnison arrived he had with him a overweight black woman dressed in pale blue scrubs. "This is Natasha, my right hand," he explained.

"I'm glad to know you, Julia," Natasha said in a deep Southern accent Julia couldn't place. Was this oncology office over run with southerners? Julia wondered.

Julia followed Dr. Pinnison's orders and moved to the edge of the table. She winced as he inserted the tools. She wasn't sure when it had happened, but she was suddenly aware of Natasha holding her hand.

She caught the woman's deep brown eyes and held her stare for support. Julia winced as the doctor explored her. Natasha nodded almost imperceptibly, encouraging Julia to stay strong.

When he was done, Dr. Pinnison asked Julia to sit up. "I see the area Dr. Lamont was concerned about. I removed some cells, basically a cervical biopsy called a colposcopy. We'll do some tests on those cells to see what we're dealing with."

Wait, she thought. What? You just did a procedure, and I didn't even know it?

She was grateful Natasha was still holding her hand and looked to her for reassurance. Why hadn't she asked David to come along? Why did she think she could handle this on her own. A biopsy. She just had a biopsy?

"We'll wait to see what this biopsy tells us. But based on what I see so far, I'd like to perform a surgery called LEEP, which stands for Loop Electrosurgical Excision Procedure. It's a simple outpatient surgery that allows me to remove the abnormal cells from the area around your cervix." And on he spoke. And on the war drums beat.

There were words and terms and important bits of

information, but again Julia couldn't hear any of it. The hollow in her head rattled like empty tea cups. She, Julie Ellis, might have cancer. She might actually die from cancer.

"While you set up a surgery appointment with Rebecca, I'll write down what we've discussed, and you can talk it over with your husband. I also have a brochure about the procedure I'll send home with you. If ya'll have any questions, just call."

How Julia got home she wasn't sure. In her empty house, the silent halls echoed her footsteps. An onlooker might have thought she was reflecting on the life she had built thus far. She touched her wedding picture and the photo taken the day her parents were married. She looked at the ugly flowers still on the kitchen table. She rubbed her hand over the top of the couch and the blanket that lay cast aside over the armchair. She felt nothing.

Walking into the closet, she took off her heels and changed into her running clothes and sneakers. She needed to feel something—anything. Even if it was the aching throb of her heart and the stabbing pain in her side. She needed to find a way outside of her head and back into the world.

She stepped into the sharp crisp air and began to move. One foot in front of the other. Over and over again. Julia's body was unused to the methodical rhythm of running. She had only been doing it a short while. The app spoke in her headphone every five minutes, thankfully forcing her to reality though she didn't follow the commands of when to run and when to walk. She knew but one pace, and it was escape.

The app concluded, but Julia wasn't done. She propelled her body forward. Not feeling the street below her feet or the cold wind against her face, she hammered heel then toe over and over. Finally her body relented, and she fell to her hands and knees in the dry brown grass of her front yard, gasping for breath.

Where she had gone she couldn't say. How far she had run, how fast and how long, she didn't care.

David must have looked through the window and seen her

in the yard heaving and sweating. All of a sudden there he was, in dress slacks kneeling on the ground next to her with his hand on her back.

"Honey, are you okay?" His eyes were concerned when she met his stare.

Her face was red from running, but there was a look about her that he had never seen before—th. frantic frozen look of a deer before the car's impact.

"Jules, talk to me."

She pulled herself to her knees. She searched into his eyes, threw her arms around his neck, and finally allowed the tears to crest the dam she had built and flood her completely.

She cried, and cried more, and deeper. He held her. Only slowly she caught her breath. When her tears were exhausted and her body drained, David picked her up like a father carrying a hurt child and took her into the house.

Cradling her protectively, he sat on the couch.

"Honey, I am freaking out a little here," David said. "What's going on?"

She pulled her head off his shoulder and looked at him as if finally realizing he was there.

"I might have cancer," she said.

His eyes were wide with shock.

"I might have cancer," she repeated. "I went to an oncologist today. They said I need surgery to see if I have cancer."

"What?. You went to an oncologist? By yourself?. Honey, please talk to me."

She crumpled again.

"You can't stop here, Jules," David said.

"Let's take a bath," she said blankly. "Like we did that time in Colorado. Remember? Let's do that now."

She didn't let David answer but pulled herself from his lap and took his hand. He was too bewildered to resist.

Julia turned on the faucet and added shampoo to the flowing water hoping it would bubble enough to envelope them. She took off her clothes and stepped in. He followed.

He sat with his back against the tub and she leaned against him, her back to his chest. She rested her head against his shoulder and closed her eyes as she allowed the heat of the water and the arms of her husband to surround her. Their warmth gave her strength.

She began the story. "I got a call today from Dr. Lamont's office. They said my Pap showed abnormal cells. I was referred to Dr. Pinnison." She took a steadying breath. "An oncologist. I saw him today at four."

Feeling more courageous as she spoke, she continued with the story.

David did not ask any questions, he did not interrupt. He just held her while she allowed the past few hours to spill from her.

When she was finally done, her body went limp from releasing the burden. He put a finger under her chin and tilted her head toward his. They kissed.

Julia hadn't known he was crying until she tasted the salt on his lips.

"You might have cancer," he said into her mouth.

"Yes," she admitted.

"You have me, and I have you," he said. "Always."

CHAPTER 16

Three nights later, at their monthly dinner, Beaty said, "Well, just three more months and your sister will arrive."

"I thought she was going to be here by now," Julia said.

Beaty shrugged dismissively.

"Mom, you know Savvy is never going to move back here. She just started this rumor so you wouldn't forget about her, or something."

Julia hadn't intended to sound harsh, but she was sick of her absent sister being the major topic of conversation.

"My, my," Beaty said giving her daughter a stare that Julia painfully recognized from childhood. "If you would rather us talk about something else then please give us a topic."

Julia and David looked at one another. They had promised not to tell anyone—anyone—about the threat of cancer until there was actual news. Holding tightly to the secret, they endure. through dinner.

It became a weight they both carried, the secret they guarded the next week at David's dad's birthday party. It separated them from everyone else in the world—and united them more closely.

During the two weeks, they made love only twice. Each time was cautious and tender, filled with tight embraces, deep kisses, and slow-building movements. Both husband and wife needed the bond of closeness sex brought, but both were also afraid of angering the cancer that might be within Julia's body.

After the first time, Julia cried from both the pleasure of

this new kind of compassionate sex and from the emotional exhaustion it left her with. After the second climax, they both cried.

Before they took her into surgery, Dr. Pinnison spoke every word to David's attention. Julia was impressed with the litany of questions he had prepared for the doctor. She had no idea he had done so much research on the procedure, on the abnormal cells, and on Pinnison himself.

Through the preparation, Julia simply sat idly by, wringing her hands and concentrating on swallowing the large lump that threatened to choke her.

Natasha was there, her brown eyes shining compassionately over the white surgical mask. She took Julia's hand. "It's gonna be all right, Sugar." Julia wanted to fold herself into the woman's confidence.

It wasn't a painful surgery, mostly uncomfortable. The nurses made sure Julia was steady enough to walk out of the outpatient surgery center before she was cleared to leave. She was still groggy, but it was her own pillow she longed for. When they got home, David opened her door and scooped her into his arms. He placed her gently on the bed and kissed her forehead. "You're so brave," he said.

The comforter had never felt warmer as Julia sank into her bed. During the surgery they had given her a local anesthetic and a high dose of painkiller. The procedure itself lasted only twenty minutes, but the two weeks of waiting was enough to give a person wrinkles and an ulcer.

Julia turned up the temperature on the heating pad, placed it on her cramping stomach, and curled into a ball. She felt the effects of the medicine as her body moved slowly to adjust the pillow. As she fell into sleep, she pictured her healthy cervix as a small, hard, wrinkled, cone-shaped organ. Then she imagined the divots that had been sliced out of it, looking as if it had been hit by shrapnel, now pock-marked and falling into dilapidation.

She woke up longing to hear from the oncologist's office. She kept a tight grip on her cell phone, waiting for the call that might change her life forever—or foretell its end.

If these are my last days, she thought, how will I spend them?

Pouring her coffee, she reflected on herself, her best self. She determined she should smile more, be more grateful and generous. She wanted to be remembered as a person who was kind and worthy of knowing. She would no longer regret the things of the past, like the time she kissed Rachel's boyfriend the summer after high school. Those things were for yesterday. Unable to forgive herself and troubled by guilt and shame, Julia had lost her friend. Today, she thought, she would call Rachel and find peace.

Stirring milk and sugar into her coffee, she decided not to lament the times she had failed to do something adventurous or wild, like that summer everyone was jumping off the cliffs at Lake Smith but Julia was too afraid. Here she was, in her late twenties, staring down a cancer diagnosis. She would no longer fear life being cut short. She promised to throw herself off any proverbial cliff and savor all the life she had left. In these moments the potential of cancer gave her power.

At the kitchen table, her phone in front of her, Julia took a sip of coffee, the liquid burning her tongue. Pain brought her back to reality, and she wondered who at work would come to her funeral and how they would act. She imagined Sarah giving a eulogy and her mother in tears. She wondered if her death would drive Beaty to drink again.

She folded her knees to her chest and thought about all the things she would miss.

Her mind turned to her sister. She shouldn't be so hard on Savvy. They were different, but they were family. If this turned out to be cancer, she would call her sister and start to work on their friendship. Someone needed to be the grown up.

She watched the steam rise from the mug and, without thinking, slowly spun her phone in circles on the table. She couldn't continue like this. She couldn't sit here trapped within herself frozen with possibilities and what ifs. She grabbed the phone, poured the coffee down the drain, and got ready for work.

David was still in bed. "The doctor said you don't have to rush back to the office," he said. "We can stay home together."

She found it hard to look at him. They had spent the weeks before the procedure enraptured with one another. Now all she wanted was space. She was pushing him away, creating distance so that it would be easier for him if she did have cancer, if she did die. Julia rationalized that the more space between them the less he would hurt, the less she would hurt.

"I can't just lie around watching my phone," she said. "Life goes on."

Then she instantly regretted those words. Because what if it didn't.

She took her lunch to a park and watched the children play. Life felt like a beautiful gift, the kids running and screaming, smiling and excited. their childhood and all the future's possibilities in its most pure form.

She couldn't believe she had ever feared motherhood, even for a short time. Seeing these women follow their children, cheer them on as they crossed the monkey bars and protect them as they slid down the slide, was a future she wanted more than anything. To hold a person created within her.

She wanted life.

Please, God, Julia silently begged. Please. Please. Please.

The call came three days later. Julia was pouring a glass of wine while waiting for the veggies on the stove to sauté.

She picked up the phone with shaking hands. "Hello, this is Julia." She didn't recognize the number but knew instinctively who it was.

"Julia, this is Matt Pinnison. Have I caught you at a bad time?" His accent caught her off guard. The world stopped spinning as she waited for the news that could change her life. She sank down onto the kitchen tile, folding her knees into her chest.

"Yes. I mean, no, you haven't caught me at a bad time. This is fine."

"We just got the results back from your procedure." She was trying desperately to decipher his tone while hearing papers rustling on the other end of the phone. Was it bad news. Was that why he was calling personally? Or maybe it was good news and he saved giving that gift of happiness until the end of his day. His life must be very tragic, she thought. Will I be one of his tragedies?

"It looks like the biopsy was negative, and we were able to remove all the questionable fibroid cells during the procedure."

She breathed out the question slowly, "So?"

"So, you don't have cancer."

She let out more voice in her relieved exhalation than she intended.

"Are you okay?" Dr. Pinnison asked.

"I don't have cancer? I really don't have cancer?"

"You really don't have cancer," he said, and Julia could hear the smile in his voice. "I'd like to see you in a week to make sure you're healing properly. And I want you to wait three months while your cervix heals before you continue trying to conceive."

"Oh, my God." Julia said. "Thank you. Thank you. Thank you." She wasn't sure if she was speaking to Dr. Pinnison, God, or some other force that deserved her gratitude.

David walked into the room as she hung up the phone. He had overheard the last of the conversation and wrapped his arms around her, swinging her in a dizzying circle, her legs lifting behind her, flying.

Life. She was given the diagnosis of life. It was as if her heart was exploding with thankfulness.

When he sat her down, she joyously clinched both her fists next to her jaws and screamed. Tension and fear released its physical hold on her body and she felt light and free.

At dinner that night, David lifted a glass. "Jules, you are my world. These last few weeks have been the scariest time of my life. There is no way I can live without you." She wiped the tears from her eyes.

"Fuck cancer," he said.

She was so surprised she spit out a laugh.

They clinked glasses and ate their dinner alone together, the secret possibility of cancer no longer between them at the table.

CHAPTER 17

Winter was everywhere now. The cold made its painful presence known in the wind that stung the skin and the frost that bit the fingers. Julia also felt winter in the vacancy of her belly. The required three months without trying had passed more quickly than she had expected, but now time crept along as it had when she was a child waiting for Santa Claus.

At the Becketts' house on Christmas Eve, Sarah gave Julia a small box wrapped in the signature gold paper. Inside was a handmade voucher for a girls' trip to the Florida Keys. She had secretly worked it out with David, and they were leaving just after the first of the year. The gift was over the top, but that was Sarah's style.

Julia had found the perfect gift for Sarah, a small white sculpture of two girls holding hands, their ponytails behind them, and their legs kicked back, running. When she saw it at a small boutique downtown, she had fallen in love with the looks on the girls' faces, as if they enjoyed the conspiracy of knowing one another's secrets. It was the perfect depiction of the friendship she shared with Sarah.

She gave Joseph a pair of "dino-riffic" pajamas, a football, and a zip-up stuffed dinosaur he could hide his treasures in. After opening the plush toy, he ran to his room and filled it with his most special rocks. He gave her a drawing of his hand that he turned into a Santa by coloring the fingers red, adding a beard to the palm, and placing eyes, nose and smile in the center, perfectly awkward and childish. It was Julia's favorite gift.

"Soon we'll be in bathing suits," Sarah said with a squeal. "But don't go looking at my big, fat, pregnant belly. The doctor said this is the last possible week I can travel before the big day."

Julia didn't need to be reminded of the pregnancy. Every time the two were together, she was fought a losing battle against jealousy. Had she and David gotten pregnant when they first set out to, Julia would be just as round and full of life as her friend. Instead, she had a busted-up cervix and nine months of emptiness.

Julia brought a beautiful bottled Merlot along to celebrate the gift exchange. When she grabbed the bottle, she honestly hadn't thought that Sarah wouldn't be able to drink it.

"Oh," Sarah said. "That looks delicious. I have to turn my head. I am so jealous." She rubbed her swollen belly and dramatically turned away.

Julia searched deep within herself to find the willpower not to scream at the top of her lungs, "You're an asshole!"

Her emotional balance, around Sarah especially, had become a seesaw with one child outweighing the other. Often, envy was the fat kid, pressing down with its girth and mass, leaving the lighter, grateful child suspended and helpless.

She knew David had okayed the trip because he had mentioned several times that "some time away would be good." He probably thought it would free Julia from her burden of barrenness. She'd let the sand and the ocean water slough off her mood swings and agitation. She'd see the joy in her friendship and be grateful to escape her daily routine.

Of course, David was a man, and men don't exactly think this deeply about emotions. In all honesty, Julia thought, he probably organized the trip to get some time away from my craziness.

On Christmas morning David awoke to find that Santa had brought him a pack of boxers, naturally decaf herbal tea, and three pair of running shorts.

"This is an interesting mix of gifts," David said.

"Getting pregnant was your idea, and I kind of feel like I am doing all the heavy lifting," she said.

"And herbal tea and boxer shorts are going to lighten your load?"

"Maybe," she said.

She had read that tighty whities might make sperm too hot and unable to swim. So boxers seemed like an easy remedy. Yes, she remembered him vetoing the boxer idea months ago. But now that they had been cleared by the doctor to try again, she thought maybe he'd be willing to have a change of heart and underwear.

Frankly, caffeine should be off limits for both of them always—since studies showed terrible effects of consuming too much. This time while they were trying to conceive would be a good trial run. And, it's true, she had stopped running. But when the new year and the warmer weather hit she was going to give it another go. She wanted David to do the same.

"I think you're getting a one-track mind?"

"We set a goal, David," she said. "These are some of the tools you need to help us reach that goal."

"I'm trying really hard not to be mad at you about this," he said. "You're being a little passive aggressive."

"Well, you're being a little stubborn," she said.

They were quiet for a while, Julia considering her next retort.

"I don't want to fight with you," he said.

"Me either. I'm sorry. I didn't do this to make you mad," Julia said. "We want this, don't we?"

"Yes, Jules, we want this," he said with exhaustion. "But making a baby is supposed to be about love and joining ourselves to one another. Not all this." He gestured to the gifts laid out on the table.

"All what, David?" she said, moving her hands to her hips. "What we've done hasn't worked. We need a plan."

"We've only been able to try for a month since your surgery. It's not like we're failing, and it's not like we're on some kind of clock."

"The hell we aren't," she said, storming out of the room and slamming the door to the bedroom.

CHAPTER 18

"Let's sit here in the shade," Sarah said. It was the last day of their long weekend in the warm Florida Keys. "With my belly this stretched out I don't want to get too much sun."

Sarah said something about her stomach every time they went outside. The solution was clear to Julia; don't wear a bikini. Even pregnant, Sarah looked like a model.

The first time Sarah made a comment, the women went in search of sun screen. The job should have taken three minutes, seeing as every shop on the boardwalk had sunscreen displays out front. But Sarah demanded something organic, and the first afternoon of the trip was spent asking, "Is this pregnancy friendly?"

The words tasted like acid in Julia's mouth.

Now, lying on her towel in the sun next to Sarah's shade, Julia rolled her eyes and then caught herself. She had been so emotionally centered for much of the trip. The first day on the island, the girls had taken a beginner's yoga class, which gave Julia a peace she hadn't expected. And from that moment on she was trying hard to channel her mother's new, weird tranquility. Thus far it had worked pretty well.

"Let's order a drink!" Sarah said, flagging down the tanned college-age pool boy wearing all white and carrying a tray.

"Tequila Sunrise," Julia said.

"And I'll have a virgin pina colada." When the boy walked away, Sarah added, "Isn't it funny that I have to order a 'virgin'.

I mean, it's not like I am one." She threw back her head in laughter.

Julia smiled and laughed for the sake of her friend. She didn't want Sarah to know how annoyed she was, how annoyed she had been most of the weekend. She was grateful for the retreat and the lavish expense, but Julia had felt the dark shadow of Sarah's pregnancy all week, and she was ready to get away from it.

She wanted to keep Sarah's friendship, but to do that she needed space.

"I'm gonna go talk to that masseuse over there," Julia said motioning to the white tent in the sand. "How wonderful does a massage on the beach sound?"

"Let me know if there's a cut-out in the center of the table, maybe I can get one too."

Swallowing hard, Julia stood up and walked toward the tent. A hole in the table, for God's sake, she thought.

Fortunately, the masseuse, Claudia, had just had a cancellation and could see Julia right away. Fearing the awkwardness of getting undressed on the beach, she looked to Claudia for help.

"Darling," Claudia said in an Eastern European accent, "we all walk upon the beach almost naked anyway. I will help you get to the table, but I have a feeling modesty is not your only issue."

Julia sucked in a breath. She would have been offended if it weren't for Claudia's voice. It wasn't just the accent; Claudia's way was kind and understanding. It was as if she was seeing the core of Julia, like a gypsy reading tarot cards, revealing her to herself.

"Lie face down, Darling," Claudia said. "Let's get to work."

Julia did as she was told and concentrated on relaxing.

"You are breathing from your chest like you have been running from a lion," Claudia said. "Slow down and concentrate on your stomach. Fill it fat with air and let it go."

Slowly in and slowly out, Julia did as she was told.

Somehow the noise of the beachgoers was slowly swallowed in the rhythm of the crashing waves and her own breathing. Time slipped away. The silent air blew lightly on her skin as it was worked by Claudia's professional, well-trained hands.

"You have much stress in your life," Claudia said, surprising Julia out of her meditation.

"No, not really," Julia lied. "I mean I'm on the beach with my best friend, so I don't have much to complain about."

"Your muscles speak to me and I can feel how worried you are. Tell Claudia."

Julia always hated when people referred to themselves in the third person, but it worked for this woman.

"I guess it's just that my husband and I are trying to have a baby, and I'm a little stressed that it isn't working." Why couldn't she admit the truth to a stranger whose judgment didn't matter? There was no "little stress" about her. It was all big stress and big tears and big fights and big anger at her best friend for getting pregnant first.

"I hear more of this story from here," Claudia pushed deeply on the muscles in her middle back next to the spine. "They say you are depressed."

"My muscles say that?"

"Yes, Darling. When we are depressed we hunch over causing this knot here. Your whole body is strong with will and determination but also with sadness."

Julia's breath began to shake and a tear slipped from her eye.

"You go ahead and cry," Claudia said placing a consoling hand on her arm. "This cleanses out the bad and makes way for the good."

By the end of the massage, Julia felt like a piece of ice that had melted. She took three deep breaths and then raised herself from the table. Claudia covered her with a towel as she dressed.

When she was done, Claudia hugged her tightly. "You choose your response, Darling. No one is in charge of your emotions but you. I believe you will find your power."

"Thank you, Claudia." Julia said with tears again.

"You are why I love this job. I will remember how much you want to bring life to the world."

She went back to lie next to Sarah, who was engrossed in a book. "How was it?"

"Better than I could have imagined," Julia said. "I think I'll take a nap in the sun."

"Okay. Glad you enjoyed it."

As Julia fell asleep she concentrated on Claudia's words: "Bring life to the world." Even in the depths of her muscles she desperately wanted it.

CHAPTER 19

Work offered little in the way of relief. Julia assumed most women in her circumstance would go to work and have the great fortune of escaping the heartache of wanting a child. A lawyer or CPA could bury her anxiety in paperwork. A nurse or therapist would be dealing with the burden of others' pain and illness. Even a teacher or nursery worker had the joy of working with children. They got to help God's tiny creations grow into good people, perhaps lessening the desire to have one of her own.

Since coming home from the Keys, Julia had had to deal with the painful truths her job provided. She organized an STD awareness campaign for the local high school and saw the number of tests for STDs skyrocket. Though they were forbidden by the school district from giving away condoms, she doled out more pregnancy tests than expected. Julia heard one girl comment, "I would just die if I got pregnant."

She worked with the elementary and mid-level schools to educate teachers and principals about spotting child abuse and neglect and submitted proper reports. The big awareness campaign would begin in April, but there was a lot to do leading up to the month.

Julia found a way to mentally cope with young kids having unprotected sex too early. Hell, if she was honest, she had been one of them. She remembered her own fear of getting pregnant in her teenage years. The abuse of a child, however, was something she could never reconcile, and the more she saw signs of trouble, the more she wanted to rip the children from their parents' abusive hands and take them home.

She watched kids come into the department, the dusty smell of poverty leaving a fog in the waiting room. She saw their thin bodies wrapped in clothes too small and too light for the weather. She watched as they cowered in fear or acted aggressively, mirroring the anger of their parents. She knew which children were rarely spoken to by their parents because their speech was so far behind. A few times she noticed bruising.

She looked into the big eyes of these children, wishing she could give them the love they deserved and angrily begging God to justify this harsh reality. Why had these parents been chosen and not her and David? The injustice was infuriating.

What threw her over the edge of despair were the teenage mothers. One particular girl in the waiting room of the Health Department was enough to boil her blood. The girl came in wearing combat boots and a cutoff AC/DC shirt. She was far too young to know either the band or their music. Her pencil-thin legs were squeezed tight in black jeans rolled over at the waist and rubber-banded together. With her white belly half exposed between black shirt and jeans, she reminded Julia of an Oreo cookie.

She chewed gum like she was mad at it. And she hadn't looked away from her phone since she sat down. Her dark hair was obviously dyed, and her lipstick was too dark and too bright at the same time. The smell of stale smoke hung in the air around her.

Returning from the restroom, Julia looked closer still. The girl couldn't have been more than seventeen at most.

"Hi," Julia said as she walked by.

"Uh huh," she grunted, not lifting her eyes from the phone.

Anger. Julia's first reaction was anger. She went to her office, gritting her teeth, and closed the door.

I don't get it, Julia thought. Why does that girl get to have a child and I don't! She wanted to scream in God's face. She wanted to take him by the gold lined lapel of his holy robes and shake him. I would be a great mom, and that girl probably doesn't even do her homework, damn it!

She knew she needed to concentrate on work, to restock pamphlets, double check staffing for tomorrow's big flu shot event, work on the grant application, verify that the newest information was on the website, and check her email. But nothing felt attainable.

It was as if her head weighed ten extra pounds. She dropped it to the desk. Her neck and upper back tightened as she held in guilt and wrath.

She took three deep breaths and tried to channel her inner Claudia. How wonderful would it be to be like her, working on the beach, helping other people heal, wearing flowing skirts and long braided hair, the only weight the ocean's breeze?

Failure. No matter how she tried to change, she was still Julia, the Type-A personality who couldn't belly breathe and liked making plans and lists.

She pulled up Google and typed in "get pregnant faster." Every site seemed to start with estimating ovulation and then listed things she had already done. She decided to stop getting angry at the ovulation kit in the cabinet and start using the dumb thing.

The ringing phone pulled her out of herself. "Julia Ellis, how can I help you?"

"Jules, it's me." Sarah's chipper voice made Julia smile. She would continue to work on setting her envy aside. "I know you said you'd order the flowers for my shower this weekend, but I just feel silly not doing anything. So I already did it."

"Ugh, Sarah . . . "

This didn't surprise Julia, and it also didn't upset her. She knew her friend well enough to know she wouldn't sit out during the planning of an event, especially one in her honor. "I'm hosting this shower. Now quit doing stuff."

"I know, I know. That's the last thing, I promise. I was just at a luncheon for the Women For Charity, and they had the most beautiful arrangements. So I found out who did them and ordered a few. Really I just want them around the house after the shower. They are beautiful, you will love them!"

"Okay. Three more people called today saying they will be there. So I think we are at thirty."

"I'm so excited!"

"It'll be great. I'll be by your house at noon to set up, and everyone will be there at two."

"Make it twelve-thirty. That way I can jog first and be ready by the time you get there."

"Shit, Sarah, you're still jogging? Did anyone tell you that you are like eight and-a-half months pregnant?"

"Oh stop. You know I can't sit still, and it's really more of a fast walk. I'm not setting any land speed records."

It would be easy to put successful, athletic, mature Sarah on one side of a room and the moody Goth girl in the lobby on the other. Their differences couldn't be more obvious. But to Julia, they were together, and she, barren, sat in her own lonely corner.

Julia pulled the covers over her head when she saw the clock on her bedside table read 10:00 a.m. Not since college had she slept this late. She hadn't even been drinking the night before. Then it hit her like acid reflux. Today was the day of the dreaded shower.

Of course Julia knew it was today—she was the host. Though Sarah had selected the invitations, Julia had mailed them, and made arrangements for the mini sandwiches and chocolate-covered strawberries. She had prepared in a typical Julia way, by making a "to do" list and checking each box after each task was complete. But she had done so on autopilot, void of feeling.

There were two things left to do, and they would take every ounce of emotional energy, a commodity that was quickly depleting. The two tasks—"Buy a gift" and "Smile at the party"—sat at the bottom of her list like a land mine waiting for detonation.

Thankfully there was a parking spot near the front door of the store and she'd be able to run in quickly. Whipping her car into the space, she read the sign posted like a warning aimed right at her—Expectant Mothers Only.

"Really," she said to the emptiness of her car. "Do they really have to make a federal case of pregnancy in the freakin' parking lot too? They have a person in their uterus, it's not like they're unable to walk."

She accelerated in reverse as her hands began to sweat. For vindication and to prove to the offending sign that she was a capable person, she parked under a light pole at the far end of the lot, spaces from any other vehicle. Getting out of the car, she slammed the door with indignation.

Like a knight at the entrance of the dragon's cave, she was going to have to dig deep for inner strength and face her dreaded nemesis—big box baby stores.

The light fragrance of baby powder engulfed Julia as the doors slid open. An attendant with an overly animated smile handed her a pamphlet about the sales and asked if she needed any help. Behind the woman a swirl of pink, blue, white, and yellow began to close in.

"Um," Julia stammered. "My friend is having a shower, and I need a gift."

"I thought so," she smiled. "Let's get her registry printed for you."

She thought so. Julia rolled the sentence around like an unwanted Brussels sprout left on her plate.

The attendant handed her the registry—four pages of descriptions, prices, and bar codes. Julia handed it back and said, "Help me spend seventy-five dollars, and then get me out of here."

The girl smiled uncomfortably and tilted her head as if trying to decide if Julia was joking. Julia mocked the girl's posture and opened her eyes wide as if to punctuate her seriousness.

Twenty minutes and $74.92 later she was out the door. Julia opted against the free gift wrapping. Another second in the store would have done her in, and the dragon would have won.

She made it to the car, put her head on the steering wheel and sulked. Composure, fickle yo-yo that it is, eventually returned. She picked up the "to do" list and checked the box.

Although she had chastised Sarah for ordering the floral arrangements alone, she was now grateful. She only had thirty minutes to pick up the flowers, and get to the Sarah's house. She would have just enough time to decorate and freshen her makeup before everyone arrived.

"Picking up an order for Sarah Beckett," she told the woman behind the counter. Nothing refreshed the spirit like the heavenly smell of a florist shop. The cut flowers, so close to one another, condensed the perfume into a transformative adventure for the nostrils. Julia breathed in deeply.

"We just finished the arrangements," the woman said. "We'll gladly carry them to your car for you."

"Thanks," Julia said, grateful for the help, and led the way.

She didn't turn to see the flowers until she opened the passenger side of her car. Her breath caught.

The woman and the two men behind her were gingerly carrying clear round bowls with beautiful stones at the bottom the water sloshing despite their best efforts. The green stems rose from the stones like a gift from the desert and blooming at the top were daffodils. Daffodils!

Seeing her response to the arrangements, the woman said, "Beautiful, right? They are such a common flower but so beautiful when bunched together like this. They haven't started growing here, but I'd say in the next couple of weeks we'll see these beauties pop up everywhere. A wonderful way to celebrate the birth of spring."

"Yes," Julia said, barely audible.

During her research into getting pregnant, she had strayed away from one single word—the word she feared would define her. She knew that after twelve months without conception, she'd have to accept that the word belonged to her. These daffodils, now seat belted into her car, reminded her of David's conception proposal. It had been one year since they began trying. The word was now hers—infertility.

CHAPTER 20

When she arrived at Sarah's, the house was already flawlessly clean, the catered food placed beautifully on the table, the mommy-to-be's dress and hair immaculate. There was nothing to be done but place the daffodils and wait.

Julia excused herself. In the bathroom she stood for a long time considering her reflection. She was hollow, an empty lifeless shell. It was as if she had been turned off. She didn't want to be here, she didn't care about these people. She wanted to lie on her couch and stare at the ceiling.

"Hi, glad to meet you," Julia said as she opened the door to the first guest. The words came from her smiling lips, but delight didn't reach her eyes. They had been friends forever, but Julia didn't know most of Sarah's work friends or the women she palled around with at charity events.

Women wearing beautiful spring colors energetically visited with one another. They clamored for positions as Sarah gave a tour of her home, including the new baby's room. They delicately ate finger sandwiches and commented on the freshness and size of the chocolate covered strawberries. In Julia's eyes it was all very plastic and superficial.

While the gifts were opened, Julia busied herself in the kitchen throwing away napkins and consolidating the remaining food onto smaller platters.

"So, what's your deal?" a woman's voice asked. It was Roxanne, the same aggressive woman Julia had met at the bar years ago when she had faked her grandmother's death to save Sarah from an uncomfortable conversation.

"Pardon me?" Julia said.

"You're the hostess and you're not in there with the gifts."

Julia wasn't sure if it was a question, and she responded with a shrug. She knew this type of woman and had learned it was best to minimize the conversation.

"You don't like babies or what?" Roxanne said.

"Funny," Julia said, trying desperately to shake free.

"I have four kids," she continued. "And I am so over the baby phase." She stressed the word "over" giving it exaggerated importance. Roxanne picked up a platter from the sink and began to wash it. Julia was stuck with her.

Rolling her eyes, Julia asked, "How old are your kids?" She knew how the conversation was supposed to go and, seeing that she had no choice, would politely follow expectations. She was grateful they were not looking at one another.

"Our youngest is three, the others are five, eight, and eleven. You?" Roxanne handed Julia the cleaned platter.

"We don't have kids," Julia said, turning her back to return the serving dish to its place.

"What's taking you so long?" Roxanne said.

Julia froze. How could a person ask such a question? Roxanne didn't know her or her story, and yet there she stood accusing Julia of taking too long—as if the timeframe of motherhood was a choice. Heat expanded within her body. She wanted to slam the glass platter on the corner of the granite counter top and feel the weight of it shatter.

With gritted jaw, Julia turned around and stared at the back of the woman cleaning the dishes. "Your youngest is three, huh? What's taking you so long to lose the baby weight?" Julia glared, as the woman turned around in shock. Julia walked out of the room still carrying the dish.

She made it to the car, slammed the gear shift into drive and made her escape.

When she hit the dirt road that led to the lake, she began

screaming a mixture of moaning sobs and expletives. A torrent of sorrowful agony overflowed its banks and rose into rapids, covering every pebble of hope and happiness, leaving Julia to drown.

"Jules," David said. "You have to get out of the shower. I'm already running late for work, and I need to get in."

She sat on the tiled floor, her arms around her legs, her head on her knees, the hot water reddening her neck and back. Her salty tears mixed with the shower water, slipped into the drain, and disappeared.

This had become her favorite place to cry. The shower allowed her to be alone and hidden, two things she had become accustomed to feeling. A life without kids now felt like a prison of lonely, helpless solitude. She wanted nothing more than to be hidden from the happy people of the world—the people fulfilled with healthy children and happy marriages. Hidden from the people skipping down the street to their next blessing.

She wanted a hot shower and raw tears.

David opened the shower door and saw his wife crumpled. She looked up at him with the blotchy face of grief. "Jules, honey," he said softly. "You have to get past this. Come out of the shower. Get dressed and I promise to take you to lunch today. We can work it out there. Okay?" He reached out his hand and she took it.

He wrapped her in a towel and hugged her tightly. "Everything is going to be okay. This is no big deal."

With a kiss on the forehead he released her and stepped into the shower.

"Nothing is okay" she said. "Nothing."

The phone rang and she went to pick it up. Her usually chipper "hello" had turned into a moody greeting the color of ash.

"Jules, it's time!. Sarah's voice was filled with excitement. "See you at the hospital!" There was a click, and the line went silent.

Wrapped in her towel, she sat on the edge of her bed and searched for a reason not to go back to bed.

The baby was born at 10:15 a.m. A healthy boy of 7lbs 4oz with dark tufts of hair and bright eyes. Both mother and baby were doing great. The baby had yet to be named, but that would come soon enough. Julia knew all of this because she saw Sarah's post on Facebook when she checked at four o'clock.

Under the post there were 112 Likes and myriad comments of congratulations and blessings.

When work ended, Julia drove to the gas station to fill up and get a soda. She picked up David's dry cleaning and dropped a package at the post office. When she was unable to avoid it any longer, she drove to the hospital.

"Jules!" Sarah said, exasperated. "Where have you been?"

She was in a mint green, buttoned-down shirt and diamond earrings. Her hair was in a messy bun that was trending now, and her lipstick was stunning. The baby, covered with a blanket, was suckling at her breast.

"Are you sure you just had a baby?" Julia said, hugging her best friend. "You look like a million bucks."

"Thanks," Sarah said, brushing her compliment away. "I've had plenty of time to freshen up. I thought when I called you this morning you'd be here right away."

"Oh, I'm sorry," Julia said, faking confusion. "I didn't realize that was what you meant, and today has been crazy."

"It's okay, " Sarah said, pulling the tiny child from her breast and skillfully recovering herself. "Wanna hold him?"

No, she didn't want to hold him. He was so very small and fragile. A whisper of a person nestled in the warmth of a blanket and his mother's comfort. What if he cried? What if she dropped him. What if she couldn't handle it?

"Where are John and Joshua?" Julia asked, changing the subject.

"They went to grab us some dinner. Now take the baby,"

Sarah scolded.

Julia did as she was told, being careful to support his tiny head with one hand and his blanket-bundled frame with the other. She sat on the chair at the end of the bed and cradled the infant, her body hunched in protection around him.

He smelled clean and fresh. She put her lips to his cheek and inhaled the heat of his breath as she kissed him. Julia rubbed her nose against his and closed her eyes, savoring the essence of him.

This is what love felt like. An ache of joy for his existence and a fearful prayer for his health and protection. She loved this little guy more than she expected. She had assumed there was no balm for her pain, and yet here it was, in the sleeping face of a newborn hope.

"I'm actually glad we're alone. I've been wanting to talk to you," Sarah said. "Roxanne told me what she said before you took off during the shower. She's a bitch. Blow her off."

Julia smiled.

"Really though. What has happened to you?" Sarah squinted her eyes. "It's like my best friend has disappeared, leaving me with . . ." and she motioned open handed to Julia ". . . this. I don't even recognize you."

Julia's high began to plunge. Her elation and spiritual uplift at holding the baby was giving way to darkness once again.

"Sorry to disappoint you with 'this,'" she said, handing the baby back to his mother as if he had become too hot to hold any longer. "I'm just barely hanging on, okay?"

"No, it's not okay. This has to stop. You have to find a way to get tough and deal with this thing you are doing to yourself. Your eyes are always swollen and you're always sad. That negativity is not good for anyone."

"So, let me make sure I hear you. You want me to 'get tough' so that you aren't around my negativity?" Julia said. "Let me help you with that." She exited the room, leaving Sarah to hear the sound of her footsteps down the echoing hospital corridor.

CHAPTER 21

"Your mother has gone vegan. God help us," Julia's dad said, opening the door. "We've missed you, Kiddo."

They had missed supper last month, the first time since Julia was in college. Going two months without seeing her parents felt like an eternity, but she had needed a hiatus from questioning eyes and uncomfortable inquiry.

"Vegan, huh?" David said. "Let's do this!"

Dinner was surprisingly good. With all her experiments, Beaty had become great with new recipes and ingredients.

When the men went outside for their beer, Julia fell in line next to her mother washing dishes. "How are you, my love?" Beaty said.

"Good, Mom. You?"

"I'm worried about your sister. She hasn't called in a week," Beaty said. "I just feel like something's wrong. The universe feels unbalanced, like we should be prepared for something. Ya know?"

Julia did know. The idea of Savvy moving home had been sitting like a rock in her stomach. Not that she'd hate to have her sister home; she'd actually like a chance to get to know her again since they were both adults now. But the reason for her move had to be substantial.

When Savvy left she said, "It will be a cold day in hell before I every come back here." Until now she had been true to her word. Julia wondered what kind of hell Savvy had fallen into.

"I was thinking about that too," Julia said. "But time has passed, and she hasn't come home. So maybe whatever it was she needed to run away from stopped chasing her."

"Now, that's poetic," Beaty said smiling. "I love you so much."

Beaty pulled her oldest daughter into a hug. It was still unfamiliar for both of them like a sweater that didn't quite fit. During Julia's childhood, James had been the hugger while Beaty remained physically distant. She was always loving, even when her alcoholic moods were unstable, but hugging didn't come naturally; it was something she had picked up in AA.

"Dinner was good, Mom." Julia said, changing the subject.

"Yes, it was," she said happily. And then looked into Julia's eyes. "As much as I'm concerned about Savvy, I'm even more worried about you. Let me in, Honey. David told me what's going on with your infertility."

"What?" Julia was shocked. David had spoken to her mother without her knowing? He had told her about their personal business. Her? He knew better, and he was going to learn that lesson again when they got home. Julia felt betrayed.

"He's worried about you. He thought you might need some depression medication. I told him about some natural solutions."

"I'm not depressed, Mom," she said feeling her body heat up. "We want kids, and we haven't had any luck. Every drunken cheerleader under the bleachers on homecoming can get knocked up, but not me. I want to see a specialist and David doesn't. What else did he tell you?"

Beaty started plucking at the air, removing unseen particles. "What the hell?" Julia demanded.

"I'm trying to clean your aura. You're filled with dark clouds."

"My aura is fine. Leave my aura alone. Tell my husband I'll be waiting in the car."

Julia marched to the front door, but then she stopped and

stood.

Why was it when she was away from her mom a small, pea-sized part of her wanted to be like her? To be freed from the cage of self-ridicule and live more in touch, communing with creation and spiritual forces. But in the presence of her mother she felt like her fur had been rubbed the wrong way. All she wanted to do was roll her eyes in annoyance.

Maybe that was why she couldn't get pregnant. Maybe God didn't want her to have a baby because she was short with her mom, bitchy to her friend, angry at her husband, and out of touch with the spiritual side of, well, everything.

Maybe, just maybe, she could make God a deal. She would eat better, quit cussing, pray more, send money to charities, something. Anything. If she could better herself, would God hold tight to His end of the deal?

Julia wondered what would be considered a handshake deal with God himself since his hand was not available for shaking. Is that what baptism was for?

Maybe that was the secret Yvette was privy too that Julia wasn't. Maybe the handshake of baptism was why Yvette understood so deeply the proverbs and parables of the Bible that read to Julia like the Spanish she had tried to learn in middle school. Picking up a word here and there but uncovering the depth and internalizing the messages was far too much work to Julia.

Maybe that was the deal she would make with God. She'd go and get herself baptized and then she'd be given a child.

When Julia opened the door to leave, she saw her sister sitting on the porch steps in the dark.

"Savvy?" Julia asked.

Savvy turned her head and looked at Julia over her shoulder.

"Hey," she said. Julia would know that voice anywhere.

She was in jeans and a tank top, the key tattoo on her shoulder easily visible. Her hair was longer than Julia had ever seen it before, and even in the dark she could see that the

California sun had lightened her sister's hair considerably.

"What are you doing out here?" Julia said.

"I was about to ring the bell and surprise everyone but..."

"But what?"

Savvy started to cry and Julia moved to sit next to her. In all their year of growing up in the same house, Julia had never seen her sister cry. While Julia was the organized one, the hard-worker, Savvy was the strong one.

And then Julia saw it. Savvy's stomach, round and full.

The sisters looked down together. "That's why I'm home," Savvy said.

Julia's instinct was to flee—she had become rather good at that lately. She closed her eyes, gathering herself. It all made perfect sense. Her sister was pregnant and couldn't handle it alone.

"You made the right choice," Julia said. "Let's go inside."

After the initial shock and questions were asked, Julia told David it was time for them to go. "Let's let Savvy get settled in," she said.

David opened the car door for Julia.

"Take me home," she said.

"Jules, are you mad at me or your sister? I can't tell with you anymore."

Even though he couldn't see her face, she glowered, a deep crease forming between her brows. "My mom," she growled. "You told my mom about our problems? You know how I feel about her. You know how she is about stuff. That was my call to make. Who do you think you are telling my mom?"

"I'm worried about you Jules," he said. "Look at me." He waited without response. "Please."

He had fallen in love with Julia because of her strength. He was upset with her now for thinking herself too strong to let him in.

"I feel like you are drowning in all this baby stuff. You've always been the one to save me with a kickboard. This time it's so different. I had hoped that talking to your mom would be a lifeline," he said. "For both of us."

"Calling my mom was like throwing me in the river. And now Savvy, too. Will it never fucking end?"

They drove home in silence and spent the following day in the pulsing quiet of unresolved anger, like magma simmering beneath the volcano.

Julia wanted to give up the frustration. She wanted to throw her arms around her husband, beg forgiveness, and cry until her body was empty. But she was prideful, and with that came an impenetrable shell of self-righteousness.

More than that, she had grown comfortable in the darkness of her hopelessness. She had still been able to see a light in the distance, piercing the forest horizon. But every time she tried to run toward it, the light eluded her and remained always distant, always unattainable. Now she had stopped chasing the light and began to accept the seclusion the darkness provided.

Through the common language of shared space, meaningful communication came again. At dinner the following night David spoke first asking her to "Pass the salt" and then said, "What do you want to watch on TV?" The next evening it turned into "How was your day" and finally back to "I miss you" and "I'm sorry."

David told her that Beaty had been phoning him twice a day at the office to check in.

"Now you see why I don't tell her anything," Julia laughed enjoying David's unintended punishment.

"This just isn't my strong suit. I was trying to do a good thing by asking for help," he said, looking down. Julia was familiar with this behavior. It was similar to a dog begging for food. The lowered head meant he didn't want to start a fight but he wanted to say something.

"I get it," Julia said. "You think I need help."

"I don't know. Maybe." He moved toward her and pulled her head to his chest. His deep breath told Julia he was thankful she had not fought the conversation.

"Maybe you're right," she said, beginning to weep. "But I don't want some kind of happy pill or something. I just want what everyone else is getting. I'm sorry it's making me so crazy."

"I love you and your crazy," he said. "You feel things bigger than me, and I get that. But you need Sarah back, ya know? How do we fix all this?"

"Just like a man," Julia said, suppressing her rolled eyes. "Always wanting to fix things."

There was no stepping over the hole that Sarah's absence made in Julia's life. Before their fight, they had gone days without speaking, but never weeks. And never under duress. The few weeks that had passed since Julia stomped out of the hospital seemed to move like lazy afternoon clouds, slowly and without purpose.

Julia longed to talk to Sarah about Savvy. She wanted to rant about her younger sister showing up six months pregnant expecting everyone to drop their lives and help her. But Sarah was no longer the friend who could understand everything. Happy in the land of babies and pregnancies, she would never understand the grief Julia was struggling with. Plus the negativity would be bad for Sarah and the baby. At the thought of Sarah's words, Julia clenched her jaw.

As they made amends, Julia again told David she was ready to see a specialist about their fertility issues. This time he didn't say no.

That was good enough for her.

They spent the evening with a glass of their favorite Cab Sav blend under the stars as the hot tub massaged their bodies, the heat billowing above them.

"Jules, can I ask you a question?" David said, as she kept her eyes on the sky.

"Uh huh," she murmured.

"Why are you putting yourself through all this? I mean"— he was obviously trying to phrase it so as not to start another fight—"why is this upsetting you so much?"

She took a deep breath, knowing he was trying to relate to her, to understand her.

"Because I want to be a mom," she said simply.

"Why?" As he asked the loaded question, she realized how important the answer would be.

Her thoughts flew like a bottle rocket into the air and exploded into a million answers.

She hadn't realized how much she wanted to be a mother until David had proposed the question eighteen months ago. At first, the idea scared her, but then she realized how wonderful David would be at parenting. She wanted to do it for him, to see his eyes glow with pride at the person they had created, to see him with a child on his shoulders watching a local parade.

She thought about how being a mother was the most basic of female drives. Women were made to reproduce. It was how we are created physically, emotionally, and hormonally. She wanted to fulfill that promise.

She thought about Claudia, the masseuse from Florida, who had said she would remember Julia because of how much she wanted to give life.

Thinking outside her own self-centered creation, Julia considered the world as a whole. It was, at times, a broken place in need of someone to fill it with joy and positive leadership. Maybe her child would satisfy that need with his or her talents and love.

At other times, the world was full of promise and beauty. She wanted to bring a child into the world to experience the sunsets and the laughter and the wind in his hair as he rode a bike.

Then, finally, she contemplated her own selfishness.

She has spent the last year and a half filling her heart with love for the child that could be and then each month the bucket was emptied and filled with pain. Through this process she realized something so very important about herself. Because of her unfailing love for the creation of a child, she would make a great mother.

She realized that the depth of love a mother got to share with her child is a bond deeper than the oceans and more vast than the heavens. Love, like the magnificent universe of stars, always expanding. The thought fell from her mind into her heart, much like a star falling from above.

Julia took it as a sign. This was the right answer. This was why.

CHAPTER 22

In proud Julia style, she researched every fertility specialist in the area. There were four. Not that she had ever thought about it, but she assumed there would be more. It seemed like women all over Facebook and blogs were going to these clinics all the time. Julia had just assumed they'd be everywhere, like Starbucks.

But four was promising. All she had to do was choose the right one, and she and David could go about their life with a new little soul to raise. Professional expertise would be the knockout punch she had been waiting for.

One of the clinics was over two hours' drive from her home, so that one went to the bottom of the list. One was associated with a rival of the state university she and David had attended. She was raised never to cheer for them and couldn't see herself going to a fertility clinic with that name on the building. As a last resort maybe, but definitely not the first choice.

The other two clinics seemed to be neck and neck in terms of services, doctors, and driving distance. Julia clicked on the Facebook pages of each office to see if the women who commented were anything like her. How could she walk into a place asking for help if the doctors and nurses saw couples that were nothing like her and David? What if they specialized in the treatment of old women or fat women or those that have perfectly diagnosed medical problems? Except for the suspect cells that Dr. Lamont said would not interfere with fertility, she was healthy.

On one Facebook site, a post had been made just three minutes earlier. "Support group meeting at Panera Bread in thirty minutes. I'll be the one in all white. See you there." The address was just up the street, and the time was her lunch hour.

All white, Julia thought. How hokey.

She turned off the computer monitor and spun around in her chair, letting the idea of a support group catch up to her as she swiveled. She couldn't possibly go. If she did, it would be admitting she had a problem, like an alcoholics' meeting. Of course, she knew she had a problem, but this felt like creating a forest fire just to roast a marshmallow.

She tried to picture the women who would choose to attend the meeting. They probably wore frowns and obnoxious red hats. They probably cried and patted each other on the backs and said worthless things like "It'll be okay."

She would never, never be one of those women.

She spun around in her chair again. She couldn't leave the idea alone. Like a dripping faucet, it nagged at her. She grabbed her keys and walked out of the door.

The parking lot at Panera was full, and she had to park down the street. She pulled down the visor and opened the mirror, illuminating her forehead. Her brows needed plucking, but there was nothing she could do about that now. She applied a lipstick and topped it with a rose-colored gloss. She pinched her cheeks and combed her fingers through her hair.

Before stepping out of the car, she grabbed a stack of papers she had been meaning to go through at home. It was a grant application prepared by a colleague, and she wanted to double check it before it went out. It would provide the perfect cover for snooping.

The restaurant was loud with the chatter of patrons, the scream of the coffee grinder, and the dinging bell of a meal ready. She loved the first step into any bakery, the smell of sugared, yeasty confection thawing memories of a happy childhood frozen by time. She could almost taste the

Christmas cookies her mother used to make.

Fortunately the line to place an order was long, and she had the chance to look covertly for the woman in white. She saw only one woman who fit the bill, but that couldn't be her. She was probably in her mid-thirties, thin and elegant, the kind of woman who could pull of all white and get away with it. There were six or seven others swarming around her table.

Without warning the woman in white got up and walked in Julia's direction. She was smiling and making her way through the crowded restaurant directly to Julia. Did she have some kind of built-in compass that pointed toward the woman with fertility problems?

Julia held her breath. If the woman spoke to her, she planned to deny her reason for being there. She'd say, "You must have me confused with someone else. I don't belong in your group." Then she'd offer her best smile.

A dampness began to grow under Julia's arms and on her palms as the woman approached.

Politely, she gave Julia a smile and said, "Pardon me." Julia smiled and was just about to speak, when the woman looked just past her said, "Rebecca, I am so glad you are here." The two women embraced.

How self-centered can I possibly be, Julia thought, as she reddened in the face.

She desperately tried not to look at the two women as they talked about how busy was and how glad they were to see one another. When finally Julia ordered she allowed herself quick glance.

Recognition hit her instantly. "Rebecca?"

"Hi, Julia," Rebecca said, excitedly moving to offer a hug. She addressed the woman in white. "Ava, this is Julia Ellis. We know each other through Yvette Williams. Julia, this is Ava, our fearless leader."

It was surprising that Rebecca had introduced her as Yvette's friend and not someone she knew from the oncology office where Rebecca was the receptionist. That was, after all, the place they knew each other from the most.

The two shook hands, Ava taking Julia's hand with both of hers.

"Your fearless leader?" Julia asked, faking confusion.

"We're in a support group, and Ava's the one who keeps us organized and inspired."

"I don't know about that," Ava said, humbly. "It's my great pleasure to meet with each of you."

Ava's formality made Julia admire her immediately. Who says "my great pleasure" like that? Old movie stars, maybe? Queens and princesses? Julia wanted to pull that into her repertoire but thought she'd come off like a schoolgirl playing dress up.

Abruptly, Julia's name was called over the speaker announcing her order was ready. She wanted more time with these women, to ask about the group, to hear their stories, to know what they knew. It took some effort to excuse herself to get lunch.

Fortunately, there was a table next to support group, and Julia snatched it. She set her sandwich in the middle and laid her paperwork to the right side, arranging everything so she could face the women and see who was speaking. She felt like the lead in a bad detective sitcom.

"Let's begin," Ava said, calling the meeting to order and quieting the buzz of conversation. "I am so glad to see that we have a couple of new faces, so let's go around the table and introduce ourselves and give just a small introduction. This is a safe place where we look to one another for ideas, support, and sanity. Share whatever you're comfortable with."

Julia could tell from Ava's body position that she made eye contact with each woman as she spoke and held it like a private, delicate thing. Rebecca, whose back was to Julia, spoke first. Though Julia strained to hear, she could not make out the words.

The woman to Rebecca's left was pear shaped and overweight. Julia assumed she had probably been pretty in high school because she had excellent hair and big, well-made-up eyes. Julia caught her name, Kristy, and the words "thyroid issue" and "ovary."

The woman next to Kristy, who said her name was Laney, had been "fighting the fertility battle for four years" and been through two rounds of in vitro fertilization after her PCOS diagnosis. Laney brushed tears away as she said this last part, but there was something about her that felt a little plastic, like she was putting on a show.

The acronym was new to Julia. She flipped the grant application over and jotted down the initials so she could look them up when she got home.

The heavy-set woman in purple next to Laney, whose name Julia didn't catch, had just finished an unsuccessful bout with IUI, but her husband didn't want to do IVF. Next to PCOS, Julia wrote IUI.

Julia could relate to someone not wanting to do IVF or other advanced medical treatments. She could hear Beaty's speech about the universe introducing itself. The woman might literally combust if she learned that Julia was interested in medical help to get pregnant.

When Julia had first brought up the idea of medical help, David squelched it, simply making an offhand comment about the "slippery slope" of medicine. Julia had instantly felt guilty for bringing it up.

"Hopefully, we'll get pregnant naturally and won't have to get into a debate," the woman in purple said, snapping Julia back into the present. "We don't need more to fight about."

To Julia's shock, the next woman, with shoulder length auburn hair, said she was a lesbian, and since neither she nor her partner had the right equipment to conceive, they had no choice but to visit a fertility clinic. She said she felt like people assumed she was infertile because she was going to the clinic, but shared, "I've been labeled my whole life, so this was nothing new." All that being said, she added that they had tried artificial insemination three times with no success, and now she feared her partner wanted to give up.

With all the gay rights battles over marriage, adoption, and hospital privileges, Julia had never thought about the difficulty a gay woman would face trying to conceive. The more she watched this woman, stricken by her inability to conceive and her expressed love for her partner, the more she saw the personal stake of those gay-rights battles.

Stephanie, a well-dressed business woman, called herself an IVF veteran. "I've been at this for ten years and have had six failed rounds of in-vitro," she said as a matter of fact. Hearing this, the only thing Julia could think of was the disappointment. Just what kind of emotional toll would six stints of in-vitro actually cost your spirit?

"I'd like to address something you said," Stephanie motioned to the woman in purple. "We obviously don't have trouble with using medical advances to further our birth plan . . ."

Julia wondered if there was about to be an argument—doctors vs. God, medicine vs. miracle. After David had made the slippery slope comment, she had thought long and hard about it. Though she wasn't under the umbrella of "religious," Julia wholly believed in God and had wondered if God would approve of them doing something invasive to conceive. If nothing else, this debate could give her more to mull over.

Stephanie continued. "Years ago when we started this, my sister-in-law told me a story that helped to shape our opinions. One day a man was at his home watching the news of an impending flood. A knock at the door was from a fireman who told him of the mandatory evacuations. The man chose to stay, saying, 'God will save me.' As the waters rose to his knees, a canoe came to his door. The man turned down the ride to safety, saying, 'God will save me.' Finally the man was atop his roof and a helicopter dropped a rope. The man refused the lift, saying, 'God will save me.. When the man died and went to heaven he had one question for God—'Why didn't you save me?' And God responded, 'I sent you a fireman, a canoe and a helicopter."'

The group laughed, and the woman in purple said she would share the story with her husband. Julia thought she might do the same. On her notepaper she wrote "helicopter."

"Well, ladies," the next woman said. "For those of you I don't know, I'm Mel. But you don't have to remember my name because this is my last meeting." There was a gasp from Ava and Stephanie, who clearly knew Mel well. She threw up her hands in surrender. "I wish I could say it is because I'm pregnant. I'm not. About a year ago we decided to adopt but continued to try to get pregnant." Her smile suddenly grew. "Our new package arrives in two months."

Several woman jumped up to hug Mel, and there were tears from several. These women really care about one another, Julia thought. She had expected to see a bunch of downtrodden, angry, hormonal women who talked about their sorry lot in life and their terrible husbands. She hadn't expected this camaraderie.

When the women finally settled back into their places, the last woman introduced herself. Sophie spoke with her hand over her mouth and leaned in as if sharing a secret. She was seated closest to Ava and so was the easiest for Julia to overhear from her spy's perch.

It turned out Sophie had some kind of illness that required her to take a medication that would cause birth defects. With her doctor she was trying again to wean herself from the prescription, but the headaches and joint pain she was experiencing were difficult, and she feared if she did get pregnant, she wouldn't be able to sustain the strain on her body.

After the introductions, health insurance seemed to be the topic of conversation. Julia ate her sandwich as she eavesdropped.

From what Julia could overhear, it sounded like Kristy had been on the phone with her carrier for two hours and had hung up in tears. Laney said the insurance company wouldn't cover any infertility treatment because she had PCOS and that was considered a preexisting condition. Stephanie commented that her carrier covered abortions under certain circumstances but wouldn't cover any kind of fertility care. The outrage was tangible.

Biting into her apple, Julia realized she had never considered the cost of the clinics she was researching. She had assumed that she'd pay her twenty-dollar co-pay and then be on her merry way, pushing a stroller as she went.

These women were talking about begging the insurance companies for thousands and thousands of dollars. Though she was leaving the group, Mel brought up the idea of scholarships, and Laney offered to do some research for the next meeting, which would be held in four weeks.

Julia added insurance to the list of things she'd look into when she got home.

The group had a strict policy of ending at one o'clock so that everyone could get back to work. "Getting fired is the last thing we need," Ava said with a smile. Julia stole glances of the women hugging their goodbyes as she pretended to work on the grant application.

Julia looked up as Rebecca approached. "Get a lot of work done?" she asked, glancing down at Julia's papers.

"Sure did," she lied, thankful that she'd turned the application over. It would have been humiliating for Rebecca to see the words "PCOS," "IUI," "helicopter," and "insurance." She could not have explained the notes without divulging the truth.

"So, I was walking in my neighborhood the other day, and I saw you running."

"Oh, my gosh," Julia said. "How embarrassing, but thank you for calling it 'running.' I tried that Couch to 5K app, and decided I couldn't cut it, so now I just have an app to track my progress. So we live in the same neighborhood?"

"Guess so," Rebecca said, taking a seat at Julia's table. "I'm on Celia—third house on the left with the black shutters."

"I'm on 21st Street. You're right around the corner." Julia hadn't met anyone in her neighborhood other than the older couple across the street. When she was growing up, she remembered, her mother and father had spent hours outside talking with neighbors as the kids rode bikes and played hide-and-go-seek.

When she and David had moved into Heather Hills, she had envisioned the same scenario. But as of yet they hadn't met anyone and didn't have the excuse of kids to keep them outside and engaged with the neighbors.

"Next time you decide to run, will you stop by and get me? I need motivation," Rebecca said, grabbing Julia's hand and leaning in conspiratorially. The gesture reminded Julia of Sarah, and an unexpected pang of loss hit her in the chest. It made Julia like Rebecca instantly.

"I'll do it," Julia said. "How does after work tomorrow sound? But afterwards we have to drink wine or something."

"Perfect," Rebecca said.

CHAPTER 23

The evening was beautiful. A light breeze blew the clouds into billowing shapes as Julia and David walked hand-in-hand around the lake.

It was a three mile track, and on nights like this, it was full of athletic girls in their sports bras running effortlessly fast and overweight men jogging like locomotives lumbering to up a hill. There were speeding bikers in spandex and parents slowly herding children with scooters and training wheels.

It was the kind of place that allowed a person to go at their own pace but, amid lithe athletes and on-looking eyes, encouraged you to do your best. Julia was certainly not ready to run here lest someone recognize her and place her in the locomotive category.

As they walked, she told David about her special-ops mission at lunch. In the moment, it had felt like research. But as she explained it she wondered if David thought her clever for spying or inconsiderate for intruding on their hallowed time.

She told David about seeing Rebecca and about their plans to run together the following day. There was no reason for it, but she left out the detail of Rebecca's involvement in the support group. Somehow that fact felt a little like betrayal.

David admitted he had never heard of Rebecca before, shocking Julia. "Didn't I tell you about her after my first appointment with Dr. Pinnison?" Of course there had been a lot going on that day, but Rebecca's holding Julia arm and walking her into Dr. Pinnison's office was an act of kindness she had been exceedingly grateful for. How could she had forgotten to tell David?

"Do you really want to join the group?" David asked. His "really" told Julia he thought the idea was a bad one.

"No, no," she said defensively. "I was only snooping."

But it wasn't true. She knew there was a kindred spirit among those women that she yearned to experience. Like it was watching the popular girls in high school laugh and joke at a separate lunch table, she longed for their attention and acceptance.

"Good. I mean we don't fit into an infertility group. We're just getting the ball rolling."

"It's been well over a year David." Her voice was quiet. But she also let his word "we" cascade down on her, refreshing her with the feeling of his companionship. It wasn't often that David spoke of their trouble, and Julia felt like she carried the burden by herself. She squeezed his hand tighter as they walked.

"Yeah, but come on. Didn't you say those girls introduced themselves like alcoholics? 'Hi, I'm Bertha and I'm infertile.'"

"Nice choice of names," Julia laughed.

"And those girls have a resume a lot longer than ours."

He was right. They had been engaged in fertility experiments and failure for a long time. They had tried multiple things multiple times. Their introductions alone were a synopsis of heartbreak. How could a person try and try so often without success and still manage to get up in the morning and put on makeup?

Maybe the slope of fertility medicine was greased with the tears of thwarted expectations. Once you began medical treatment and it didn't work, the natural response was to slide into the next medication and procedure, moving ever forward until you attained the summit of live birth or toppled over the cliff of failure.

Maybe playing the percentages of success was like putting your chips on a Las Vegas roulette table and waiting for the ball to stop in your one special number.

But an infertility regimen has to start somewhere, with some motivation. The moment Sarah turned up pregnant, she felt her own urgency double. With Savvy knocked up and thrust back into her life, she felt it triple.

"Don't go again," David said. "Not until we're ready for all of this."

Deflated, Julia agreed.

"What's the news with Savvy," he asked.

"Don't get me started. She is a hot mess."

"Has she said who the father is yet?"

"Nope. Still refuses," Julia said. "And get this, she got a job as a barista at Flavors."

"Good for her."

"What do you mean 'good for her'?" Julia asked. "She's going to have a baby in three months. She has no money so she gets a job making coffee. And apparently the apartment she had fell through so she's living with Mom and Dad."

"At least she came home," David said.

"To mooch!"

"You are way too mad at Savvy. I think you need to talk to her. She is your sister, and family matters. You need to at least be civil. Go to the coffee shop to see her or something."

"Can't you ever be on my side, even for a second?" Back came the beast of betrayal Julia met when she learned David spoke to Beaty about their fertility problems. How dare he tell her how to handle her sister? How dare he act holier than thou? How dare he tell her she couldn't go to that fertility group? She was his wife, not his slave. He wasn't the king of all righteousness.

Julia was glad the walk was over. She was done holding his hand.

When he got home from work the following day, David told Julia he didn't feel right about going to a specialist yet. He had spent his lunch with Brian discussing it. He determined to give their bodies another chance before doctors and medicines clouded what was supposed to be natural.

Julia could picture the conversation—David saying, "We're thinking of seeing a fertility specialist," and Brian saying, "Hmm," and David saying ,"Yeah, I know," and then magically things were understood. The grunting of male bonding was a foreign language indecipherable to the fifty percent of the population with boobs.

"So Brian is calling all the shots in this family now?" she said, simmering with anger and frustration.

"It's not like that," David said.

"Sounds like it to me."

She left the room, restraining the hateful words that, if spoken, would start a war.

She seethed. He hadn't discussed anything with her, his wife. Instead, he discussed their most private and personal decisions with a friend. David didn't give her a chance to tell him about the effort she had put in when, earlier in the day, she had phoned Dr. Lamont to request a referral.

He obviously didn't realize how difficult it had been for her to hear the receptionist's voice and then say, "I'd like to get a referral from Dr. Lamont for a fertility specialist." It had been exactly like admitting she was an alcoholic—she recalled David's analogy—and this particular step had been excruciating.

When the receptionist recommended she first speak to Dr. Lamont in person, Julia clenched her teeth and closed her eyes. Nothing was easy. Not even a referral. She imagined sharing this at the support group . . . if she ever went.

Fine. If David was going to make a decision without consulting her, then she was going to do the same. This was supposed to be a partnership, damn it. He was not going to control the partnership without her input.

The appointment with Dr. Lamont was scheduled for five weeks from now. After hearing David's snarky view of the support group and now his change of heart about a specialist, she would keep the appointment and keep it secret.

Julia knew she was flash-in-the-pan angry with him now, and she made a vow to herself not to make a habit of keeping secrets. Maybe David would come around to the idea, and she'd look like a genius for not canceling. They were talking about how to conceive a baby, after all, not having an affair. It was a tiny secret, and she wouldn't allow herself to worry about keeping it.

Julia figured there were several options for couples in their situation. The large woman in the purple shirt at the support-group meeting had said they had just done IUI—Julia still needed to look that up. Maybe it was something David might do. She'd visit with Dr. Lamont and maybe even the specialist, and then come to David with the options. All he'd have to do is pick a path.

She would take these five weeks to do everything she possibly could to conceive. And if that didn't work she'd research their options and formulate good questions for Dr. Lamont. She'd seek comfort in intimacy and information and find a way to increase the odds in their favor so that when David did come around to the idea of medical assistance, and the roulette ball finally did stop, they'd be left with a healthy baby. The gamble of the secret would be worth it.

Thus far, Julia had not looked at their situation as a contest she wanted to win but as a personal assault on her character. That would change today.

CHAPTER 24

Hoping it was right, Julia rang the doorbell to the house with the black shutters on Celia street. To her relief, Rebecca opened the door.

"Still wanna go for a jog?" Julia said with a smile.

Julia was invited in while Rebecca got her shoes. From the entryway, she could see that the living room flowed into the kitchen and breakfast room. Where Julia's sink was full of dishes awaiting the dishwasher, Rebecca's was spotless. The house smelled of lemon, and Julia assumed she had just disinfected the kitchen.

Rebecca's home was decorated in a plush contemporary style. The living room walls were painted a deep maroon that warmed in the afternoon light shining through the wall of windows at the back of the house. Modern curtains hung from the ceiling by five pearl-colored finials on each side. The couch looked sleek but comfortable. The art and accessories had obviously been selected by someone with discerning taste and an eye for style and scale.

Julia stepped closer to the wedding portrait hanging on the wall inside the door. Rebecca, with an overjoyed, gummy smile and wearing a timeless dress, strapless and without lace or bravado, was looking into the camera. Her hair must have been longer then because it was pinned at the crown of her head and surrounded by a tiara. Cascades of dark curls fell around her strong jaw, the black hair contrasting beautifully with the pure white of her dress. Her husband, more round in the belly than Julia had expected, looked at his bride with pride and amazement, as if he thought she might at any moment run away laughing at him. He looked to be about ten years older than his bride.

"It was kind of a fun day," Rebecca said, motioning to the photo. "Brandon loves that picture. I think it makes me look kind of squinty."

"You looked beautiful," Julia complimented. "Ready?"

"Take it easy on me," Rebecca said, twining her arm with Julia's.

She expected the touching this time and warmed to the persistent closeness it demanded. Julia understood it to be a physical declaration of friendship and knew she'd grow to appreciate it as part of her new comrade.

"I say we do more of a fast walk and pat ourselves on the back for being so athletic," Julia said with a smile.

As they walked the women laughed about drunken family members at their weddings and compared mother-in-law stories. They gave overviews of their husbands, and Julia was refreshed to be around another woman who seemed to truly love her husband. More and more often she had come across women who wanted to point out inadequacies and belittle their spouses. Julia often heard things like, "if he doesn't pick his underwear off the floor I'm going to scream," or "All he wants to do is sit on the couch and watch another damn football game."

True, Julia and David were in a battle of wills even if he didn't know. But that was not something you tell a new friend. Every couple had something they kept behind closed doors.

Five miles and an hour-and-a-half later, the women said goodbyes and parted ways. They had expected to be gone for a third of that time, but the conversation moved their feet. Julia discovered they liked to read the same authors. They agreed that Charleston was a crazy choice for Yvette to name her baby but that somehow it completely worked.

Julia had feared that their conversation would be weighed down if the subject turned to infertility and that more pounds would be added as she fought with herself about what to share and what to keep hidden. She didn't want Rebecca to know she had spied on the support group, and she wasn't ready to share her struggle. But the conversation never turned that way, and the walk seemed weightless. In fact, it was uplifting.

If Julia hadn't known Rebecca was in the support group, she would never have guessed she was dealing with fertility issues. Rebecca was the kind of woman who wanted to know about friends lives rather than share the burden of her own. Though it made her even more curious, Julia admired this. She seemed to be making a mental list lately of the characteristics she wanted to absorb. Asking questions of others as a way to drive conversations was definitely going to make the list.

Their growing bond was like a gem being unearthed—bright, substantial, and real. Once uncovered it would show the way to the understanding of greater things. But new friendships are delicate and worthy of care, and the unveiling process had to be slow and thoughtful.

Before promising to walk again soon, Rebecca brought up the idea of participating in a mud run. "It's a 5K full of muddy obstacles," she had explained. "And it's in a few weeks. Please say you'll do it with me. It's for charity after all."

Julia had barely run one mile without stopping. The idea of three miles and change sounded insurmountable.

On the other hand, Julia thought, this is the month I'm going to play to win. I can do this.

"I'm no runner," Rebecca continued. "But I'll be thirty that weekend, and I need something to take my mind off my birthday."

There was a load of things Julia wanted to get her mind off as well. Back at home, she got in her car.

She wasn't the kind of person to drink coffee at night—in fact, she'd never been to Flavors after 1:00 p.m.—but Julia knew she needed to see her sister. Since leaving her parent's house, she had only heard about Savvy through her mother. And though she hated to admit it, David was probably right. She was way too angry, and it the poison would affect Julia alone.

Behind the cash register, her sister looked the same as the day she left her at home. Her skin was beautiful, a point of jealousy Julia always carried. Her hair, though longer, was thick and dark. It was only when she left the register to make a drink that a customer would notice her expanded belly. She carried beautifully.

When they made eye contact, Savvy gave her customary "Hey."

"Hey," Julia said back.

Julia wasn't exactly sure what she was doing there. She didn't want to reconcile with Savvy or maybe didn't know how. There was no true substance to their lifelong dispute; it was more like cross-currents of hostility that began to combust, like a storm system, when the two were together.

But circumstances were changing, and Julia wanted to be the bigger person.

Julia glanced around, half expecting to see the old man with the pageboy hat. The crowd was light, mostly late teens and early twenties with papers in front of them. She imagined them studying for a college calculus test.

When the customer in front of her cleared, Julia approached the counter.

"What can I get ya?" Savvy said.

"Nothing really," Julia said. "I just wanted to come by and check on you."

"I'm pregnant, not damaged. I'm fine."

"Savvy, stop." Julia said. This was the point in their conversation when the thunder heads swelled. Each woman so used to defending herself. "I'm not here to get old fights going," Julia continued. "I care about you."

"I'm sure you do," Savvy said. "You want to walk in here

and tell me I need to get a job more fitting for a mother. You want to tell me to move out of Mom's house and stand on my own two feet. You want to bask in your perfect marriage while I am going to have to do this as a single mom. I won't let you judge me, Julia. I don't need that right now."

"I came by to start over. I came by to see how you are, and there you are putting words in my mouth. Who do you think you are. You don't know anything about me. You don't even know what a blessing you have. Forget you, Savvy. I'm done."

Julia left the coffee shop and marched to her car. Of all the responses Savvy could have had, Julia had never expiated that. How dare she.

CHAPTER 25

Most of the participants jogged through the first pool of mud, willing to let the wet brown dirt to coat their shoes and socks up to their knees. Rebecca, however, a warrior ready for battle, reached two fingers in the mud and drew them across each cheek. Then she charged. Julia, loving the liberation she saw in her friend, followed suit.

The entire experience was otherworldly to Julia. During the first hundred yards she questioned her ability as well as her sanity. But after passing a cheering crowd holding pink-ribboned signs of thanks at mile one, she found her groove.

At the second mile she caught the eye of a teenage girl, ordinary in her makeup and dress, except that she was completely bald. Her poster read, "Run For Me." Julia felt a surge of emotion that both clutched her heart and propelled her forward. She had the overpowering understanding that this experience was the culmination of a full life in which exertion and love grow for the benefit of others. She wanted to scream in thankfulness at being here.

Like military trainees, Julia and Rebecca crawled under barbed wire, their knees, arms, and stomachs coated with thick mud as they tried to keep from ripping their shirts and skin. Together they ran through hanging tires, slogged through a muddy stream, and climbed knotted ropes up and over walls. Whooping like a couple of children, they slid down tarp-covered hills while being sprayed with a fire hose.

They ran up more hills than either had thought possible. Admittedly, they walked several times. But at the finish line, they jumped over a line of fire holding their hands triumphantly in the air.

Heaving, with her hands on her knees, Julia looked down at the medal around her neck. She hadn't touched it yet, and the copper medallion was the only thing on her body not covered in the thick paste of brown mud.

She had second-guessed herself as she handed over the seventy-five dollar entry fee before the event began. But in this moment, fatigued but victorious, it had been more than worth it.

Rebecca threw her arms around Julia, and their muddy, exhausted bodies fell into the grass, the girls laughing uncontrollably. Rebecca took off her shoes and peeled down her socks. The line of clean skin was a surprise, and the girls laughed again.

A young girl approached them confidently. By the looks of her, she was eight or nine. With one hand she held a sack and with the other she pulled along a younger boy.

Julia looked around for a parent and spotted a woman under a shade tree watching the kids intently. The woman gave a small smile and nodded.

"My name is Grace," the little girl said, her voice high and clear like the call of a springtime bird. "And this is Elijah. He's my little brother."

"I'm not that little, Gracie," Elijah said, defensively and with the adorable lisp of a young child. "I'm this many old." He proudly held up four fingers.

Rebecca sat up straight and crossed her legs. "Well, how do you do? I'm Rebecca, and this is my friend Julia." Rebecca teasingly held out a muddy handshake to the children. Grace and Elijah giggled as the gingerly touched the muddy hand.

"Did you run?" the girl asked.

"We sure did, and now we need a bath," Rebecca said, playfully.

JULIA'S FIGHT A battle with infertility

"There is a fire truck over there that will spray you down, and if you don't want those shoes any more there is a pile over there you can throw them in." She pointed in each direction as she spoke.

"Is that right?" Rebecca asked. She had a comfortable, natural way with kids.

"Yep. There is a place that cleans the shoes and socks, and they give them to the homeless shelter downtown. Cool, huh?"

"Very cool," Rebecca said. "Did you run?"

"Nope. I'm just a kid. You have to be thirteen to run this race, and I'm eight and three quarters."

"Is that right?"

"Yep. I came here for my Grammy."

"That is great. Is she a runner?" Rebecca asked.

"No, she died right before Elijah was born. She had breast cancer. But my Grammy loved jewelry, so we come to these runs and pass out beads so people know we're glad they're running. Want one?"

It was a marvel to see this little girl speak so easily of her grandmother's passing. Truth to a child was simply fact and nothing else. The sky is blue. Dinner will be spaghetti. Grammy died. It was a beautiful and heartbreaking thing.

Julia made eye contact again with the woman under the tree. She thought the mother's simple smile must be a mixture of pride for the bravery of her children and sadness at the loss of her mother. This was such a powerful day, and Julia sucked in a ragged breath, trying to cover her emotions.

"We would love one," Rebecca said, without missing a beat. Julia assumed the ability to deal with the news of tragedy was both God-given and grown in the environment of Rebecca's job. It must take great strength to look at people every day and see them as both cancer patients and regular people. How difficult to share a smile with so many and know they are fighting for their life. The dichotomy would be painful.

Grace opened the bag, and Elijah reached in and pulled out two strings of pink Mardi Gras necklaces. The women lowered their heads as Grace put one around Rebecca's neck and Elijah slid one over Julia's muddy pony tail.

Unable to look up, Julia heard Rebecca say, "Thank you," as the kids ran off to the next group of muddy participants.

Suddenly Julia felt tired in her bones, as if the only thing holding her together was the covering of mud that had begun to dry and crack on her skin. The ache under her breast bone seemed to flow and swell throughout her body until the tears began to fall.

"You okay?" Rebecca said, with her hand on Julia's back.

"I just didn't expect all of this." Julia was unsure how to explain herself. "I mean, the run, the exhaustion, the posters, the little girls with the dead grandmas. I'm just so overwhelmed."

There was silence for several moments, and Julia saw that Rebecca was crying too. She was thankful to have found Rebecca. They had been friends only a few weeks now, and in that time Julia had begun to see Rebecca as a temporary replacement for Sarah—a casual friend to fill the void until its rightful owner could reoccupy the space.

But after today, she realized Rebecca wasn't a replacement, temporary or otherwise. She was a true friend, in whom Julia could confide and with whom she could cry.

Rebecca sniffled. "Tomorrow I'll be thirty, and all I want for my birthday is a child."

Julia had been waiting for this talk and was relieved it was finally coming. Since their first walk together, Julia had felt guilty for secretly knowing something so personal about Rebecca. It was a splinter, and Julia was ready to extract it.

"I feel so damn selfish being here and experiencing this, seeing these signs of hope and tragedy, and all I can think is, I'm healthy. Where are my children? What's wrong with me?"

Julia knew her duty as a friend was to point out Rebecca's positive attributes and tell her that there wasn't a thing wrong with her. She was supposed to give the "Everything is going to be all right" speech. But in this moment, staring at the raw truth of life—that it took loved ones with cancer and forced high school girls who should be worried about prom to instead worry about chemo—Julia didn't want to sugar-coat her response.

In the voice of a frightened child, Julia said, "Me too." She looked directly into Rebecca's eyes searching for her response, her surprise.

Julia had envisioned this conversation with her friend a thousand times. Rebecca would finally talk about her struggle and Julia would say "me too" and then Rebecca's mouth would gape open in shock.

But there was no bewilderment on Rebecca's face. Instead she began to laugh.

"What?" Julia said, thoroughly confused.

"I knew it. I knew it. I told Brandon after I saw you at Panera that day that you were in the same infertility boat."

"You did?"

"Yeah. I mean who brings all those papers into lunch and never gets past the first page? I thought you were listening to our conversation, but I wasn't sure."

"Shut up. You knew I was a spy?" Julia laughed.

"I knew because I did it for three months before I officially joined."

"David says we're not far enough along for me to go," Julia admitted, ashamed. "He's right, of course. I just wanted to see what the other people looked like. Is that so tacky?"

"It would be if I hadn't done the same thing."

They shared their stories, hitting the highlights and lamenting the way fertility problems consume you body, mind, and soul. When a mud-covered woman with an elated smile walked slowly by, they fell silent. The woman held the hands of two small children, who held the hands of two more children. A mother surrounded by her four kids.

"What makes her so lucky?" Julia asked. "Why is she so blessed and here we sit without children."

As the woman passed Julia read the bold word on the back

155

of her shirt—Survivor.

The friends looked at one another, both experiencing the same emotions of jealousy and then regret.

"We all have our battle," Rebecca said.

"Let's go get in that fire hose," Julia suggested. They linked arms to face it together.

CHAPTER 26

The next week, Julia was eager to arrive for dinner at her mother's. She was still living on a high from the run and wanted to share it with her family—she'd just ignore Savvy. When the door opened, her mother appeared dressed in a blue and white flannel shirt tied at the waist and a knee length, tight fitting jean skirt. Julia couldn't take her eyes off Beaty's exposed waistline and the shapeless white skin hanging there.

She knew her mother had lost a lot of weight and gained a healthier, more shapely figure. But she hadn't anticipated the shell of skin that wouldn't tighten and conform to her mom's fitter body. She couldn't decide if the saggy skin made her proud of her mother for losing the weight or mildly disgusted.

"Have I landed in Kansas? Did you steal Dorothy's clothes?" Julia asked, kissing her mom on the cheek.

"For months I've been making dishes from around the world. I thought it was time I made something from the heartland."

Savvy wore her long hair braided over her left shoulder and tied with a ribbon. She's pregnant and still trying to look like a juvenile, Julia thought.

The meal was chicken fried steak, mashed potatoes with gravy, and corn so slippery with butter it glistened in the dining room light.

Since deciding to win the war against infertility, she had seen her weight as an obstacle to victory. Asserting every ounce of willpower, Julia had neglected her stomach's begging and pared down her caloric intake. She drew a ragged breath at the temptation before her.

Deciding to go all in, she cut a generous portion of the deep fried meat and scooped a lump of potatoes on top. When the first forkful hit her tongue, she closed her eyes and relished the flavors. If it wouldn't have been completely inappropriate, she'd have moaned in delight.

David told the family that Julia had run in a race for breast cancer and then sat back to allow his wife to have center stage.

She described the logistics of the race—the five thousand runners, the atmosphere of loud music mixed with powerful support.

"But most of all, Mom," she said, looking Beaty in the eye, "I was moved. I felt like I made a difference, and I felt like a difference was made in me."

Speaking more rapidly than usual she explained about Grace and her brother, about the bald teenager, about recycling the shoes. She wanted her family, gathered around this home-cooked meal, to experience the powerful thing she had been a part of.

"I will definitely do another race," she said, when her dad asked. "But it's more than that. It's like I want to volunteer at the animal shelter. I want to give blood. I even want to recycle."

Beaty abruptly pushed herself from the table, ignoring her soiled napkin as it fell to the floor.

"You have finally seen the light," Beaty said. And like a big-top preacher, she threw her arms around her daughter.

"Next it'll be yoga and composting," her dad said, smiling. "Get ready, David."

"As long as we don't go vegan, it's okay with me," David said. The group laughed, and David beamed at his wife. He had missed this side of her.

The group moved on to other topics, and James asked David how work had been treating him.

"It's death by meeting at that place," he said. "I've actually put out a few feelers to see who's hiring."

For the last few months, David had come home from work more frustrated than usual. He'd talk about leaving the company and going to work for a smaller firm where he'd have more influence and mobility. But Julia knew he loved what he did and assumed the remarks were nothing more than a release of pressure, a way to escape the dissatisfactions that come with every job for greener pastures somewhere else. People needed the opportunity to believe themselves greater than their current status, which is why the run had influenced Julia so much. It made her feel more important. She thought David's ramblings about work were the same kind of outlet.

When they made eye contact across the table, Julia read the hopefulness in David's eyes. It was much like the look he gave her as he placed one knee in the sopping wet grass at Walter T. Landry Park and asked her to be his wife.

As they pulled into their garage that night, Julia leaned over and kissed David on the mouth. She allowed her lips to soften and stay with his longer than the usual peck of "hello" and "goodbye" that signified years of marriage in comfortable intimacy. His lips followed hers and opened to accept her tongue.

With passion he grabbed her hair, increasing the intensity. She clutched her hand high on his thigh, seductively massaging him, encouraging him. They made love that night in a fury of heat and urgency, clothes pulled off for fear they might catch fire in the friction of pulsing urges.

It had begun to feel like the last year of lovemaking had been about outcome and not romance or love or fun. They had begun to look at one another over the dinner table like a chore that needed to be done. Tonight was a reminder of erotic passion.

"I like it when you take charge," he told her when they had freshened up. "Let yourself go."

"How could I not let myself go with a man on the brink of a new career," she said.

"So you're not mad about the job search?"

Before he even asked, she forgave him for not sharing the details of his search. His eyes were looking toward a bright future, and so were hers.

"Mom, it is five in the morning," Julia said. "Why are you calling me?"

"We're with Savvy. He's here!"

Julia sat up and clicked on the lamp light. "What? Mom, who's there? Where? The father?"

"At the hospital. We're at the hospital. The baby is here. She went into labor around three this morning and the baby is already here."

"We are on our way," Julia said.

Half of Julia wanted to ignore the birth. The other half wanted to see her nephew for herself, to hold him, to savor him. She wondered if this would make her resent her sister more or less.

When they walked into the room an hour later, Savvy looked exhausted. The baby was wrapped in a blue blanket, and Beaty proudly said, "May I introduce Talon James Meyer, my perfect grandson."

Julia knew the answer now. It made her resent her sister more.

It was as if she had sat on a cactus - the adrenaline in her body had calmed her before it allowed the pain to traumatize her.

"Do you want me to come over?" Rebecca asked when she called after Julia didn't show up for their walk.

"I'll be fine. It'll be fine," Julia said, her voice betraying her.

"Want a drink?"

"Yep."

When Rebecca got to her house, she found Julia sitting on the floor. It wasn't until the shot of vodka and the glass of red wine appeared that Julia allowed the cruel reality to soak in.

"This is ridiculous," Julia said.

"True, but I didn't know if you wanted something hardcore like a shot or something classy like red wine, so I went with both."

"Not the drinks, but they are pretty ridiculous." She downed the shot and drank half the glass in one gulp. "My sister is ridiculous. How dare she."

By the time David got home from working late, Julia was lit like a candle and talking as unsteadily as a flickering flame.

"She's all yours," Rebecca said, passing the baton to David.

Julia just couldn't make sense of it. Why, if God was just, would He choose to allow Savvy to have a baby? What kind of life would that kid have with a mom who only works random jobs, who now lives with her parents, with no father, and no college degree. Sure, women have done it under worse circumstances, but why would it happen in her family?

Maybe life really is nothing but a card game that can't be controlled. If you have a terrible hand then you just fold. Savvy's pregnancy made Julie want to do exactly that. Fold. Quit. Hide under a blanket of self-pity and snuggle with the heartbreak.

She wanted to shake her sister by the shoulders and ask why she would do something like this. Why she would break her sister's heart. Why, as Savvy had said, would Julia be the smart one, the settled one, yet she, Savvy, end up being the beautiful, fortunate, fertile one?

The injustice tasted like metal, and Julia wanted to spit it out.

Julia walked into Dr. Lamont's office with a chip on her shoulder. She and David had been having sex like breeding rabbits. She had even used the obnoxious ovulation kit, two actually, and the second her levels spiked, she jumped on David like a new trampoline.

She had eaten so well that she had lost four pounds—since the chicken fried steak. She had taken a baby aspirin every day for two weeks, but her skin had started bruising easily and she decided to nip that practice in the bud. Other than the celebratory bottle of wine that she and Rebecca had shared with their husbands after the race, and the wee nip after Talon was born, she hadn't consumed an ounce of alcohol.

The month had felt like punishing deprivation, but if it resulted in a positive pregnancy test then it would all be worth it.

Then, as it always did, her period came along with cramps and fatigue that had her curling on the couch like an old cat, comforting herself with a heating pad and a chick flick.

Julia rolled her eyes as she sat in the waiting room. All she wanted was a referral to a specialist. The doctor should have been able to provide that over the phone. Instead, she had to pay another twenty dollar co-pay and sit among all these pregnant women, one of whom was complaining about her backaches and swollen ankles.

Just like my sister, you don't know how lucky you are, Julia's thoughts growled. Then she remembered the woman in the survivor shirt and felt a pang of guilt. *We never know another's story as well as we think we do.*

She didn't want to sit in this waiting room thinking about the truth because the truth was she still hadn't told David about this appointment. The truth was she was here when he expressly told her he was not ready. The truth was she was lying to her husband.

A few days before, she had asked a leading question, hoping to assess David's current position on the idea of a fertility specialist. "So, Rebecca told me she and Brandon have tried in-vitro already. Has Brandon ever said anything about that to you?"

All he said was, "Nope." She figured his yo-yo was still on the downslide, and until he was on an upward arc, she was not going push.

"Julie Ellis," the nurse called.

"It's Julia," she said, following the nurse into the examination room. She had expected to be in Dr. Lamont's office—she Julia didn't need an exam, she needed a single piece of paper with the name and phone number of the pregnancy wizard.

"I'm sorry about that," the nurse said. Her pen poised above Julia's file, she asked, "What are we seeing you for today?"

"Actually, I was just hoping to get a referral to a fertility specialist."

"I see that you came in a little over a year ago. Is that when you started trying?"

Julia shook her head. She had actually started several months prior to that, but she didn't feel the need to be too specific with the nurse.

"And what have you tried thus far?"

She couldn't control the uncomfortable smile that grew across her face. How was she supposed to explain what she had tried. She could only imagine saying, "Well, we've had sex six times a week except when I was on my period. I've put pillows under my butt and literally stood on my head. I've added more veggies to my diet, started running, and stopped alcohol. I've purchased more than three hundred dollars worth of lingerie to keep things spicy. I bought vitamins and supplements and added and subtracted foods to my diet like a high school math problem. I've been in a terrible fight with my best friend because she is more fertile than me, and my new hobby is crying in the shower. All I want is a remedy, here. Send me home with a prescription to pluck a chicken and dance around a fire naked for thirty minutes, and I will absolutely do it."

"The usual," Julia replied, thankful she was able to bite her tongue.

After writing, the nurse double-clicked her pen. "Okay," she said, smiling. "The doctor will be in shortly."

She needed a better plan than to say "the usual." The doctor would never refer her to someone if she hadn't been actively working on conception. It would be like the time she flippantly went to the high school volleyball coach and said she wanted the starting position. She'd been second string for two years, but she wanted the chance to shine in her senior year. It was demeaning to sit on the bench while some sophomore with "potential" took the spot. The coach asked, "Have you been practicing?. "Sorta," she answered. And she really had. She'd spent hours in the backyard bumping the ball in the air and setting it, repeating the moves until the ball moved without rotation and her neck ached from watching it ascend before gravity brought it back to her. She'd practiced hitting the ball into the garage, snapping her wrist to strengthen her spike. She'd read magazine articles about Gabby Reece, her beach volleyball career, and tips she offered.

She was not given the spot. And later she heard that the sophomore had grown into an amazing talent and actually went to a Division I college on a volleyball scholarship.

History would not repeat itself today. She would not allow an inaccurate answer about "practice" to keep her from her goal.

On the exam table, Julia made herself as comfortable as a person could be sitting on the paper, every reposition a loud crinkle. She rolled her eyes up to glimpse the poster on the ceiling—three kittens in a basket. Stupid.

Then the manila file caught her eye. The nurse had left it next to the sink instead of hanging it on the door like usual. She saw the blue, green, and red stickers on the tabs and read her name from her spot on the exam table. It was spelled correctly, the nurse had just been lazy reading it.

Eyeing the door, Julia wished she had S-ray vision to make sure the doctor was not about to twist the handle. There was no reason she had to sit on the paper table like she was confined to it, but approaching the file, she felt like she was breaking the law.

She ran her first finger over the letters of her name. The file technically belonged to her even though it was the property of the office. She had every right to look but something tingled up her spine and she was stricken with a pang of conscience.

If Dr. Lamont walked in, she'd be caught red-handed and would have to explain herself. He'd think she was a snoop, the kind of person you invite to dinner and then suspect of rifling through your medicine cabinet and bathroom drawers.

The last time she had been in the office was for a follow-up after her ordeal with the abnormal cells, the oncologist, and the LEEP procedure. She had been given a clean bill of health, but reading the notes about the ordeal might prove interesting.

The temptation was too great. She flipped open the chart. The first page was for today's visit, her name and the date noted. Below she saw her weight, blood pressure, and date of last menstruation, all of which the nurse had checked before leaving.

Below these were a series of questions and blank lines. The first question read, Reason for visit. The nurse had written "Infertility." Julia felt as if she had fallen and someone was stepping on her chest.

No longer caring if the doctor caught her, Julia grabbed the folder with both hands and took it to the exam table. The entire time her eyes couldn't leave the "I" word.

Clearly written letters slanted to the right. The black ink labeled her. With only the whir of the industrial air conditioning, there was nothing to do but stare at her definition.

Yes, she had seen the word on the Internet. And yes, she had eavesdropped on the support group. But those were actions within her control. Those were missions in search of answers. This was entirely different. It was like she had been reading about the history of war and now she was fighting on the front line.

This word, coming from a medical professional no less, hit her like an unexpected, whiplash-inducing, airbag-exploding crash to her psyche.

"Mrs. Ellis," Dr. Lamont asked. "Are you okay?"

He had entered the room without her noticing. She turned the file his direction and pointed to the accosting word.

The paper crinkled loudly as he sat down next to her. "It only means that you have attempted conception for twelve months without success. But I understand this is what you came to discuss."

Her eyes felt dry, and she imagined the rim around her lids to be already red. She felt herself shrinking, shoulders folding, compacting her into something safe, like a roly-poly.

"What can you do?"

"I know you want the name of a specialist. You don't actually need a referral, but I'm glad to give you my recommendation." He rose from his place next to her and pulled a prescription pad from his lab coat pocket. "I know the doctors at this clinic and have heard good things about their success rate. If you're willing, however, there are a few things we can do here first—some tests we can run and a few simple medications we can try."

On all the blogs and searches, she had never realized a general OB/GYN had access to these medications and the knowledge to prescribe them. Julia was thankful she wouldn't have to call another receptionist, introduce herself, and declare she needed help . . . not yet.

Accepting Dr. Lamont's care, Julia took the prescription as he gave her specific instructions about taking the medication. Together they hovered over the calendar and determined that, based on her cycle, she'd start taking the pills in ten days. She'd take the pills for five days, and then hopefully her ovulation would be stimulated and the job would be done.

In his lumberjack voice, Dr. Lamont explained, "This does increase the possibility of twins and has a success rate of thirty percent in the first month of use."

Though the thought of twins gave her pause, Julia reflected that up till now she'd had a zero percent success rate. Any little bit would help. Twins! She couldn't imagine a more wonderful solution.

As he was leaving, Dr. Lamont put his hand on her shoulder and said, "Keep your chin up."

Somehow she made it to the car without shedding a tear. She turned the key, and the radio blared the Madonna song, "Papa Don't Preach." She twisted the volume control with rage to the mute position and put her head on the steering wheel.

She knew the song by heart. She loved singing it into her hairbrush. "Papa don't preach, I'm in trouble deep. Papa don't preach, I've been losing sleep. But I've made up my mind, I'm keepin' my baby."

There had been two times in college she had run to the store to buy a pregnancy test. Her period had been a day or two late, and she imagined her future turning into vapor and disappearing all because of lust and beer.

She had been taking birth control for so long that she assumed the moment she flushed those tiny pills, a baby would immaculately land in her womb. Never in all her hairbrush-singing days did she picture herself crying in her car with the opposite problem.

The sobs shook her chest. She picked up the phone to call Sarah. Staring at her name in the favorites list she shook her head. Sarah abandoned me when I needed her most, Julia thought. She should have wrapped her arms around me and helped me make a checklist or something. She should have encouraged me or got me drunk or eaten chocolates with me while I bawled.

Julia threw the phone into the passenger seat. Sarah had called three times yesterday but didn't leave a message. She was probably ready to apologize, but Julia wasn't ready to hear it.

She deserted me and got pregnant and rubbed it in my face with that stupid trip to Florida, she thought.

On the verge of hyperventilation, she grabbed the phone again.

She dialed David's number and heard the first ring before realizing what she was doing. She pressed End and looked at the phone.

It illuminated and began to vibrate almost instantly. "ICE

David Ellis" displayed on the screen. She took two quick breaths to steady herself.

"Hi, Honey," she said more cheerfully than she thought she could. He couldn't know she went to the doctor. If he found out, he'd be livid. They had finally found a place in their marriage that didn't feel like the knife's edge of a fight.

But now, here she sat with a prescription in the cup holder. Maybe she could plead naiveté. She had wanted information, not medicine, and the doctor gave her a prescription without her request.

It was a lie and she knew it. She knew he'd never believe her. She just needed more time to breath before she told him the truth.

"I just missed your call," he said. "What's up?"

"You missed my call? Are you sure?" Another lie. Julia was amazed how easily they multiplied.

"You good?" he asked. "You sound a little funny."

"Fine. Just working through some stuff here. Can we chat at home tonight?" She hoped he'd assume the stuff she was working through was work-related. Her response was vague. She hadn't lied, other than saying she was fine.

CHAPTER 27

Julia got home before David, cinched up her hot pink Adidas, and wrote a note—Went for a walk with Rebecca. Home soon.

The rap of her knuckles on the black front door felt good. She was angry at the fertility cards she had been dealt and hitting something, even a door, felt therapeutic. Maybe she'd get one of those karate punching bags shaped like the head and torso of a naked man. She could punch it and let all the energy explode from her fists to be drilled into someone, something, anything but her.

When Rebecca answered, she was already pulling her short black hair into a tiny pony tail at the top of her head, a serious look in her eyes. "Got your message. Let's go."

She had found a soul mate in Rebecca. The text had just said, We are walking at 5:30. She hadn't explained that she needed to walk off the "I" word. She could have wanted to walk out of joy because something wonderful happened at work or because she ate two slices of cake for lunch. But Rebecca's face conveyed a fierce mood of determination. It was exactly what Julia wanted to see.

"It's official," Julia said. "I'm a big fat infertile."

Their matched pace was rapid and their steps exaggerated, as if each length of pavement pushed them to the truth of their shared situation.

"Welcome," Rebecca said. "The club sucks."

"I saw Dr. Lamont today. His stupid nurse wrote 'Infertility' on my chart for the whole wide world to see. INFERTILITY!" she screamed. "I HAVE INFERTILITY!" The words tasted like bile, doubling her rage.

"The whole wide world may not have the chance to read your chart, but Roger Phillips now knows," Rebecca said, nodding to the man pushing the lawn mower around the yard. The women giggled. "A tip for club membership," she continued. "You don't have infertility. You are infertile."

"What?" Julia asked.

"You should have said, 'I am Infertile,' Rebecca explained. "It's not like the flu that you catch and then you have it. It's like something you check on the census, like being Caucasian or your income level."

"How did this happen? How the hell did this happen?"

No matter how fast they walked, Julia couldn't escape the emotions running after her. She stopped and let them attack her.

"My freakin' sister gets pregnant with some loser boyfriend she won't even name and now she has the most beautiful baby. I just don't get it. I just don't understand."

Sitting down on the curb she put her head on her knees. "What if he leaves me?"

"Who? David?"

"Yeah, what if when her hears I'm infertile and he leaves me?"

Julia didn't realize she was afraid of this until the words came out. But the truth was there now like a thief who'd been hiding in the closet waiting to steal everything you owned.

He had left his college girlfriend because she couldn't have a family. What if he left her for the same reason?

"It's a real fear. I get that. Oh, how I get that," Rebecca said. "But your relationship wasn't built on procreation. You need to remember why you fell in love and fight like hell to stay that way. This gets harder before it gets easier."

If anyone else had said those words, they would have felt as empty as Julia's womb. But Rebecca was wise from experience.

"Oh, my gosh," Rebecca said, suddenly, as if remembering something important. "How is Sarah holding up?"

"It is so funny you ask. She called me a couple of times yesterday but I didn't answer."

Just as Rebecca understood seeing the "I" word for the first time, she understood Julia's rift with Sarah. Rebecca's best friend from Kansas City had jilted her in the same way. Apparently when the friend heard Rebecca was struggling, she compared it to her own difficulty. The friend had tried for "two whole entire months" before it finally worked. Rebecca had slammed the phone down and cursed out loud for an hour.

When she had told the story, Julia died laughing. Rebecca could barely say "poop" without whispering. Julia pictured Rebecca in a cartoon with a bubble above her head filled with asterisks and pound signs and percent marks.

They had since made amends. Rebecca mailed her friend a long letter of apology and a book with dog-eared pages explaining how a friend should respond to a someone battling with fertility.

Although Rebecca had continued encouraging Julia to do the same, she wasn't ready.

"You have to call her back," Rebecca said.

"I just can't. I needed her, and she told me my negativity wasn't good for anyone, and I had to stop doing this thing to myself. To myself!" Julia huffed. "Like you do infertility to yourself."

"Oh honey, you don't know," Rebecca said with the patience of a kindergarten teacher.

"Know what?" Julia sat up, an electric current suddenly flowing down her spine, cautioning her that something was about to happen.

Rebecca took both her hands and squared Julia's shoulders. "I saw Yvette and she told me that Joshua was hit by a car yesterday. I just assumed you knew. They took him to the hospital in an ambulance. From what I heard, he's still there."

171

Her feet were running before she knew she'd stood up. Over her shoulder Julia yelled back to Rebecca, "Tell David I went to the hospital."

Her home was a mile away in one direction and the hospital only three miles away in the other. She couldn't imagine running home, getting in her car, and driving this same mile over when Sarah and dear sweet Joshua were in the other direction . . . hurt.

She couldn't feel her body. Her mind reeled at the possibilities and questions. How badly was Joshua hurt? Where? Was he going to be okay. What could she do to help?

Oh, precious Joshua, she began to repeat in her mind. Be okay. Be okay. Be okay. Chanting the mantra held her together.

She pictured Joshua's face as he told his mom, "Aunt Jules is here to play with me." She saw him in the navy blue dinosaur pajamas, brown hair sticking up at the cowlick, slightly off from the crown of his head. She saw the proud smile he wore when she took him to the park and pushed him on the swing until he swore he touched the sky.

She imagined a car slamming into his tiny frame. The bumper striking his young body sending it forward into the air. She saw his eyes wide with fear, heard him call desperately for his mommy. She saw Joshua hit the unforgiving pavement, hard. The bounce of his torso, his limbs, his head before he was sent sliding across the road.

And Julia ran.

She could almost hear Sarah's scream, a terror so great it was beyond human. She saw Sarah run to her son and kneel beside his twisted body, afraid to touch him but unable to keep from pulling him into herself.

Julia pictured the people that would come to observe the horror of a young child sprawled on the road. Someone would have called 911 as Sarah rocked her unconscious child, tears falling from her face onto his.

Picturing this was like living inside a nightmare. Please God, let him be okay.

And Julia ran.

She had ignored the desperate phone calls of her best friend. Not one but three. Her pleas for comfort unanswered because of Julia's stubborn selfishness and unwillingness to forgive.

She could not forgive herself for not being there. For not protecting this family that she loved so much.

Julia wanted a child with ever fiber of her being, but she had not yet been given the chance to experience the kind of pain that is experienced when someone, born from your body, is hurt . . . or worse.

Her body ached to comfort Sarah, to see Joshua, to be there for this family when she had failed them so deeply.

And she ran.

Her chest heaved when she reached the receptionist desk. "Joshua Beckett's room, please," Julia said.

"Are you all right, dear?" the elderly woman asked, her grayish-blue hair a thin helmet atop her head. The name tag read, Agnes.

Julia explained why she was here, and making a call, Agnes received permission for Julia to visit.

Agnes pulled a pink sticky note from the pad and retrieved a pencil from the pencil cup. She licked the tip and began to write in a slow, careful hand. She handed Julia the paper. Room 316.

Julia swiped the paper and raced to the elevator—and waited. The elevator didn't arrive and didn't arrive, and Julie ran to the stairs taking them two at a time.

As Julia burst from the stairwell, Sarah was waiting—the surprise on her face would have been comical had the situation not been so serious.

"What the hell?" she said, pulling Julia into her arms. "Did you run here?"

Julia squeezed both of Sarah's hands. "What happened? How's Joshua? Oh, my God, Sarah, I am so sorry I wasn't here."

And finally she cried. They held each other, and they cried

together. When the elevator opened and a stranger exited, neither woman felt any need to hide her pain.

Finally, Sarah told Julia that Josh was fine. "He was riding his bike when a neighbor hit him," she said. "It was dusk, and he was darting from one driveway to another. Mrs. Robertson couldn't see him in the setting sun. Fortunately, she had just pulled out of her driveway and was going very slow. Joshua landed in the grass.

"He broke his right arm and sprained an ankle. The doctors kept him overnight for observation. This morning, they did a few tests to make sure there was no internal bleeding or anything else. Everything is good, and he's being discharged within the hour."

Julia listened with wide eyes, absorbing all the information. When Sarah said the word "discharge," she broke out into tears again, each drop falling like a prayer of thankfulness.

They held hands and Sarah led Julia to Joshua's room. "I wanted to tell you about it out here because he was so shaken up," Sarah explained. "He's pulled through it like a champ, but we don't want to keep reliving it for him and give him nightmares."

Julia understood and began to feel a little silly for her frantic appearance.

"Seriously, did you run?" Sarah laughed.

"Of course I ran. I just heard what happened, and I took off. I love you, and I'm so sorry I wasn't here for you."

"I knew you would be," Sarah said. "Will you forgive me?"

"I love you," Julia said. "Will you forgive me?" She felt the Sarah-shaped hole in her heart begin to fill and hoped it would heal with an even deeper friendship than they had shared before.

When she walked into the hospital room, Joshua was sitting on the bed with his tiny brother swaddled next to him. Joshua was explaining to Kyle about how cool casts were and how maybe one day he could have one too. John, Sarah's husband, was sitting in a chair opposite the boys recording the conversation on his phone.

Joshua swung his head around and, his green eyes alight with innocence, said, "Hi, Aunt Jules!"

Her heart soared.

CHAPTER 28

"Come in," Rebecca said, her face spotted and swollen. The women had fallen into a pattern of walking on Wednesdays after work and Saturday mornings. It had become their time for friendship and support. Though Rebecca had encouraged Julia to come to the infertility support group, she still didn't feel like a viable candidate, and the walks were what Julia really needed. Plus, she still hid the truth about the gynecologist appointment and the fertility medication from David. She was trying not to add to the list.

Today, however, Rebecca suggested they walk after dinner instead of before. Julia didn't question the shift—things came up like doctor appointments, eyebrow waxing, and grocery shopping. But Rebecca's face, heavy with sadness, and her oversized sweatpants gave reason for concern.

"I have to test your friendship," Rebecca said, pulling Julia into her home by the forearm.

The couch was covered by a crumpled quilt, its color and condition aged by love and wear. Atop the quilt lay a box of Kleenex and several crumpled, used tissues. The television was showing the movie Sweet Home Alabama.

Once, during a walk, Rebecca had mentioned she watched the same movies over and over again when she needed comfort. She lost herself in the predictability of the stories. Julia could relate to this. If a movie was new to her, she felt obligated to give it her full attention—she'd pause it if she needed to use the bathroom or take a phone call. But if she loved a movie like Rebecca loved her blanket—movies like The American President or Ever After or even Shanghai Noon, which had her falling in love with Owen Wilson—she could relax, even fall asleep and reawaken without feeling like she'd missed anything.

Julia turned to Rebecca, who was now holding a large syringe and a square of antibacterial cleaner.

"I need you to shoot me in the butt," she said, "with this."

A look of confusion must have crossed Julia's face because before she could respond Rebecca had placed the needle in her hand and said, "We have five minutes. Do it now, and I'll explain."

The size of the needle was daunting, and it was heavier than Julia had expected. Her eyes grew wide as the serum, a clear, thick liquid, moved sluggishly in the barrel of the syringe.

"What is this?" Julia said, not masking her shock and fear. She had never administered a shot before and wasn't comfortable doing it now. Neither did she understand why she had to give the shot this minute. It just didn't make any sense.

"It's my trigger shot," Rebecca said, collapsing on the couch and pulling the quilt around her. Something about the way Rebecca folded into herself reminded Julia of an abused dog seeking solace. "We're doing another round of IVF, and this is the big shot."

From the little research she had done, Julia knew that in vitro fertilization required a lot of shots. She wondered how many her friend had gone through or if this was the first.

As if reading her mind, Rebecca pulled up her shirt to expose her lower stomach. Spots of blue, black and red covered the area below her bellybutton.

All of this time Rebecca had been doing this to herself and hadn't said a word. Julia looked from her stomach to her eyes and read the pleading.

"Tell me what to do," Julia said.

Rebecca bent over the armrest of the couch and tugged

down the right side of her grey sweatpants exposing her rear. Julia cleaned the area with the wipe. With one hand, she squeezed the area of skin Rebecca had pointed out. Holding the needle with her other, she removed the cap with her teeth and spit it to the ground.

"Ready?" she asked.

Rebecca's body stiffened as Julia counted to three. With a stiff inhale she plunged the needle into her friend's bottom. As she compressed the syringe and the fluid was ejected so was Julia's breath.

She removed the needle and Rebecca stood up and threw her arms around Julia's neck, catching her off guard. "Thank you."

"I shoot all my friends," Julia said. "What's going on? Why am I giving you this shot and not Brandon?"

Going back to her quilt and favoring the other hip, Rebecca began her story. "He was supposed to give it to me. The whole IVF thing is all about hurry up and wait. The trigger shot has to be given within a two-hour window. I waited and waited for Brandon to get home. He called at six." She started to cry.

"Apparently, he had some kind of meeting at The Polly Wog at five. They each ordered rounds, and there were several people at the table. The first few guys ordered shots. I mean who does that at a meeting in the middle of the afternoon?"

Julia couldn't remember what Brandon did for a living, but she imagined how she would have felt if David had the same story.

"I reminded him that tonight was the trigger shot, and that I needed him to do it. I've been doing all the work here. I've taken who knows how many shots, and all he does is go out for drinks. He says he is praying this will work, but I never see him praying."

She blew her nose and added the tissue to the growing pile.

"I tried to call Natasha from my office. You remember her, right?" Rebecca said.

Julia nodded her head. Natasha had been such a comforting

presence when Dr. Pinnison performed the procedure. Natasha's eyes, the only thing visible between the mask and hair cover, never left Julia's.

"She was out to dinner and couldn't get here in time," Rebecca continued. "And I couldn't possibly call Dr. Pinnison. I couldn't think of anyone else I could trust."

Julia wondered if she meant "trust" with the injection itself or "trust" with the knowledge that she was taking the shot. Probably both.

Julia grabbed for her hand, offering encouragement in a language Rebecca would understand.

"This has to work," Rebecca said. "It has to."

"Why didn't you tell me?" Julia asked softly.

"That is the thing with infertility, there is no triumph in it. There is so much joy in having a baby, in being fertile, that it makes it even harder to express any grief if you're not.

"I wanted to be the friend who could announce 'I'm pregnant' and everyone would cheer. Then later I'd tell the everything I went through. The suffering would all be worth it. You know? Plus you know how I feel about our struggle. I talk to people all day who are battling cancer. Mine is a choice, theirs isn't. They struggle with life or death, mine is only the desire for more life."

Rebecca worked the Kleenex in her hands, rolling it around, tying it in knots.

"I feel so frivolous, so worthless when I tell people the truth. Even you."

Julia understood this more than she wished to. She didn't feel comfortable at work, surrounded by pregnant teens. She didn't feel comfortable with Sarah as she nursed her healthy baby boy. She didn't feel comfortable around her nephew, Talon. She didn't feel comfortable at David's grandpa's house, thinking he may never get to see his great-grandchild.

She was angry and sad one moment and filled with fight and encouragement the next. She cried when it was sunny, thinking the rain would comfort her. She cried when it rained, feeling like the sun would never shine.

And all of this she was doing to herself. A baby may not be a necessary condition for happiness or a requirement for moving forward in life, but it sure felt that way. She felt like her dreams were a source of heat and energy and infertility was a cube of ice. She wondered what would come to pass. Would life melt the ice, or would she live forever with a frozen emptiness?

"And what about Brandon?" Julia asked. "How is he with all of this?"

"He is the love of my life, and I hate him," Rebecca said, without a flinch. "I'm afraid if this doesn't work he'll leave me. And I can't say I blame him."

Again she blew her nose. "Who wants a broken wife?"

CHAPTER 29

And they waited.

Infertility was an all-encompassing orb of empty time. There was nothing to do except suffer through the pain of waiting. It was dire and traumatic. Julia felt like a tiny ant pressed by a thumb into the concrete sidewalk.

For the next two weeks, Julia called Rebecca several times a day for updates. Rebecca seemed to be in a state of high alert. "The eggs have been harvested and mixed in a Petri dish with Brandon's sperm," she reported. A few days later, the embryos were transferred into Rebecca, and she spent an afternoon on her back hoping they would find a comfortable spot in her uterus to grow.

A week after the transfer, Julia found her friend lying with a pillow under her bottom watching Sweet Home Alabama yet again. Rebecca thanked her for the chocolate mint cookies she had baked and proclaimed, "As of this moment, I am pregnant!"

Her elation was contagious. Sperm and egg had met and mingled, they had divided and multiplied, the beginning of creation had been accomplished. It was beautiful to imagine what was happening within Rebecca's body. They were both overcome with optimism and promise.

The doctors had procured six healthy embryos. Rebecca and Brandon had to decide how many to insert for incubation and how many to freeze for future use. "One or two?" they debated. If they only put in one and it didn't take, they feared they'd regret their choice. Two, however, would greatly increase the chance of multiples, increasing risks at birth.

In the end, two embryos were introduced into Rebecca's body and cheers erupted from Brandon when the procedure was complete.

As the week marched forward, Rebecca felt shadows of doubt about her pregnancy. She relived the emotional toll of her first failed attempt, and fear began to seep into the cracks of her expectations.

Today, however, she told Julia of her painful breasts and cramps. In one hope-filled breath she was positive a baby or two had taken hold. "Women always say their breasts hurt when they're pregnant, getting ready for nursing. And the cramps could be implantation. I've even heard women say they have spotting."

In the breath, she'd say, "But these are exactly the same symptoms I get when I am about to start my period." And her hopes would deflate again.

"Becks," Brandon said. "Let's not borrow trouble. Until they tell us otherwise, you are pregnant. Have faith."

Julia hadn't asked her friend what happened when her husband finally came home on the night of the trigger shot, and Rebecca hadn't offered an answer. When Julia told David about the situation, she called Brandon a "rat bastard for ditching his wife at a time like this."

David, ever the peacemaker, offered Julia guidance. "An onion has many layers, and this one is not yours to peel. Trust your friend's judgment in her husband. She knows him beyond the surface."

Seeing Rebecca and Brandon during these weeks, she understood the breadth of their relationship. And the best Julia could assume was that Brandon's own stress had built up to the point of a small explosion.

The timing of Rebecca's pregnancy test couldn't have been better. In secret, Julia had taken the Clomid prescribed to her by Dr. Lamont. She had used an ovulation kit, even though he had said it wasn't necessary. And when the stars of procreation aligned, she had made love to David, twice.

Her plan was to take a pregnancy test at home over the lunch hour, the same time Rebecca was getting her news. Hopefully they could celebrate together.

Julia placed the stick in her urine stream as the phone rang. She sat the test on the back of the toilet and ran to answer the phone. This distraction would allow the test time to work.

"Hello," she said, thinking how gross it was that she hadn't washed her hands.

Before Rebecca said a word, Julia sensed the failure.

With a slow gait she walked into the bathroom and looked at her own pregnancy test. One pink line, not two, appeared.

She dropped her head, defeated again.

Driving back to work Julia realized she hadn't eaten lunch and pulled into Flavors. Surely a chai latte and a cinnamon roll could be considered lunch.

As she approached the door, the old man in the pageboy hat was leaving. He held the door for her and she passed through. "Good afternoon," he said, tipping his head. If his thick accent had been food, it would have been a dense, warm lasagna that melts apart at the touch of a fork.

But it hadn't been a good afternoon, and Julia wasn't in an emotional state to return his greeting. She smiled a simple smile and met his eyes. He blinked slowly and nodded his head slightly as if he understood her plight.

Even if his grace was imagined, Julia wished everyone responded they way he seemed to.

"Hey," Savvy said.

"You're back to work?" Julia asked.

"Only a few hours a day," Savvy said. "It give me some space, and mom gets Talon."

"Oh," Julia said. "How is he?"

"The best thing that ever happened to me," Savvy said.

Julia wilted further.

CHAPTER 30

The months of autumn were a series of bleak changes.

For the first time, Julia agreed to go to the fertility support group, but only because Rebecca didn't feel like she could speak aloud the devastation she was feeling. She and Brandon had run out of money for fertility treatments so their frozen embryos would remain that way until they could save enough to try again.

The support group's table at Panera was alive with packages and baskets of every shape and color. Brightly colored tissue paper exploded festively from gift bags.

Ava, again dressed elegantly in all white, greeted the group. "I am so glad we have such a large turnout for our Lucky Sock Exchange."

Julia looked at Rebecca confused.

"Each woman was asked to bring two care packages," Ava continued. "In each of these baskets we've put socks, nail polish, journals, chocolate, books we love—whatever we felt would make a nice gift of support for a woman struggling with infertility. The twist to this year's event was Rebecca's idea."

Julia thought about what she might put in a care package to help empower the preg-not. Without question, the pink hair dye she had used when she learned of Sarah's pregnancy would make the list. So would Kit Kats and wine. Too bad you can't package a hot shower or a hot tub. Those two things gave her more support than anything else.

And daffodils, she would certainly add daffodils. The flower had bloomed when she started the fertility journey and had been there as a sad reminder of the passing of time. Nonetheless, the flower had been a symbol of hope in a desolate winter. Maybe another woman struggling with infertility would recognize the special meaning.

Rebecca set two bags down on the table, then turned to the group. "Ladies, it was my idea to bring two baskets this year, and I hope you didn't mind the extra work and money. But the idea came to me because of my friend, Julia."

Julia felt heat rush to her face. Her plan was to come to this meeting and sit in the shadows, absorbing information like the sunlight. Now, however, she was being used like a prop in Rebecca's speech. She wondered if she had been invited for this specific purpose, and the thought planted a seed of resentment in her heart.

"Julia has become my dearest friend," Rebecca continued. "She struggles with the same problem as the rest of us, but she hasn't felt comfortable enough to come to our group. I've watched her cry at failure and thrive in hope."

All eyes moved between Julia and Rebecca.

"I am sure many of us know women who are struggling and are afraid to seek comfort from a group like ours. So as we leave with our baskets today, please take two, one for yourself and one for a friend."

Ava jumped in. "It's a beautiful idea. And we are delighted to have Julia with us today." She turned to Julia. "You are always welcome."

The words, spoken sincerely, touched her deeply, and she knew instantly that she would be back if only to glean some of what made Ava so spectacularly genuine.

"The socks are to be worn during your next procedure, shot, medical appointment, or time of need. Most of them are fairly ridiculous, and it is our hope that they will bring a smile or laugh in your difficult time."

On that note, the meeting started. When the introductions

came around to Rebecca and she related how her number of IVF treatments had increased, the ladies gasped and sucked in a collective breath. Hands flew to hearts and mouths alike.

While, to an outsider, the gesture might have seemed a little like the Southern woman's bless-your-heart-as-I-stab-you-in-the-back, it was entirely the opposite. These women, Julia saw, didn't need to be told the depths of Rebecca's heartbreak, nor did they need the details. They knew firsthand and with deep empathy exactly how Rebecca felt. This was true support, and Julia was glad she was there as a witness.

Stories of emotional breakdowns ensued. Ashamed, Kristy, the heavy-set girl with the thyroid issue, told of her response to her mother-in-law's pressure for grandchildren. She had intended to slam the dinner table with her fists, outraged. But before the table, she hit the spoon in her bowl of peas, sending tiny green bullets flying across the room. Her embarrassment was still raw, but Julia knew she would laugh about it later . . . the way everyone at the table did now.

The one-upmanship began, and story after story painted infertility as the catalyst to crazy behavior.

Sophie, the frail girl, told Julia's favorite tale of the afternoon. She had become so angry with her insurance carrier and their inability to show any human compassion that she yelled into the phone, "Fine. I don't need your help! Maybe I'll just steal a baby from Walmart!" And then slammed the receiver.

Sophie had tried to call back and apologize for her aggression and make sure the insurance rep wasn't calling the authorities or putting her on some kind of secret insurance watch list for crazy people. However, she hadn't written down the agent's name or gotten her ID number.

Sophie said, making large gestures with her hands, "What was I supposed to do. Call this giant company and say, 'Hello, I would like to say I'm sorry to one of your employees. Which one, you ask. Oh, she'll be the one on the phone with the police.'"

Julia could relate. Just after Sarah's baby shower, when she was feeling so vulnerable, she had stopped at a convenience store to grab a few Kit Kat bars when she saw an obese woman in short shorts carrying a crying infant like an afterthought as she lugged a carton of cigarettes and a six pack of beer in the other hand. She had to restrain herself from marching up to the woman, slapping her in the face, and running off with the child.

Regardless of the reason for her invitation, the support group meeting was a success, and Julia was glad she had come along.

While leaving, Laney, the one who seemed too plastic, pulled Rebecca aside. Her body language told Rebecca it was a private conversation. When they were done, Laney wiped her eyes and handed her a slip of paper.

"What was that all about?" Julia asked.

"Laney and Kent are getting divorced," Rebecca said.

Suddenly, the pieces fell together for Julia. The reason Laney had seemed to be phony the first time Julia saw her was because she was covering up the truth, wearing a mask of protection. Yes, the women were privy to her struggle with infertility, but they weren't fully aware of the toll it had taken on her marriage.

Fear hit Julia in the chest like a blow from a heavyweight champion. The very same thing could so easily happen to her. Life without David would paralyze her.

"I'm so sorry to hear that," Julia said. "What was the paper all about?"

"Apparently there is a scholarship at our fertility clinic that I might qualify for." Rebecca pulled out the note and read. "The Raftopoulos Fund."

"The what?"

"Raftopoulos," Rebecca said again. "My maiden name is Papadopoulos. My dad came here from Greece when he was a child. Laney said she thinks the fund gives extra attention to applicants with a Greek background."

Julia was surprised. She had always admired Rebecca's

dark black hair and olive skin but never expected her lineage was Greek. The only thing she could think of was the movie My Big Fat Greek Wedding.

"Does your dad squirt Windex on everything?" Julia asked.

Rebecca only laughed.

When Julia got home, she opened the care package. She had hoped to get one prepared by Ava, but instead pulled the name of Stephanie, whom Julia remembered from the meeting she had spied on. Stephanie had called herself an IVF veteran because she had had six failed attempts in ten years. With that many treatments and years of difficulty, this woman probably knew exactly how to prepare a gift bag.

She pulled a handwritten note from its envelope. "Dear Sister. I am so sorry you are struggling. Please know you are not alone. I pray for both of us daily. I apologize for the stupid socks, but hopefully the wine will help you forget your humiliation at wearing them."

Julia reached in the bag and pulled out a bottle of Flip Flop Moscato. An inexpensive bottle of dessert wine, but with a twenty-five dollar gift limit, it was perfect.

She found a bag of individually wrapped dark chocolates by Ghirardelli and a pair of bright yellow Sponge Bob Square Pants socks. Finally, Julia removed a beautiful leather-bound journal in a deep purple so rich it could have been mistaken for black. The gold embossed lettering asked Julia's fingers to experience their depth.

She thumbed the pages, enjoying the soft feel to the unevenly cut edges. Though it was new, the book had a medieval quality. It was as if, through the journal, Stephanie was communicating that infertility was timeless. It had existed through the ages and affected women of all generations.

Stephanie had written an inscription on the inside cover: "Romans 5: 2-5. And we rejoice in the hope of the Glory of God. Not only so, but we rejoice in the glory of our sufferings, because we know that suffering produces perseverance; perseverance, character; and character, hope. And hope does not disappoint because God's love has been poured out into our hearts through the Holy Spirit, who has been given to us."

"Hope," Julia said aloud in the silence of her living room. It was as if she were tasting the word for the first time. Would it be bitter, causing her to pucker with disappointment? Or would it be sweet, like the wine and chocolates that accompanied the gift?

"God, give me hope."

Julia was not the kind of person to save things. She didn't have her high school report cards. She gave gifts the moment she bought them instead of waiting for an occasion. She figured that at any moment of the day she could be hit by lightning and life would end, and someone else would have to throw away the report cards and the gift would never be received.

The same was true with wine. There was no sense in letting a perfectly good bottle of wine, even if it was white, sit in the cabinet until the perfect occasion arrived. She popped the cork and poured a glass.

She watched the bubbles rise as she slipped her feet into the socks. Turning on Pandora to the Plain White T's station and turning up the volume she began to make dinner.

Chopping a yellow squash and singing to "Hey There Delilah," she suddenly felt arms squeeze her middle. The grip was strong and she screamed in terror.

"Oh, my God, David," she said, breathless. "You almost killed me."

David was smiling but his arms had flown up into the posture of surrender. "I think you almost killed me."

Julia realized she was pointing the knife at him and lowered it immediately.

"Sorry," she smiled. "But now you know I can take care of myself."

"In those socks?" he said. "I'm not so sure."

"Like 'em?" she asked, feeling the adrenaline flush from her muscles.

"If I say 'no' will you point the knife again?"

She told him about the fertility group and the gift basket and about how wonderful Ava had been to invite her back.

Julia had always appreciated the way she could read David's face. His expressions had become so familiar to her that they spoke a language that only she could understand. The twitch of his right eye meant he might be feeling amorous. The furrow of his brow meant he was thinking something through and needed a bit more time. The clench of his jaw told her his stress had hit a dangerous level.

But the face he made now was new. The furrow was between his brow but he held his jaw in a different way. The light of eyes was like a halogen lamp when it's first turned on and needs time to warm. She couldn't understand.

"Why did you go to the group?" he asked. "I thought we talked about that."

"Huh?"

"The support group," he spat. "It is like you're telling everyone that we're having trouble. We don't even compare to what those women have been through. Plus, I'm looking for a new job and you're telling the whole town that we're infertile. How does that make me look?"

His words felt like blades stabbing into her.

"I went to the support group for me. Not for you. Plus," she said, mocking him, "we've been through some stuff that you don't even know about."

The words had been cast from her mouth, and she couldn't reel them back. There was no turning back, she would have to tell him.

"What's that supposed to mean?" he said, squinting in indignation.

She took a deep breath and closed her eyes. She would have to give him the truth. "I have been taking a fertility drug called Clomid for the last couple of months."

"What?!. The word felt like a slap.

She bowed her head, submitting. She didn't want a fight. "I should have told you, but I thought if it worked then you'd be happy and you'd forgive me."

"Well, I don't forgive you. This was supposed to be a choice we make together, Julia. What the hell do you think you're doing?"

She was asking for forgiveness and he was unyielding. The gloves were coming off, and that was fine with her.

"At least I'm doing something!" she yelled. "At least I've been eating well and working out and taking medication. You just sit on your ass eating crap."

It's true that she stole a few too many calories every day, but she was doing better than a year and a half ago when they had begun trying. And she didn't work out every day, but she walked and even sometimes ran with Rebecca, which she never would have done before.

Ever since the mud run she had begun resenting David's laissez-faire attitude about health and fertility. It was as if he had discovered an acorn and named it "It Will Happen." Then she had planted it hoping one day it would take root and grow into their family tree.

But thus far, It-Will-Happen was still just an acorn sitting in the dirt.

The clock on the wall ticked loudly as the couple stared at one another, as each accumulating second opened more space between them.

"I'm going out," David finally said.

"You do that," she rebuffed and grabbed her wine and went to the bedroom.

CHAPTER 31

She abandoned the dinner plan and instead made a pot of macaroni and cheese. She longed for comfort food and planned to eat the entire bowl. She wished she had some of her mother's chicken fried steak. It had been a while, but she could taste the warm goodness on her tongue.

But she couldn't eat out of worry and let her mac and cheese to grow cold. She anticipated the worst—that he'd be so angry at her deception he'd be unable to forgive her, that he'd lose trust in her honesty and faithfulness, a staple to their relationship, which, if broken, might never heal. She feared he would ask her to leave and her world would dissolve.

The best-case scenario, she thought, would be that, still enraged, he'd march back into the house and belittle her poor decisions.

Regardless of her intention, she had lied to him for months. And banishment from her home, from his love, from their future, seemed inevitable.

This would be the end of their marriage, she knew it would.

The clock read 10:27 p.m., when she heard the garage door open. He had been gone for hours. She sat frozen on the couch, waiting. She assumed he had called Brian and gone drinking.

He walked into the living room and sat on the chair opposite her, his head down, studying his shoes. She expected him to be stiff and defiant, to look her in the eyes, challenging her to a fight. But his posture was crumpled, almost slack.

This could only mean her fears would become reality and he would ask her for a divorce. She tasted bile, and her ears began to hum.

Waiting for him to speak, Julia forced herself to concentrate on the clock for the second time that day. She would take the batteries out tomorrow, if she was allowed to stay that long.

When he finally looked at her, she could see from his swollen, squinted eyes and blotched skin that he had been crying. Her heart tore, knowing she had broken her husband with her lies.

When he finally spoke, his tone was raw, as if he had also given voice to his anger and bitterness, his shredded vocal cords not yet healed. "I met Stacy half way," he said.

Visiting his sister could not have been a good thing. She and Julia had the kind of personality conflict that kept friendship at arm's length. Surely her advice to David would have been to run.

Julia swallowed in anticipation. When he told her to leave, she would not put up a fight. She would simply say, "I love you, and I'm sorry." Then she would walk to her car and find a hotel room.

"We met half way and talked in the car for a while and then she got a call." He began to cry. His inhalations were ragged, and Julia sat forward with concern. "Pops had a heart attack," he said. "He's dead."

She moved quickly to him and knelt at his feet. She put both hands on his knees and bowed her head, full of pain and pity. The lump in Julia's throat threatening to choke her.

She recalled the moment she had met Pops. They had gone to dinner at Red Lobster; it was the first time Julia met any of David's family. Her palms clammy and armpits sweating, she could not control the fluttering nerves in her stomach.

Before opening the door, David put his arm around her and said, "They'll love you, the way I do." It was the first time he had said those life-changing words. And while it brought her great joy, it made her eyes and her mouth fly wide open.

"You love me?" she said.

"You know I do," he responded with the smile she could not resist.

Then David turned as if feeling a presence and hugged the man behind him.

"Pops, this is Julia," he gestured, presenting her like royalty.

When she offered her hand, Pops smiled and said, "I'm a hugger." His embrace contained all the warmth of every story David had shared about the man. She was enveloped by him.

Pops stayed quiet through dinner, and Julia worried that her first impression hadn't been up to his expectations or standards. David's reverence for his grandfather meant that his opinion of her was paramount. She feared she had ruined her future with David by not dazzling Pops.

When the meal was over and the family said their goodbyes, Pops walked the couple to the car. He opened Julia's door and hugged her again.

"It was so nice to finally meet you," Julia said.

"It was entirely my pleasure. My grandson will live a happy life with you, Miss Julia. I love you."

She pulled away and looked into the old man's eyes. This was the second "I love you" she had heard in an hour, and both were so tremendously sincere that she wanted to capture their warmth and cradle it.

He winked at her before closing the door.

"What was that about?" David asked.

"Jealous?" Julia had teased.

"Maybe."

"Pops said he loves me," she said sheepishly, feeling silly.

"Welcome to the family," David said before kissing her on the cheek.

Julia came to learn that Pops was always like that, always positive and eternally endearing. David thought that when his grandma died Pops must have felt like he missed the chance to tell her he loved her, and so now he gave praise and affection to his family daily.

David's mom, however, said that her dad had been that way since she was a little girl. Once, David's mom admitted that the difference she felt between Pop's exuberance and her husband's choice of work before family had cultivated many of the underlying difficulties in her marriage.

Pops loved his grandchildren so much that when David's family moved to Chicago, he went along. His wife, Gerty, had died before David was three, and family was the most important part of Pop's life.

As the kids matured, they learned that Pops had come to Chicago to help babysit David and Stacy. David's mom and dad were having marital trouble and had worked hard to revive the marriage. They had gone to a two-week retreat and followed it with counseling twice a week for several years.

All that time, it was Pops who cared for the kids, sheltering them from the difficulties of their parent's marriage. He had done such a brilliant job that, if asked, David and Stacy would have no memory of those two weeks or of any fights between their parents.

If a scuffle broke out over dinner, Pops would look squarely at the kids and say something like, "Ah, grownups, so much passion. Let's go to the shop and get some ice cream."

To this day, David attributed his stability to the love and constant presence of Pops.

He was the strongest male influence in David's life. During his school years his father was often too busy at work to attend athletic events, but Pops was always there. He'd wear the school colors and clap his large, strong hands in jubilant praise at his grandson's performance.

He was equally good to Stacy. David remembered sitting outside his sister's room while Pops consoled Stacy about a breakup with a boyfriend.

"Oh, my sweet angel," Pops had said in a voice as distinct as a fingerprint. "I am so sorry you are in pain."

David had peeked his head around and saw Stacy curled

up in Pops' lap. He was rubbing her back as she cried.

"I too know great loss. When your Grandma Gerty died, I thought the world would stop spinning. She was my one true love. But I found so much happiness in loving you and your brother. So I know that this boy will stay in your heart forever, but you will find other great loves soon."

He had not belittled the heartache of a fifteen-year-old girl. He had inspired her to love again.

The family often joked, "Pops, what would you do without us?. But the real tragedy would be what the family would do without Pops.

And now they would have to find out.

Julia and David went to bed that night curled together like newborn kittens, seeking life and warmth from one another. Little had been said as they spent time quietly mourning and remembering the life this great man had lived.

As dawn broke, Julia heard the rusty hinge of the steel trap of her heart. While Pops' death was tragic and unexpected, it did not alter the judgment that David had to make about her lies.

Losing Pops and her husband at the same time would be a price too expensive to pay.

"Pops will never meet our children," David said, as brightness began to warm their bedroom.

Her heart hammered so loudly she feared David could feel it. "I'm sorry I lied to you."

"I know," he whispered.

Like the light, silence slowly filled the room again.

"I forgive you," he finally said.

Relief washed over Julia like a baptism, and she promised never to put herself in a situation that tempted her to dishonesty again. How could she have been so nearsighted in her desire to get pregnant that she got to the point of almost losing her husband?

"I'm ready to do the treatments," David said, surprising

his wife.

"Really?"

"I can't believe my children won't know Pops. By waiting this long to get aggressive . . ." he trailed off. "I couldn't give him great-grandkids. And my children—our children—will miss knowing the greatest man I've ever known."

Together, united by grief and what could have been, they cried.

CHAPTER 32

"Hello, Sweetheart. What are you doing here?" came the familiar voice. The hospital hallway echoed, and Julia turned to see her mother walking toward her.

Embarrassment, like bats from a cave, rushed to her.

Beaty was in all white, accented by several gold necklaces. Julia thought of Ava and wondered if, when she turned fifty-five, Ava would still wear only the color of purity. At least her mother wasn't in a sari or a gold jogging suit.

"Hi, Mom. I'm surprised to see you." Worry suddenly grasped her and she spoke quickly. "Is everything okay? Where's Dad?"

If something was wrong with her father and he was in the hospital, if, God forbid, she had lost him like they had Pops, Julia would not be able to handle it. The older men in her life were a brace that kept her wavering of sanity stable. Now that she had been looking at her father with new, parental eyes, she loved him more deeply than ever before, with a new love built on a mature appreciation that she hadn't had before.

Please, God, she thought. Don't let anything happen to my daddy.

"Oh, Honey, everything is fine. I'm getting my thyroid checked. I do it every couple of months." She leaned in closer relaying a secret. "They want to make sure I'm still alive."

"Are you?" Julia joked.

Her mother smiled hopefully at her. Conversations

between them had not been smooth since Julia stormed out of supper several months ago and Savvy showed up pregnant. Their relationship was further strained when Talon was born and Beaty gushed over her "first" grandson as if, Julia felt, conception was a competition and Savvy had won. Beaty knew she and David were struggling, but she continued to vocalize her desire for more grandkids which left Julia wounded. Julia was beyond disappointed in her mother when she so easily agreed to help Savvy raise him. Julia saw this as enabling Savvy's reckless behavior.

Mother and daughter had tried several times to reconnect, but, like a tree without leaves, the substance was missing.

"Why are you in such a good mood this morning?" Beaty asked.

Julia's good mood was undeniable—her body was still glowing from exercise and satisfaction. What her mother couldn't see was that it was the happy result of morning sex.

Julia had taken four unproductive cycles of Clomid and was now doing a series of tests with Dr. Lamont. At their last appointment, he told Julia and David that the next step in their fertility assessment was semen diagnostics. The couple was instructed to "collect a sample" and bring it to the hospital within an hour—the sooner, the better—and today was the day.

When they had awakened this morning, both were thinking about the task at hand, but they were unsure whether David was to retrieve the sample on his own or with Julia's help. The decision turned out to be simple—and mutual.

In the heat of the moment, David pulled out early and grabbed the sample cup from the bedside table. The doctor had told them to keep the sample warm, so while Julia brushed her hair and put on mascara, he sat on the bed with the cup warming between his legs. He had an early morning meeting and wouldn't be able to make the special delivery to the hospital. So Julia kissed her husband, took the cup, and nestled it against to her belly, and drove to the hospital giggling to deposit the goods at the lab.

"No reason," Julia said to her mother. She needed to cut the conversation short. With only fifteen minutes to spare, she had to find the correct lab and get the specimen delivered.

"And what are you doing here," Beaty asked.

Her mother already knew they were trying to conceive and failing miserably. Maybe the truth was the leafy olive branch they both needed to repair the relationship.

"I'm taking David's sperm to the lab," Julia said, taking the plastic cup from under her shirt and showing her mom, hoping to elicit shock.

"Now that I did not expect," Beaty said, laughing. "Go ahead, then let's have coffee." It was more a question than a statement, as if Beaty were dipping her toe in the lake before diving in.

Since their fight, Julia had begun to feel that, like a child outgrowing a beloved stuffed animal, she had moved beyond the need for her mother's counsel. But standing before her now in the stark hallway, she realized that could never happen.

"I would love to, Mom," she said.

They went to Flavors, of course. "The usual, Julia?" the barista asked. Julia tried to come in only when Savvy was off work—it made the place feel like her own instead of another place her sister had invaded and taken over.

"Yes, please," she said. "This is my mother, Beaty Meyers. Mom, this is Sasha, who somehow remembers everyone's name and order."

"What can I get you?" Sasha said, moving a strand of green hair from her eyes.

Julia watched her mother take in Sasha, with her tight black jeans, flannel shirt, black-rimmed glasses, and piercings. She worried that at next month's dinner her mother would be wearing something inspired by this hipster and wondered what she would serve to complement the ensemble.

"I'll have what my beautiful daughter is having," she said. "And I must say, I love your look."

Julia playfully rolled her eyes and said, "Come on, Mom."

"Oh, you love me," Beaty said.

"Yes, I do," Julia said with floods of sincerity. And with that they were back.

Since their impromptu coffee date, they had grown closer than ever before, speaking almost daily about the most irrelevant things, from new window treatments to recipes with quinoa. It was nice.

During one of these conversations, Julia told her mother about her friendship with Rebecca and how, through the roller coaster of trials, Rebecca had been a stabilizing force. She also admitted to her mother that, while Sarah was still her best friend and their history dictated they always would be, there was a frayed edge to their relationship.

"She wants to support me, Mom," Julia said, "but discussing the battle of infertility with a fertile woman is like trying to describe a beautiful melody to someone who has never heard music. It just doesn't work very well." Julia realized as she said this that she wanted her mother to understand she, Beaty, fell into the same camp.

Beaty gave Julia a card for a yoga studio, and she actually thought about trying it. "It makes you feel strong and grounded," Beaty said, "like the roots of a tree that grows to touch the sky."

It was the first time Julia hadn't rolled her eyes at her mother's eccentricity. It was as if they were, for the first time, starting to understand and accept one another.

CHAPTER 33

As it turned out, morning sex had been the wrong choice. The lab tech called to say that since Julia's fluids had been mixed with the sample, the test would need to be re-administered. The formality of the words made Julia laugh under her breath. They were talking about sperm and masturbation, not chemistry or auto repair. She felt like a middle school student in sex ed.

David was to take the test at the hospital and provide the sample immediately. "Is there like a special room or something?" Julia asked.

"There is a private bathroom across the hall from the lab," the tech said. "Just be sure to lock the door."

With an unquenchable smile, Julia paced outside the bathroom while David preformed the task at hand. In the silent hallway the only thing she could do was imagine her husband's shame behind the door. She didn't mean to smile, she just couldn't stifle it.

When the door finally opened Julia burst into laughter.

"Oh, shut up," David chuckled. "You could have offered to help."

Holding hands, they delivered the sperm.

"Someone will call you later in the week with the results," the woman said, unflinching as she took the sample. Julia thought of all the things she had to physically handle on a daily basis and wondered how much Germ-X she should use.

"You need to find your center, Darling," her mother said later that morning. With the gift certificate from the yoga center burning a hole in her pocket, and her mounting anxiety waiting for the test results, now seemed as good a time as any to give it a try.

Beaty had often told her daughter that she went to yoga for the exercise but came back for the grounding. If the class offered some kind of emotional stabilizer, Julia wanted to be a part of it. She felt like she was angry all the time. Angry at her sister, mad at the loss of Pops, angry about Rebecca's failed attempts, frustrated that David took so long to get tested, and most of all furious at her own body.

She was apprehensive when she stepped onto the second floor of the office complex and headed toward the yoga studio. The red door, the smell of lavender, the sound of birds and Indian bells wafting through the air—all let her know she was in the right place but also elevated her flight instinct.

What kind of Zen-inspired exercise studio was next to a CPA firm and above a law practice, she thought. But she had promised her mother she would do this, and she was going to stick it out. After all, it was only a forty-five minute class.

She was surprised with the mixed bag of attendees— several slightly overweight women in their fifties, two men in respectable shape, a forty-year old woman who looked like she was chiseled from marble, a few college-age girls, and a woman who had to be in her mid eighties. When Julia decided to go to the All Ages All Fitness Levels class she hadn't honestly expected this variety.

The instructor, a pigtailed woman of five feet, greeted Julia. When she admitted to being a yoga virgin the instructor's eyes took on an angelic understanding, as if she knew what Julia was about to experience.

"My mother got me a gift certificate," Julia said.

"Ah, Beaty is a precious and balanced soul. We are delighted to know her."

Julia smiled at the comedy before realizing the instructor

wasn't joking. "Thank you," she said. "I'll tell her you said that."

"We haven't seen her in a while. I hope she's well," the instructor said.

"My sister moved in with them and has a new baby, so mom has been pretty busy," Julia caught herself. This woman didn't need to know any of this and hadn't even asked. "But I'm looking forward to trying this out."

Julia was instructed to remove her shoes, then to get a mat and a foam block from the back wall.

The instructor's voice was measured, calm, and fluid. It was obvious that for some the discipline of yoga went far beyond the contortion and balance of the exercise and took on a metaphysical quality. Julia began to realize yoga was more an act of being than doing.

During the initial step of quieting the body and listening to her breathing, Julia closed her eyes and decided to give in and take this yoga thing for a spin. She didn't know any of these people, so why not succumb to the entire experience. If it was working for her mother, and had made the instructor into this kind of serene creature, Julia wanted in.

She breathed slowly and deliberately through each motion and into each posture. She felt muscles in her shoulders and legs she didn't even know existed. Her entire body shook trying to stabilize and sweated as if she had just run a mile.

During the final moments of quiet, each person was to lie on their mat, palms toward the ceiling, feet falling to the side, eyes closed. The lights and music were turned off so that the class could follow where their minds went.

Julia left the yoga studio realizing her body and mind were fully satisfied. Now, sitting in her car, she understood why her mother had raved about yoga.

During class there were several pieces of wisdom the instructor shared with the group, and Julia tried to make a checklist in her mind. In the car, she pulled out a piece of paper and a pen to jot down the four items she didn't want to forget. She wrote:

Number 1: Thank yourself for being here.

It was a revelation. She had been grateful for people and things her whole life, but had never once said thank you to herself for something. It felt awkward but so right.

Number 2 . . . Her pen hovered above the paper. How had she forgotten so quickly? She'd come back to that one later.

Number 3: At heart center the female needs the male for balance.

It had been during a pose in which Julia was on the toes of her left foot, squatting low to balance her bottom on the heel of that same foot. Her right leg was folded up high on her left thigh. She squeezed her toes into the floor, begging for the strength to stay upright. The instructor told the class to remove their hands from the floor and bring them into a prayer position, so called heart center.

Julia attempted the move, carefully releasing her hands and then instantly putting them back on the mat. Finally the instructor told them to "bring the left hand up first. This is the female side of the body. Then have the masculine right side meet it at heart center. When the two match, you will find your balance."

Julia desperately missed her balance with David. She hoped their fertility tests would provide some kind of answer and together they would find their center.

She focused her eyes on the mirror in front of her, and with determination she quieted her shaking body and balanced. If she could do this here, she could do it anywhere.

Number 4: Strengthen the mind-body connection.

They had done a sequence of moves lying face down on the floor. The class was told to tighten all the muscles of the leg, elongating them toward the back wall, and then suddenly lay them limp on the floor. Her head lay on the mat as if she were going to sleep. They repeated this several times.

The instructor told the group, "We pause between exercises so the mind will tell the body what to do. We become more deliberate in our motions, allowing the mind to lead, strengthening the mind and body connection."

What more in life did Julia want than for her body to hear and respond to her mind's requests for a baby. She loved this wise guidance and underlined it on the paper.

Driving home, she didn't crave a latte or even a soda. She wanted a giant ice water and a handful of nuts. If only yoga were was something she could do every day.

At the stop sign she pulled up the yoga studio's website. Classes were available only during working hours with the exception of this one on Saturday morning. She'd ask Rebecca to come with her next week.

CHAPTER 34

The urologist's call came on their home phone two days later. Julia had been feeling poorly the last couple of days and decided to stay home from work to flush the bug out of her system with fluids, rest, and Ever After, her favorite Drew Barrymore movie. Nothing kills a virus like a movie on repeat and chicken bouillon in a coffee mug.

"Mrs. Ellis, I have the results of your husband's test." Her stomach flipped. If they said nothing was wrong, then it would be back to the drawing board, extending their search for a problem and a solution. If there was a problem, however, then that could mean terrible things.

"The test confirms that your husband has an average sperm count. However, he has low motility, Grade B—meaning his sperm are shaped correctly and move their tails appropriately, but instead of swimming straight, they move in a more curved or crooked motion."

The words swirled in Julia's head like a ribbon dancer.

"If he had a high sperm count, the unusual swimmers would not matter because there would be more volume to work with. But, since the sperm count is average, it makes conception more difficult."

Those words stopped the dancer and brought her to the floor with a crash.

"This is not a death sentence," the nurse said. She had obviously given this kind of news before. "Low motility doesn't mean you'll be unable to become pregnant. It just makes it more tricky."

As she hung up the phone, Julia looked at the television screen and saw Drew Barrymore pick up an apple and throw it at the head of the man stealing her horse. Struck, he fell to the ground clutching at his injury.

This news was the apple, and she would have to throw it at David.

Julia shrugged off her blanket and walked to the guest bathroom. The nautical decor—starfish and sailboats on light blue walls—was supposed to remind them of an unhurried seaside vacation. She looked in the mirror.

"David," she said, practicing, "the results showed your sperm have low motility." She watched her mouth move over the words "low motility," repeating them several times until they didn't sound like words at all, but a jumble of incomprehensible sounds.

With both hands on the sink's edge, she closed her eyes and let her head droop like a wilted rose.

This may very well be the reason they had been unable to conceive. It may not have been Julia's fault all along. The thought gave her peace, but she wondered what the news would do to David.

Would it make him question his manhood the way she had questioned herself? Through the last two years Julia's self-confidence had slowly deflated at the idea that her body was unable to perform the very foundational task of procreation. She felt worthless that she was unable to satisfy their longing for a family. She worried that David would suffer the same painful turmoil.

How can I relay this kind of news in a way that will cause the smallest waves, Julia thought. Maybe a phone call so he'd be alone and wouldn't have to wear a mask of indifference but could react honestly.

Julia picked up the phone and dialed the first six numbers to David's cell phone. She pictured him answering the call and getting the news. He'd be sitting behind his desk working frantically to finish his one last project and leave his thankless job behind.

Since his decision to look for new work, his current job had felt even more oppressive, more confining, and he had grown more unhappy. There were two offers on the table, and his excitement when he talked of future possibilities was infectious.

Julia cleared her screen on her phone, realizing it would be wrong to call David with the news at work.

What if she didn't say anything about the motility problem. After all, the urologist said it wouldn't make conception impossible, only more difficult, which might mean that low motility wasn't the sole reason they hadn't gotten pregnant. They could search for another culprit with David never knowing the truth, never having to suffer the pain of thinking his manhood was compromised.

Flashbacks of the ramifications of Julia's last lie struck her like a burning cattle prod. She had promised herself she would never lie to David again, and she meant it. Plus, this was his body and he needed to understand its limitations.

She settled on telling him the moment he came in the door.

When Julia's attention finally came back to the television, Drew Barrymore was dressed like an angel and standing atop a staircase. Everyone at the masked ball was staring in her direction as she reminded herself to "just breathe."

It was the advice Julia needed too.

Julia had been unable to keep much food down over the last few days and so had paid little mind to her appearance. Today was no exception, but if she was going to deliver this kind of news to her husband, she was going to do it freshly showered and in a clean shirt.

When David got home, Julia kissed her husband and hugged him tightly. It was their greeting ritual, but today she savored his scent and the warmth of his body a little longer than usual.

"Does ts mean you're feeling better?" he asked.

"Not really. It was just time to freshen up." She paused. "Plus, I heard from the urologist today."

"And?"

Doing her best to use the exact words, she told him what the doctor had said.

"What does that mean?" David asked. Julia could tell from the withdrawn look in his eyes that he was rolling the information around much as she had done.

He finally looked at her. "So my sperm aren't good at swimming?" he asked, a sad smile forming at the corners of his lips.

"That's right." Julia reached for his hand and squeezed.

"Well," he said with an unflappable calm, "they swim like I do. We'll just have to get them a kickboard."

She had been impressed with her husband hundreds of times over the years but never more than now. Never more than this moment when he had every right to be broken but instead chose confidence and humor.

The metaphorical kickboard would be expensive and difficult. But they would handle it together.

CHAPTER 35

The two new jobs David had been offered sat on the table. They were polar opposites.

The first, Flagmont & Winnelson, was a large company with hundreds of employees and satellite locations all over the country. The Human Resources Director had taken David and Julia both to lunch. Over steaks he explained expectations of the position and the compensation plan. Promotions would be based on performance and longevity with the company. David would meet his team and get his gold-embossed business cards on the first day.

On the way home, Julia thumbed through the beautiful packet that outlined David's employment package. The Health Department hadn't given her a benefits package nearly this inclusive, much less an expense account or a car.

The second company, Ripperland Products, a start-up LLC with a successful, albeit short track record, made their offer to David the following day. The company had three top-tier execs and twenty-five additional employees. The president of the company, Will Watkins, had David and Julia over to his home for dinner. His wife, Claire, prepared a beautiful casserole with more side dishes than necessary. Their two children made a plate of brownies for desert and played with toys while the grownups talked.

"David," Will said, over the salad greens. "I know you have to have several options to chose from. You're talented and respected. Today, we can't compete with a corner office view and a secretary. But what we can promise is a solid team where everyone matters. Our office is full of excitement and full of people ready to come to work and make an impact on the industry. I've been looking for someone to push us to the next level, and you are that man."

Julia could see the pride in her husband's face by the way he raised his chin at the word "respected," as if the word itself, when placed upon his shoulders, made him stand taller and prove himself worthy of the compliment. She was grateful to be able to see David through the eyes of his peers.

It was clear to Julia which offer David should choose. Who doesn't like embossed cards? Though this was David's career, she thought it her wifely duty to insert small suggestions into his thought process.

"I insure Flagmont & Winnelson," Sarah told Julia when they got together for a shopping spree. "It's an incredible company. He'd be a fool not to take the job. They lavish their employees with Christmas bonuses that make me jealous."

"Honey," Julia said to David during their Sunday morning ritual of newspapers and coffee on the back patio. "I know it's not my place to recommend which job you take, but I really liked the Flagmont place."

"Really?" he said. "You didn't like Will and Claire?"

"I liked them fine," Julia defended. "It's just that I like the security of Flagmont."

"That's the thing I don't like," he said kicking his socked feet up on a chair. "We're so young and in a good place to shoot for the moon. If Ripperland hits, we'll look like a pair of geniuses. And if it doesn't, I can always find another company."

"But the benefits at Flagmont are great."

"Who cares about the benefits," he said. "At Ripperland my opinion will matter, and I won't have to sit through endless meetings to finally be heard. If I took the Flagmont job, I'd be walking through a different door into the same job I have now."

Without knowing that Ripperland was hiring or that David was looking, Brandon, Rebecca's husband, had introduced Will to David during a golf game several weeks back. By the end of the four-hour game, both men realized their complementary talents and began to dream of the future.

"Wait." She was confused. "Do I really hear you? Are you going to take the Ripperland job?"

Julia hadn't seen this coming. She thought the whole dinner routine was cute but wouldn't lead to a legitimate possibility. David had negotiated an almost equal level of pay, but there was no way the start-up could afford the benefits of a major employer.

"I think I am," he said, smiling at his decision.

"You can't," Julia stood up and looked down at her husband, in a posture of authority.

"And, why not?"

"Because we'll need good medical coverage for the fertility treatments."

"You want me to choose a job because of our fertility problems? Are you crazy? Getting in at the beginning is a huge opportunity me. For us."

"But I thought we agreed that us was going to include a child." She meant her voice to be full of sorrow and compassion. Instead it came out like an accusation.

"It still does. This job doesn't change anything."

"Like hell it doesn't. Don't you get it? Fertility treatments are expensive, and you're treating it like it's no big deal."

"Don't talk to me like this, Julia," his voice firm. "I get it. But I will not jeopardize every day of my working life for a treatment we may or may not need."

She opened her mouth to speak, but David got to his feet and met her eyes. "This is my decision, and it's final." He turned on his heels and walked into the house, leaving Julia like a teenager who had just been grounded.

She followed him. "This isn't over," she said. "You don't get to walk away like this doesn't affect us both."

"It's my job, Jules. It is my choice." He wasn't harsh but neither did he sound malleable. "I am trying to provide for us here."

"Well, you aren't doing a very good job with the for us part, are you?" she said.

It was below the belt, and she regretted it instantly. Other than the one discussion about the kickboard, they had never spoken about their fertility problems as being one person's fault. But with this comment, she had done exactly that.

A wash of hurt and anger passed before his eyes.

"I'm sorry," she backpedaled. "I didn't mean it."

"So you just wanted to hurt me?" he said. "You have taken something I am excited about and turned it into a fertility decision. I am sick and tired of this obsession."

"I'm sorry if you are mad about my obsession," she said with all the sarcasm she could muster. "But I do want kids, and if I remember correctly, it was your idea in the first place."

"I wanted to have a child with the woman I love. If you see her, will you please remind her of that."

It was as if the bell had rung and the round was over. David fled to the study, and Julia made her way to the bathroom, each finding a separate corner to cool off, replay the battle, and formulate a better strategy for the rounds to come.

The sickness Julia had felt earlier again reared its nauseating head.

CHAPTER 36

Julia had gotten the flu vaccine the first day it was available at the Health Department—mandatory since they never knew what kind of illness would walk through the door. Over the last month or so, many people in the office had been complaining of a stomach bug accompanied by diarrhea and vomiting. One woman had become so dehydrated she was sent to the hospital for fluids.

So when Julia still did not feel well after a few more days, she made an appointment with her general practitioner, just to be safe. She told Dr. Hofster's nurse, a young round woman with a pointy nose and full lips, that she had been throwing up and because of that was lacking in energy.

"Let me check with Dr. Hofster. He may want to run a simple blood test to rule out the flu," she said, while pumping the blood pressure cuff.

Blood was drawn and Julia was to wait a few minutes while the test came back.

Turning to her phone, she texted David. "I miss you." It had always been their language of apology.

His reply was instant, "Me 2."

"Let's rent a movie tonight and snuggle," she wrote.

"Will there be foreplay?"

She smiled as Dr. Hofster walked back into the room.

"I have your test results," he said. "You were right, it's not the flu," he said, looking at the open file in his hand.

Julia was distracted watching his mustache move up and down. The upper lip had always seemed such a strange place for hair—gross actually, in that a mustache was basically an extension of nose hair that sat on the lip waiting to sweep up food and drink.

In college she had gone on a date with a guy who had a well-groomed goatee. The date had been pleasant enough, but while they stood at her door saying goodbye, he leaned down for a kiss. It had been like kissing a freshly mowed lawn. She never returned his calls, and eventually he gave up.

There were only a few men in the world who could properly wear a mustache, including firemen and first basemen. Dr. Hofster was not among them.

"But it is a stomach bug," he said, looking up from the file to meet her eyes.

She waited for him to explain that she needed an antibiotic. She waited for him to tell her to get some rest and drink plenty of fluids. Instead, he said, "It's the kind of bug that will be cured in nine months."

Furrowing her brow and tilting her head with confusion, Julia very slowly began to understand.

"I'm . . ." she stumbled. "I'm pregnant?"

"I take it you weren't trying," he said.

"No. I mean, yes. We are trying, but we have an appointment with a fertility specialist coming up and we never thought . . . I mean I never thought I was pregnant." Julia nailed Dr. Hofster to the wall with a stare so strong he couldn't move. "Are you positive? I mean absolutely sure."

"Yes. The blood work shows all the right elevated levels. Mrs. Ellis, you are going to have a baby."

With those words, Julia felt her body begin to grow light, as if all her matter were evaporating into pure joy. Tears fell from her cheeks and she reminded herself to breathe.

CHAPTER 37

According to the period tracker on Julia's phone, her last cycle had begun six-and-a-half weeks ago. Dr. Hofster looked at the wall calendar and estimated the due date for April.

To her surprise, the first thing Julia thought about was the daffodils—those beautiful yellow flowers peeking their heads out of new, vibrantly green growth or already be in full bloom, bursting with yellow beauty in the most unusual places.

It was very appropriate that their fertility journey would begin with the daffodils and, three years later, would end the same way. Maybe, if the baby was a girl, David would consider Daffodil for a name.

She smiled to herself, hugging her middle.

There was so much to decide now. How would she announce it to David? How would she tell her mom and dad? Sarah would be ecstatic, and they could have their big announcement at Ringo's over the salad, just the way Julia had imagined so long ago, just the way she had done with Sarah.

And then the most natural thought followed. Rebecca. How would she tell her new best friend? How could she break her already broken heart? The guilt of a successful pregnancy began to taste bitter as she thought of the sadness the news would bring her dear friend.

Julia knew she couldn't accept the joy of her situation until she had loved Rebecca through the injustice she was sure to feel. Their friendship had become tightly braided together through their shared misery and supportive understanding. She owed her the truth and would give her the freedom to be angry, to be sad, to be begin pushing Julia away.

Immediately after stepping out of the doctor's office, she called Rebecca and scheduled lunch.

They met at Flavors. Savvy had worked the morning shift and would be gone already. The place was known for its coffee and not its food, but Rebecca had been bragging about an Asian Chicken Wrap she'd eaten several weeks ago, so it seemed like the perfect destination.

As Julia walked in, Sasha winked at her while setting a cup of coffee she had just made on the counter. The place had become like the old sitcom Cheers, where everybody knows your name.

"Mr. Raftopolis, your coffee is ready," Sasha said in her bluesy voice. The call of an order ready was the alarm that had started Julia's day for so many years. Now, with a baby on the way, she'd have to forgo her double-shot cappuccino with Splenda and whip and discover the joy of decaffeinated drinks.

Julia watched as the older gentleman in the pageboy hat walked to the counter to get his coffee. She had seen him at almost every coffee outing for the last several years and never knew his name. Mr. Raftopolis. It was familiar somehow but she couldn't pinpoint why.

Rebecca walked in full of smiles and warm greetings. The pain Julia was about to inflict began to burn her stomach. Anticipating the difficulty to come, she had already ordered them both a wrap sandwich and secured a table in the corner.

"I'm so glad you called. How have you been? Are you feeling better?"

Julia bit her lip, thinking of how exactly to say the words. "I'm okay."

"Oh, good. I've missed you. So, have you tried the yoga class yet?"

Julia put her hands on her knees under the table and took a shallow breath. She noticed the scent of roasting coffee, the sounds of friendly chatter, and the clatter of porcelain cups set on porcelain plates.

A terrible thought entered her mind. Had she chosen this public place to relay the news hoping minimize Rebecca's reaction? Julia had been so hurt when Sarah told of her pregnancy at Ringo's. In pain, she had had to fake excitement and composure.

Had she become so concerned with herself that she didn't think to offer solace to Rebecca by letting her fully and openly express her grief?

For a moment, Julia thought about not telling her about the pregnancy and then decided that was a selfish idea too. If Rebecca found out from someone else, it would destroy their friendship. And if she realized Julia already knew she was pregnant and didn't share it right here, right now, she'd think of her as an untrustworthy friend.

There was nothing else to do but tell the truth.

"Becks, I just went to the doctor." She paused and looked into the stricken eyes of her friend.

"Oh, no. Is there a problem? Are they afraid you have cancer again?" Rebecca's hands shot across the table ready to console. Julia accepted her kindness and used her warmth and strength for the next words.

"I'm fine. But I'm not sick. I'm pregnant." Julia held Rebecca's gaze, trying to read her deep brown eyes.

Rebecca's grasp grew tighter around Julia's hands as slowly tears began to form in her eyes.

"Please don't cry," Julia said. "I'm sorry. No one knows yet. I had to tell you before I told anyone else. You are my person, and I am so sorry to hurt you. I'm sorry."

"Oh my gosh, Jules." Rebecca said in a low voice.

This is where it starts, Julia thought, releasing Rebecca's hands so she could wipe her eyes. She will let go of my hands now and keep pushing me away until we don't even say hello in passing.

Rebecca continued. "Don't you dare apologize. I couldn't

be happier for you. This is what we have been working for."

The women stood up and embraced, holding on tight, one squeezing with a request for forgiveness, the other with a promise that no forgiveness was needed. The hug was the enactment of their friendship—form-fitting companionship.

When their wraps arrived, both women were engulfed in happy tears.

"How are you going to tell David?" Rebecca asked.

That was the big question. Their relationship has been so tense since the fight about his new job and the insurance ramifications. They had gone about their days as if on autopilot. Julia knew he would be elated with the pregnancy, and with the news the rapture of their relationship would return. But doing something elaborate to tell him didn't feel right.

After lunch, the secret inside of her built like a hurricane. If she didn't allow it to hit land and dissipate, it would grow to catastrophic size, consuming her.

Julia had not been to David's new office. He had not asked, and she had not offered. As she parked outside the one story white-brick building, she felt as unimpressed as she had when the offer came in.

Taking a deep breath, she opened the door into the reception area, which sat empty. The decor was modern, a little more cold than her taste, but hip. There were plaques and awards on the wall, and she could see a ping pong table down the hall. The furniture was white leather and there were accents of red throughout the room.

She heard the sound of David's laughter from a nearby office and realized that this was where he needed to be professionally, not stifled by upper management in an office as stuffy and standard as that of every other large company. He belonged here—in a place where he could stand out, in a place where he could laugh while doing what he loved.

David's back was turned and she knocked on the open door. Will Watkins and David stopped talking and looked at Julia.

"I'm sorry to interrupt," she said, suddenly conscious of her intrusion.

"No, no. Come in," David said. "You remember Will, of course."

"Of course I do," Julia said. "Hello. I hope I haven't interrupted something important."

"We're done," Will said kindly and then addressed David. "The conference call is at three." And he walked out the door.

Julia hugged David and took a seat in front of his desk. His eyes smiled, and she knew he understood the apology in her gesture of coming to the office. "What brings you by, my lovely wife? Want a tour of the place?"

"No. Actually, I just came from the doctor."

His posture and expression changed immediately, just the way Rebecca's had done. She didn't realize that her brush with cancer had put so much fear and concern into the people around her. Seeing them afraid for her was heartwarming and reminded her that love was a gift.

"It's not cancer," she said with a smile, as the hurricane made landfall. "It's a baby."

David jumped up so fast his chair shot out from behind him and wheeled into the wall with a thud. "A baby?!"

Julia nodded giddily as he picked her up and spun her around. He was a kid at the carnival overwhelmed with the cotton candy and balloons and blinking lights.

"A baby," he said again. He reached for his phone and hit the intercom button, "My wife is going to have a baby!. And the halls of the office erupted with claps and whistles.

David kissed her deeply, the kind of kiss that should be reserved for private getaways on moonlit nights. Her knees buckled, and she fell into his exuberant passion.

The intercom buzzed in the office, interrupting their kiss. "Great news. I'll handle the call," Will's voice said. "Go celebrate with your wife."

Julia invited her mom and dad for supper the following

evening. She even asked Savvy to come and bring Talon. David's parents were going to join too. When they asked about the occasion, Julia told them David's birthday was in a few weeks and this was the only time she could find on the calendar to have a get together.

She made buffalo wings, David's favorite, as well as bruschetta on neatly sliced baguette bread, stuffed mushrooms, cheddar cheese puffs, and chipotle-lime bacon-wrapped shrimp.

"Tapas," Beaty said when she looked at the food on the table. "My favorite."

"Topless?" David's dad said. "What?" And they collectively laughed. Julia hoped she would hear that sound every time she thought of this moment.

"It is kind of a strange meal," David pointed out trying to encourage the family to get the point. "We were hoping you would enjoy all this tiny food."

Their parents collectively furrowed their brows.

"Tiny," David said again pausing for them to get it. "Itty bitty maybe."

Just then Talon crawled in wearing the new shirt his Aunt Julia had put on him. When he entered the room Savvy read the shirt aloud, "I'm a cousin."

Beaty grasped her mouth and flew at Julia. Everyone else followed. The food may not have communicated the message, but the response was priceless.

When the dinner party was over, Savvy pulled her sister aside. "Congratulations, sis. I hope this brings us all together."

Julia looked at her sister in shock, unsure she had heard correctly. Was Savvy actually reaching out to her? She had been so cold and angry at Julia at the coffee shop before Talon was born. Since then, Julia had given her sister a wide birth just as she had when they were children.

Before she could respond, Beaty tapped Julia on the shoulder. "Did you learn about this two days ago?" she asked.

"Yesterday. Why?" Julia said.

"Because I felt a tightening of the earth that day, and I knew something was going to happen. I must be out of touch, though. I thought it was a bad something, not a wonderful something like this."

Julia hugged her mother again. The crazy talk of the earth tightening was becoming something Julia looked forward to, like being introduced to a new culture while on a vacation. She didn't necessarily want to become indoctrinated into the society but instead enjoyed visiting for the eccentricities.

CHAPTER 38

The appointment with Dr. Lamont was set. According to the calendar that Julia and Dr. Hofster had created, she would be eight weeks along. David, in turn, created a countdown calendar for their home computer, and each morning they'd rise, make coffee, and see the glorious shrinking of time until Baby Ellis was born.

They signed up for a weekly email from BabyCenter.com to tell them the details of the miracle forming inside Julia's womb. Their life, once marked by the frustratingly slow passage of time, was now moving forward fast toward a bright future.

They decided to wait until the official appointment with the doctor to spread the word about the blessing. Rebecca was the only person outside of the family who knew. It became a glue in their friendship, securing their closeness.

Julia was impressed with Rebecca's grace. There were times Julia could see the weight of hurt that burdened her friend, and they would talk openly about her difficulty. But they understood one another in a beautifully comfortable way and because of this were delicate to one another.

Julia still could not believe the pregnancy had finally become real. She found herself, a Christian in philosophy but not a churchgoer in practice, praying over her growing belly. Please, God, let this baby be healthy. Please, God, let this child grow up happy and safe. Please, God, keep this baby under your care.

She had no longing for alcohol or unpasteurized cheese, or the number of other things to be avoided that she and David had mocked after Sarah announced her pregnancy. She was happy to oblige the websites full of suggestions for fostering a healthy pregnancy and baby. She was tired, but snuggling with a blanket on the couch made her feel maternal, as though she was doing her best mothering job by protecting the fetus and focusing all her energy on its growth.

She and David held hands as they left Dr. Lamont, who had given them a happy handshake and a positive pregnancy test. Julia was put on a schedule of appointments and told to take prenatal vitamins, which she had already gotten from Beaty.

When they got home, Julia set out the little red shoes she had just purchased. Pinterest had hundreds of clever ideas about how to announce a pregnancy, and the little-red-shoe idea spoke to her.

Outside, in the garden, next to the tiny shoes, she placed a pair of her favorite pumps and David's work shoes. Julia snapped the photo with her cell phone and posted the picture immediately on Facebook. The caption read, Arriving in April.

It was exactly three minutes before her phone rang.

"Jules, has someone hacked into your Facebook account?" It was Sarah.

"Why, what ever do you mean?" Julia said, using her best Scarlett O'Hara voice.

"You are pregnant!?. Sarah's enthusiasm bounced off the wall like a rubber ball. Julia heard her sniffle. "I am so happy this is happening. I love you so much."

Julia knew it was true. And she deeply loved her friend too. There had been a strain between them like the stretch of a rubber band. But with this pregnancy, Julia hopped they would recoil toward one another again.

By day's end there were 112 Likes on the post and a litany of congratulations. She received phone calls from aunts and uncles and college friends.

Near dinner time a gold-wrapped package appeared on the front porch with a tag that read "Mom and Dad To Be." Sarah's signature wrapping paper and calligraphy shimmered with excitement. Before she slipped her finger under the tape, Julia knew what was in the box.

When she held up the tiny socks, she smiled. There was a pair in every color of the rainbow, bright in the smallest size. Julia put them to her nose, as she had done years ago at Yvette's baby shower, and breathed in the fact that these socks belonged to her.

The pride in Julia's heart swelled as her womb soon would. The moments of telling David, of telling their parents, of telling the world had all been worth the struggle. This was real.

When her grandparents called from Iowa, she walked into the other room to tell them what they had already heard from Beaty. Julia saw the muscles of David's jaw clench as she mouthed "grandma." Pops had obviously been on his mind, and the reminder that he was not here to see his great-grandchildren was painful.

The euphoria faltered on Friday evening. While eating a celebratory dinner out with David, Julia's back began to hurt. Each intake of air brought a stabbing pain at the bottom of her ribs. She tried to hide the discomfort, but David read her grimace.

"You okay?" he asked, taking her hand as the waitress delivered the check.

"Just a little pain," she said. "Probably just my body reminding me I'm pregnant." She loved saying those words and didn't want to alarm him, or herself for that matter.

"Let me take you home and give you a massage," he said, with raised eyebrows.

Julia read that many men were afraid to have sex with their wives when they were pregnant. The idea of a penis and a baby sharing the same small space made them either disgusted or afraid they'd harm the child. Everything she read indicated there was nothing to fear, and David certainly wasn't afraid.

A massage was probably exactly what she needed and agreed with a seductive wink.

Julia woke up the following morning grabbing her back in the same spot. The intensity slightly increased, she got up from bed not wanting to disturb David.

The clock read 6:27. Sarah was practiced with pregnancy and could probably give excellent advice, but her household didn't wake up on the weekend until after nine. Her mother would overreact and tell her to go to the hospital, or she'd give her a crazy recipe for healing, like eating a purple flower from the garden and staying in downward dog for twenty minutes. Rebecca would be up in a few minutes and Julia would call her for counsel and comfort.

"Pregnancy is different for everyone," Rebecca said. "You probably just need to rest."

"But I can hardly stand up straight," Julia said. In the small amount of time it took the clock to reach 6:30 her pains had morphed into a full attack throughout her abdomen. Everything in her uterus hurt and she doubled over on the kitchen floor.

"Want me to come over? You know I have movies, and I make a mean cup of coffee. Even decaf," Rebecca offered.

They decided to call one another at nine. If the pain was still there, Rebecca would bring over her arsenal.

As Julia stood up to wake David, she felt a warmth between her legs. She reached down and saw her fingers tipped with blood. Her ears grew hollow. The echo of her heartbeat was all she could hear.

CHAPTER 39

Panic stricken, she woke David, who quickly called the emergency number at the gynecologist's office. It was Saturday, and they knew no one would be able to see them today.

David put the doctor on speaker. "Dr. Lamont, this is David Ellis," his voice was flustered, and Julia realized he was afraid. "Julia is having back pain and just woke up to find blood."

With simple calm the doctor asked questions like "How much blood" and "rate the level of pain." Though not cold, he was formal and solid in his demeanor like a wall around a fortress of information.

"Spotting is a very natural response to pregnancy," the doctor said. "In the first trimester your body is confused by the hormone spikes and the foreign object taking up residence. That is why many women experience morning sickness, diarrhea, and headaches."

Julia looked into David's face as he stared at the phone between them, he was hanging on every word like a juror at a trial.

"You need to take it easy today," the doctor continued. "Prop up your feet and let David do all the work." They all laughed a strained laugh.

"If something is wrong, what should we look for?" David asked.

"If you continue to have spotting and the clots of blood are large, then make an appointment to see me on Monday. Worry doesn't solve the problem, so please try not to."

When the call was over both David and Julia felt less concerned. At nine o'clock Rebecca showed up with movies, a smoothie, and fingernail polish. While they enjoyed the girl time, David went to the grocery store.

By the end of the day, Julia felt like herself again. The pain in her back had subsided completely. In fact, the sore breasts and nausea had vanished also.

When she lay her head on the pillow that night Julia felt restored if a little silly for the whole episode. The pain had been like a splash of cold water waking her to the reality of pregnancy and motherhood. She had been full of pride about being pregnant, like crossing the finish line of a race. But the spotting had forcefully reminded her that pregnancy was not the finish line but rather the starting gate.

The fight against infertility had not been about getting pregnant. It had been to have a child. The ultimate goal was a healthy pink baby nursing at her breast.

Fear of a miscarriage brought home the truth, and she grew thankful for the child within her womb.

As she fell into the beautiful place between wake and sleep, Julia imagined a little girl with long hair skipping toward her with open arms, smiling. It was the little girl she and David had created in their shared dream after their first night of trying to conceive.

Peace like a babbling brook closed Julia's eyes and allowed her to sleep.

She hopped out of bed Sunday morning with a new perspective. She made a four-egg omelet with tomatoes and mushrooms, cut it in half, placed it on two plates, and topped the breakfast with an avocado, salt, and pepper. She set the breakfast on a tray along with coffee and carried it into the bedroom.

"Rise and shine," she announced, softly letting the smell of morning bring David out of rest.

"Wow," he said covering his mouth so as not to allow his

morning breath to overtake the room. "You must be feeling better."

Julia sat on the bed and kissed his cheek. "I am. I think yesterday was just a scare to remind us how precious life is and how lucky we are."

They ate in bed as David complimented her culinary creation. When they were done, he got the newspaper and went to the back porch to read of yesterday's events while Julia got into the shower.

As the warm water fell on her body, cleaning away the worry of yesterday, she hummed. Pouring shampoo into her hand and cleaning her hair, she swayed her hips. She felt like her old self again, carefree and happy.

Suddenly the feel of hot egg whites on her legs stopped her in mid motion. Julia knew in her heart before she looked down. Blood ran from her body down her legs, mixed with the shower's spray, and flowed into the drain. Swallowing the rising lump in her throat, she stared at the stream, unable to tear her eyes away.

David's voice came from the bathroom. "I forgot to brush my teeth," he said. "How gross is that?"

When she didn't respond, he peeked into the shower. "Oh, my God."

CHAPTER 40

Lightheaded, Julia found herself in the emergency room. David must have gotten her out of the shower, dried her off, and put clothes on her, though she couldn't exactly remember.

A nurse spent twenty minutes trying to put a needle in her arm. Vial after ruby red vial of blood was drawn. Julia was sent for an ultrasound. Crimson spots and the smell of metal accompanied every stop.

It was like Julia was watching it all on television. The hospital, the nurses, the people waiting—all felt like a drama she was seeing but not personally experiencing. As if everything was emotionally removed.

The ultrasound technician wouldn't allow David or Julia to look at the monitor and gave nothing away when asked what she saw. Julia had never seen David so erratic.

"Damn it. Why the hell won't you tell us anything?" he demanded of the young woman.

"I'm not a doctor," she said patiently. "I'm sorry. I understand you're worried. I'll get this information to the doctor as soon as possible so you can have some answers."

"You don't understand," he said. "My wife is covered in blood." Covering his face, he looked small and helpless, like a lost puppy hungry for food and comfort.

They were shown into a room, a sheet of a curtain between them and the family on the other side. From the conversation Julia could overhear, the child must have broken his arm while jumping on the trampoline. The eavesdropping helped the endless time pass.

What seemed like hours later, a doctor arrived. He apologized for the wait as he looked over Julia chart. She was nothing but the next stop on his rounds. A clipboard full of blood tests, observed facts, and ultrasound photographs, a name and a Social Security number. The doctor was probably thinking about his kid's little league game that afternoon.

"It looks like your beta numbers are low," he said, without looking up. It was reminiscent of Dr. Hofster only a few weeks ago, announcing that it wasn't a stomach bug making her sick but a baby.

The ER doctor continued, "It's possible you're having a miscarriage. You need to go home today and rest. In the morning, call your OB/GYN and make an appointment."

Like a bad magic trick, hope vanished.

They were discharged and sent home. David wrapped his arm around Julia and helped her limp, exhausted body walk to the car. She was unresponsive to him, so he leaned across her and fastened her seat belt. "It's going to be all right, My Love. It's going to be all right."

Their eyes met, sad and hollow. He kissed her cheek, salty with tears.

When they got home, David carried his wife to bed. He had laid out several towels under her body at her request. She has spent months looking for the right color sheets and didn't want blood to ruin them.

Julia didn't want to watch television or read a book. She didn't want to talk or cry or scream. She felt like a death-row inmate, lying in bed waiting for the end to come.

She heard David in the next room calling the doctor again. He made an appointment for the following morning.

She heard him call his parents and then hers—the words blood, emergency room, and miscarriage repeated during each phone call.

Somewhere in the fog, she had fallen asleep. When she

awoke, Sarah was at her side with a cup of chicken broth and a Kit Kat, her painted lips smiling a sad smile as the steam from the cup rose in front of her.

"What are you doing here?" Julia asked, her voice groggy.

Her best friend should have been a welcome sight—solace in the darkness closing in on her. But Julia didn't want a safe haven, she didn't want love or comfort. She wanted to be left alone. She wanted the baby, and she wanted answerers.

"David called to tell me what was going on," Sarah said, handing her the mug. "I'm here for perspective."

Julia curled her face into an unpleasant scowl, angry with her friend for the assumption that perspective was the balm. When a person is hungry, it's not the menu that makes them full.

"The ER doc didn't say this is a miscarriage. He said it's possible. I don't want you to borrow trouble."

It was just like Sarah to find a positive spin on any situation. She could be in the middle of a deadly tornado and say, "At least it's rain and not lava." Most of the time Julia admired the characteristic; today it felt like salt.

"Before I came, I read online about vanishing twins. Have you heard of this?"

Julia sat up just enough to accept the coffee cup, the warmth and weight of it welcoming.

When she didn't answer, Sarah continued. "Basically, it means you're pregnant with twins and one of them dies. It usually happens in the first trimester, which you are in. And usually it involves vaginal bleeding."

"Vanishing twins?" Julia asked.

"It's sad to think of one baby lost," Sarah said. "But it doesn't mean there's no hope of a baby at all. Honey, the power of positive thinking is important."

"You sound like my mother."

"Thank you," Sarah said. "I think that woman is fantastic."

"Of course you do," Julia said. "You think everyone is fantastic."

"And no one more than you," Sarah said. "Now, I have a pack of cards. Let's play a drinking game."

Julia let out a little laugh, knowing her best friend would never play a drinking game at three in the afternoon in bed. "How about gin rummy?" Julia suggested.

Vanishing twins. She let the idea grow in her mind, take form. Until she received the official results from Dr. Lamont tomorrow she'd harbor the possibility like a ship at port, waiting out the storm.

Sleep that night was fitful. But in the morning, the towels below her were clean, and hope found a tiny crack.

The appointment was set for eight. Intentionally, she and David were the first patients to arrive at the medical practice. Neither wanted to deal with the pain of sitting in a room full of pregnant women who were awaiting the good news of their baby's healthy growth and looking forward to a happy future.

David slipped his hand into Julia's and squeezed. His fingers felt large and warm enclosing hers. Julia tried to squeeze back but the effort was small.

David turned to look into his wife's eyes. Swollen from yesterday's tears, they had little life. It was as if a cloud had settled on her, removing the color and casting a ghostly shadow.

Without warning, Julia began to scream. The muscles in her abdomen clenched so tightly she was pushed forward, almost falling out of the chair. Her hand, still in David's squeezed without relenting.

The cloud on Julia suddenly broke, clearly revealing her piercing eyes and her unmistakable anguish and fear.

A nurse appeared and helped David get Julia to her feet.

Julia's breath caught, unable to be released, as if all her energy was concentrated on withstanding the compression in her abdomen. Maybe if she couldn't breathe then her heart would stop too. Maybe the pain would grow so intense that it would take her life, letting her escape from the torture and the terrible news to come.

"It's okay, Honey." David said. "It's going to be okay."

There was nothing left in her body to fight him; it was too busy fighting within itself. A battle raged, increasing in intensity. Stabbing and burning. Advance and then retreat and then advance again. Blow after internal blow, her body was ravaged.

She was taken to an examination room and placed on the table. Looking up at the poster on the ceiling, Julia realized she was in the same room as last time. The last time—a time of joy and hope, of forgetting the painful past of infertility and moving into the blessed future of pregnancy.

If there was an ounce of strength remaining, she would have stood on the table and ripped the poster down.

The doctor arrived instantly and asked Julia to remove her lower clothes and told David to knock on the door when Julia was ready, he would be waiting.

She put a hand on David's shoulder as she pulled down her sweat pants and underwear, thankful that the cramps had subsided if only momentarily.

"I'm sorry, Jules," David said, kissing her temple. "I'm so sorry."

Of course none of this was his fault, but the emotional pain he was experiencing didn't register with her. I'm sorry is something said when a person bumps into you at the mall or when a dish of spaghetti is dropped leaving the floor a mess.

It isn't something you say to a woman when her body is attacking itself for the sole purpose of destroying the gift within. I'm sorry doesn't stop the catastrophe.

The doctor took Julia's hand. "I have the paperwork from the hospital. I'd like to do a vaginal exam and then we can discuss everything."

Julia shook her head in agreement.

With her feet in the stirrups and knees fallen open, she heard the doctor snap on his gloves and grab for an instrument. The metal was cold and intrusive.

As soon as it found its place inside her, Julia saw David and the nurse, both shielded from the view of her body by a paper drape, step back. Pools of blood began to fall to the floor.

Julia's body went limp and her head fell to the pillow. As the blackness took her into its comforting quiet, she prayed she would not wake up.

CHAPTER 41

David told her the baby, though only an embryo, was their angel. And now it would be with Pops in heaven. She knew he was trying to comfort them both, but she didn't want it.

Months ago, they thought it had been David's sperm that kept them from getting pregnant. It had been a hurdle they could clear with time and medical help. They had joked about kickboards and swimming lessons. There was no longer any joking.

This time it was not something that could be stopped or helped or fixed. This was Julia's body rejecting the pregnancy. It was a loss so great the weight threatened to crush her.

Her body had killed a baby. Their baby. Her baby.

Like leaves in autumn, Julia's heart dried and fell. Winter settled with unyielding cold upon her.

People continued to tell Julia that time heals all wounds. Her office sent flowers. A few cards came in the mail, but all were left unopened on the kitchen counter.

Julia wanted to tell them the exception to that rule was infertility. It is the one tragic circumstance that actually worsen with time, like a shadow lengthening and deepening in the late afternoon, bringing more and more darkness.

In December, David asked Julia to sit on the back porch with him. He had made a fire in the chiminea and set out a glass of wine for each of them.

Wrapped in a blanket, Julia sat next to the fire. They had hardly touched since the miscarriage. She wouldn't look at him. Instead of home-cooked meals, which Julia used to enjoy preparing, she turned to take-away suppers or a bowl of cereal.

Work had gone from a daily pleasure to something Julia was forced to lumber though like thick mud. She never asked about David's new job, and didn't much care.

She refused to return calls from Sarah and Rebecca. And they hadn't gone to dinner with either family in several months.

In silence, the couple sipped the wine. Julia looked toward the stars, glassy-eyed.

"What are you thinking about?" David asked.

"Nothing," she said.

The fire crackled and threatened to go out, David poked in some newspaper and added a small log.

"I miss you," he said.

It had always been the beginning of their forgiveness. No matter what they had quarreled over, one would admit to missing the other, and the bond would begin to mend.

This time, however, there had been no fight. There was nothing to forgive. There was only Julia, lost.

"Did you hear me?" David asked.

Julia nodded, a small gesture.

"I miss the way we talked. The way we snuggled in front of the television. The way you'd kiss me hello. I miss your smile. Please, Jules," he begged. "I miss you."

The fire flickered again and shadows danced erratically.

Julia got up and walked into the kitchen. David hung his head in defeat.

When she returned, she held the stack of mail, a journal, and the Sponge Bob socks she had gotten from the support group. She placed the pile on her lap.

Sliding her finger under a sealed envelope, she removed the first sympathy card. It was from Yvette. She looked at it briefly, reading a Bible quote from Ecclesiastes 3. "There is a time for everything, a season for every activity under the heavens: a time to be born and a time to die, a time to plant and a time to uproot, a time to kill and a time to heal, a time to tear down and a time to build, a time to weep and a time to laugh, a time to mourn and a time to . . ."

There was more, but she had read enough.

She placed the card and its envelope in the fire, then watched it curl and char at the edges before glowing until it burst into flame and was consumed.

She did this slowly with every card, watching each one burn completely until they had all disappeared.

David sat back, without movement or voice, watching his wife burn the kindness sent to her by friends. She had done it all without anger or sadness.

When the stack of cards was gone, she laid the Sponge Bob socks on the embers and watched until they were ablaze. The socks were intended to lend humor to a difficult situation. Julia was done with humor.

Finally, she held the deep purple journal, its title embossed in gold, the leather soft in her hand. Opening to the first page she read the quote handwritten by Stephanie. At the time, the words of Romans 5 were a treasure. The idea that suffering brings perseverance, which brings character, which brings hope used to hold a promise; it now sounded like a silly school-girl fantasy.

She tore the page from the book and crumpled it in her hand. Carefully, she lay the page in the fire and sat back in her chair.

"Did that feel good?" David asked.

"I guess," she said without commitment.

"Talk to me Jules," he said.

"I'm tired. I think I'll just go to bed," she said, leaving David alone in the cold.

In February the trees were nothing but naked sticks protruding from the earth. Like Julia, they remained without life or growth, dormant.

David came home to find Julia lying in her bra and panties on the tile kitchen floor. Her body lay crumpled as tears ran down the side of her face into her ear.

When he knelt beside her, she held up a piece of paper. Glued on the front was a colorful road map, the edges jagged as if ripped from an atlas. On top, attached by a spring, was a baby blue and yellow airplane.

It was an invitation to Kyle Beckett's third birthday party, to be held at the park on Fifteenth Street at noon the following week.

David was confused. Why would the invitation make his wife lie nearly naked in the kitchen. "I don't get it," he said.

"Sarah got pregnant the same time we started trying," Julia said. "Now Kyle is three. He is three." She enunciated the last word, stressing the amount of time that had passed.

"And you are naked because?"

"Because I can't feel anything," she said. "I wanted to lie here and feel the cold tile. I wanted to feel how hard it is. I wanted to be naked and exposed and cold and uncomfortable."

David furrowed his brow.

"Don't you get it?" she yelled getting to her feet. "I don't feel anything." She hit her open hand into the wall. The sound reverberated in the room.

"Honey, we have to . . ."

Julia cut him off.

"I can't do this David. I can't live like this. I'm not the same person I was before we lost the baby. I cannot offer you what you need in a wife."

She squared her shoulders to her husband looking him directly in the eye, hoping the gravity of her next sentence would be felt.

"I think we should get a divorce," she said.

"We are not getting a divorce," he said, grabbing her around the waist.

She pushed him off. "I think we should. I can't make you a father. I can't have children. I don't want to be touched or held or anything. I want to be alone."

He cupped his hands around her face. The gesture was so sensitive she faltered a bit, remembering he had done the same thing when he proposed so many years ago.

"You are the love of my life," he said. "No one said you can't have children. And we can adopt if our bodies don't like the idea. I want you." He kissed her on the right cheek. "I miss you," he kissed her on the other cheek. "I love you," he kissed her mouth.

And for the first time since the miscarriage, she let him. And she felt him around her.

CHAPTER 42

Several weeks later, Rebecca called asking for a walk. Relentless, she had asked every week. This was no different, except this week Julia said yes.

Rebecca was the kind of person who didn't let a challenge stop her, not in the pursuit of friendship and not in the pursuit of a family. Julia envied her friend's willpower and wished for a small seed of it to fall from Rebecca and land on her. She hoped the seed would take root and blossom within her, giving her the determination not to be destroyed by life's trials but empowered by them.

"I got it!" Rebecca said with overflowing energy. She grabbed Julia's arm and began literally jumping up and down. Julia had never seen her friend so hyper. "I mean, I knew we had a shot. But we got it. We actually got it."

"Got what?" Julia asked, wishing she could put her hand on Rebecca's bouncing shoulders and stop her.

Julia had hidden from the world to limit exposure to this kind of overly anxious excitement. She didn't want to celebrate a birthday, didn't want to drink to a new promotion, didn't want to be in the presence of yet another woman announcing her pregnancy.

Work at the Health Department allowed her to sit in the dark and surround herself with illness, dysfunction, and spectrums of normalcy. Shielding herself from other's joy became a matter of perspective. She chose not to see a young pregnant girl's showing love and concern for the child growing within her but instead saw her as an object of pity for her bad choices and lost future. She saw hundreds of sick children and thought about the barrier she needed to erect between the illnesses and herself, focusing not on the care the child required but on the bodily fluids the child was spreading all over the lobby.

"The Raftopolis. I just got the call," Rebecca said.

"What?" Julia asked. "Have you gone mad since I saw you last?"

"Remember last year when you gave me the trigger shot?" Rebecca explained. "That was our last chance. When it failed we were devastated because we had run out of money to try again. We've had our last four embryos in the deep freezer at the hospital ever since."

As if she had explained everything, Rebecca stopped.

"And?" Julia asked.

"And . . . we applied for the Raftopolis Scholarship that Laney told me about at the support group, remember? Well, we got it!" She began to bounce again. "We get to try again."

Rebecca's smile had always been a bit too big for her small face, and her exposed gums were something Julia interpreted not as a flaw but as kindness in a smile too big for its confines. Today, Rebecca could not have been more happy, and Julia had never seen her so beautiful.

Julia felt dizzy. She didn't understand. Why, failure after failure, would Rebecca put herself out there again. Why would she open her fragile heart and allow pain to pierce the already bruised and broken places?

In confusion, she congratulated her friend.

When she got home, Savvy was sitting on her door step. Julia approached slowly. The last time she found her sister on a doorstep Savvy had been pregnant. Julia feared that same bombshell was about to be dropped.

"What are you doing here?"

"I came by to talk," Savvy said.

"To me? Why?"

"Because we always start like this," Savvy motioned between them. "And I want to be done with it."

"Okay." But Julia was not convinced. "What do you want to talk about?"

"I wrote something for you." Savvy handed over a folded piece of paper.

Julia accepted it without opening it. "You wrote something?"

"Yeah, Jules. That's what I do. I'm a writer."

They looked at one another, confused. Julia knew her sister used to write journals as a child, but to actually call herself a writer seemed presumptuous. But Julia wanted to handle the situation thoughtfully. Savvy was there to make amends, or so she said.

Julia joined her sister on the steps. "What do you mean, you're a writer?"

"I'm not just a barista—is that what you thought?" Savvy laughed. "God, no. No wonder you've been so uptight about me moving in with mom and dad. You thought I was going to live there forever and mooch off them. Damn, that explains a lot."

"You mean that's not your plan."

"Jules, really? No. I like working at coffee shops because it gets me out of the house and into real people's lives. It gives me ideas for my projects. I have a contract to write for two monthly magazines, and I have my first book coming out soon."

"What?!" Julia couldn't believe her ears. Savvy, the free-as-a-bird, poor-decision-making queen is a real writer with a book on the way. She has a steady job and a plan. Julia was blindsided.

"Yeah, I have a novel being published by a firm in New York. The advance was enough for a down payment on a house. I figured with Talon around I needed to grow some roots. We're actually going to be less than a mile from you."

"I don't know what to say."

Julia felt like a person who had just been told the world is not actually flat but round. She needed some time to examine this information for herself, look at it from all angles to make sure it made sense.

"No wonder we never got each other," Savvy said. "We've never really talked."

"Yeah," Julia said. "Should I read this now?"

"No, wait until later," Savvy said.

They sat in silence. Years of dust isn't blown off with a single gesture, and the sisters didn't yet know how to communicate smoothly.

"You know my tattoo," Savvy said, "the key? You've always given me a hard time about it."

"Yeah."

"You never asked me why I got it. Want to know?"

"Sure."

Julia had no idea where this was going. She had assumed the key was an easy choice, put at eye level in the tattoo parlor. She figured her sister was trying to rebel against her parents and got the first thing she could see.

"A key is a metaphor in all kinds of ways. The key to success. The key to happiness. The key to the universe. I got the tattoo to remind me that I hold the key. No one else. I'm in charge of my world, and I have the power."

Julia looked at her sister. She had never been so surprised by a person or more impressed.

"Want to stay for dinner?" Julia asked.

"I'd love to."

The next morning, Julia was stuck thinking through Rebecca's choices. On autopilot, she went to Flavors before heading to work. Over the hum of conversation and the gravelly voice of a woman singing in the speakers, she ordered her skinny double-shot cappuccino from Savvy.

"The poem was beautiful," Julia said. "I read it like a

hundred times. It was like you found me and were trying to help me out."

"Glad you saw my heart," Savvy said. "We all want to help but know we can't. And your heartache affects us all."

"Thank you," Julia said, her eyes growing misty.

She took a seat to wait for the coffee when she saw the older gentleman shuffle up to the door, his gray pageboy hat atop his head like a cherry on a vanilla ice cream. Julia got up and held the door for him.

"Thank you, Julia," the man said.

Her eyes snapped to his, caught off guard. "You know my name?"

"But of course. We have frequented the same restaurant for years. When they call for the coffee I like to see who gets up." She couldn't place his accent, though she liked the way he swallowed the R sound and how he pronounced every syllable in the word restaurant.

"May I buy you a coffee?" she asked. It was completely uncharacteristic but she felt drawn to this man and this conversation as if an invisible line were reeling in a catch.

"It would be my pleasure," he said with a smile.

Savvy must have overheard the conversation because she nodded to Julia and continued preparing the orders.

Julia walked to the old man's usual table, and he pulled a chair out for her. She hadn't expected him to be such an Old World gentleman, but it delighted her. Over the smell of roasting beans, she caught his scent, a mixture of musk and citrus.

He shuffled to the seat across from her and sat down. As he did so, Julia studied him. His bushy gray brows nearly masked his eyes. Though his body wasn't spry, his eyes told a different story. His skin was leathered and wrinkled, but she was certain that he had been quite handsome. Julia had always seen him sitting but now realized he was quite a bit taller than she expected. His shoulders, drooping forward with age, were broad and his physique under the button-down dress shirt was solid.

"You don't sound like you're from around here," Julia said.

"I am Greek," he said, gesturing with his hands, his thumb and first two fingers together. "I come from the most beautiful land in the world, surrounded by blue waters, fresh fish. The most delicious baklava ever made. So very beautiful."

"When did you move here?"

"I came with my wife before our daughter was born," a storm of emotions moved across his face. Julia was unable to interpret this—she hadn't meant to upset him. She was relieved when he seemed to settle back into his smile.

"Tell me about you, Julia," he said.

Simple as it was, it felt like a loaded question. How would she introduce herself in one brief sentence? What defines a person? Is it profession or education. Is it homeland, the only thing she knew about the man in front of her? Is it religion or political affiliation. In countless arbitrary ways we have chosen teams the might pit her against him. Is it hobbies and activities? Is it marital status or, God forbid, motherhood?

She had spent the last three years defining herself by the last of these—a woman married without children. Childless had become the first adjective she thought of to describe herself, even if only to herself.

Julia assumed the same storm must have just crossed her face that had crossed his.

"What do you want to know?" she asked, embarrassed by her lack of confidence.

"We all have a story Julia," he said. "I can tell you need to share yours."

A shiver crossed her shoulders and caught in her throat. Unexpectedly, it moistened her eyes. She would love to tell her story to someone who would neither judge her nor try to fix her. She longed to be free, if only for a moment, of the burden of her sadness and circumstance, giving it to another person to hold and keep until she was able to take it back again.

Savvy's voice broke the magic. "Mr. Raftopolis," she said.

"Your coffee is ready."

When he began to stand, Julia reached across the table and put her hand on his. "You're Mr. Raftopolis?"

"Yes," he said.

"Of the Raftopolis Scholarship?" Her eyes must have been as wide as the ocean itself.

"Ah, you know my fund?" He shook his head as if the puzzle pieces had just fallen into place.

"You have just made my friend Rebecca incredibly happy." Julia could not believe her luck. It was not every day that you are given the opportunity to thank the person who had possibly changed the life of someone you love.

"Rebecca Papadopoulos. Yes. My best friend from grammar school was a Papadopoulos, may he rest in peace," he said looking up. "They are not related. She seems like a fine young woman. I am glad to help."

"Her last name is Johnson now," Julia said, not sure why she was correcting this gracious stranger. "She's Greek on her father's side."

"I am glad to help," he repeated with little emotion.

Julia went to get his coffee, still awestruck by the amazing grace of fate.

"May I ask you a question?" she said, handing him the mug and a yellow packet of Splenda. She must have unintentionally watched him make his coffee for years because she knew exactly how he took it.

"Of course," he said, ripping the packet. "As a younger man I used to take my coffee black. Then one day I realized I did not like the bitter taste and decided to add sugar. When the Siren sang to me to try Splenda," he motioned to Savvy behind the counter, "I was hooked. My coffee has been much sweeter since."

She loved the way he spoke and could listen to his whimsical wisdom wrapped in a beautiful accent all day.

Biting her lip, Julia was unsure how to ask the question without seeming to pry. She wanted to be as respectful as possible because Mr. Raftopolis was both her elder and her friend's benefactor.

"Why do you have a fertility scholarship? I mean, is it for all health issues of people with Greek descent or just infertility?"

The word dried on her tongue.

Though his smile didn't falter, his eyes changed. "I can see why an old man with a fertility scholarship must seem unique. As I said, we all have a story."

"Will you tell me yours?" Julia asked. She felt as greedy as a child asking for a Christmas gift.

"This one is not a long story," he said, taking a sip of his coffee. "But I will share it with you.

"When my wife and I were married in Greece, we had the world at our fingertips. I was a fisherman with my own boat. A prestigious suitor, I promise. Her father had goats and was very happy that I had my eye on his daughter—not many boys my age had their own boat." He winked at Julia and she smiled.

"She was so smart and studied to be a nurse, the first in her family with an education. We lived in a marvelous little house by the ocean. One day I was in the water near the house and I heard her scream. I jumped from the boat and swam to her. She was losing our baby and we didn't even know she was pregnant. It happened three times, and each time she cried and I cried with her.

"Eventually we decided we must get help, so we came to America. Here a doctor gave her medicine to carry a baby. Delia was born in June, and she was the most treasured baby in the world.

"We had only planned to stay until the baby was born, but we made friends with neighbors, and I got a beautiful job. The doctor's office tells my wife she can come work as a nurse for him when she is ready. So we stayed here to raise Delia in America.

"We were so happy. My wife retired from the infant crisis wing of the hospital when Delia got married and told us she would have a family.

"She had three miscarriages also. The fourth one took my daughter to heaven."

Mr. Raftopolos looked down, composing himself. Julia reached for his hand and squeezed it, tears falling silently on her cheeks as she tried to absorb the pain this man must have felt losing his only daughter and so many grandchildren.

Something in the center of her being opened and she felt heat radiate from within her. It was not pain. It was empathy.

Mr. Raftopolis put his finger under Julia's chin and raised her head to meet his. "Do not be sad for me," he said. "I had thirty-two wonderful years with Delia and sixty with her mother. I am happy God gave me them for the time He did."

"But how did you deal with their loss?" She asked looking for the answers to her own pain.

"I have watched you, Julia. I know you have had pain. But I give to others with my scholarship so they can experience life and hope. This scholarship gives me life too."

"I just never pictured my life like this," she said, knowing she didn't need to explain herself to him.

"My sweet girl, life is as perennial as the grass. We must live during the growing season."

CHAPTER 43

Julia left Flavors and sat in silence for a long time in the parking lot.

She thought about Rebecca and her excitement for another chance. Delia had not been given that chance, but Delia's father gave it to strangers.

She thought about Claudia, the masseuse on the beach in Florida who said she would remember Julia because of how much she wanted to give life. At the time, she assumed Claudia meant giving life through birth, but now she realized that she could give life not only though conception but also through the love we give to others.

In her depression, Julia had forgotten to be a life-giver to her husband, to her friends, to her family. To herself. The way Mr. Raftopolis had done.

She thought about Sarah's prescription of perspective and the importance of a positive attitude. And she thought about Savvy. At eighteen her sister had realized something that Julia was just now learning. You hold your own key, the power to open the future.

She reached for the phone that had fallen to the floor of her car. She wanted to call Rebecca and tell her all she had learned, when next to the phone she found a crumpled piece of paper.

Unfolding it and smoothing out the page she read her own handwriting: "You are never too early or too late. You are when you are supposed to be." It was the quote from Mitch Albom's book that she had balled up and thrown aside after an appointment with Dr. Lamont so long ago.

She held the paper to her chest and breathed. In, slowly. Out, slowly. Beaty had always told her, at the bottom of difficulty, to "just breathe." And so she did.

This discarded note reminded her of the journal page, now white feathers of ash in the chiminea at home, with ghostly words reminding her to lift suffering into perseverance, perseverance into character, character into hope. Maybe today she would set aside suffering and discover perseverance.

She called David.

"I'm ready," she said full of confidence. "Let's try again."

SAVVY'S POEM TO JULIA

A life-giver's challenge,
a contest not to be won.
She lives with anger and depression,
a tragedy not for one.
But the whole who know her struggle,
with her bitterness and strain
for we cannot provide to her
the longing she has in vain.
The darkness begins to eat her,
we contribute without power.
For it is she who must control the beast
or the beast will devour.